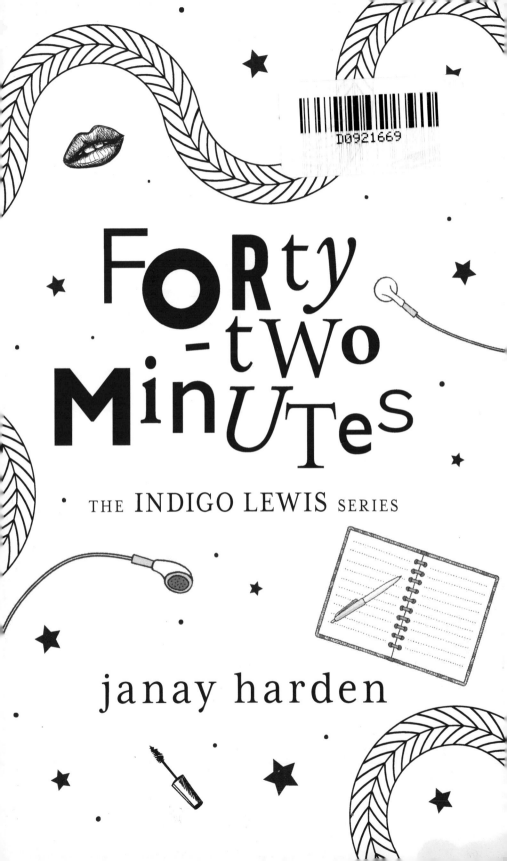

FORty-two MinUTes

THE INDIGO LEWIS SERIES

janay harden

Forty-two Minutes
The Indigo Lewis Series

ISBN: 978-1-7365412-2-7 (eBook)
ISBN: 978-1-7365412-3-4 (print)

Thank you for choosing to read *"Forty-two Minutes."*
Please join my email list by scanning the QR code or going to
www.naywrites.com for notifications of new releases.

To 2020:
Thank you for showing me parts of myself that I had forgotten.
To 2021 — thank you for receiving the baton.

PROLOGUE

THOUGH THE INCINERATOR still hummed, his cries died down long ago. My breath was ragged and my heart beat in my ears. "Think, Indigo, think," I whispered to myself. The incinerator was still running; its loud hum reminded me of easier times, like just a few hours ago. Could that be considered easier times? I don't know. Today, it became my savior. My only choice. In a sea full of different outcomes and scenarios replaying in my mind, this had been my choice.

My reading glasses lay off to the side on the floor, and I'm not entirely sure how they got there. From what I could see from here, they were a shattered mess. Do you know how expensive eyeglasses are? Damn. I just bought them too; I saved my money from working here at Dennis and Sons Funeral Home. Mr. Dennis, the Funeral director and my boss, would know something had happened. He noticed everything and being that this was a funeral home, he could smell death a mile away. He said it lived in his blood, in his soul. How could someone smell death? He said his job was to "see for the dead." I wondered what he would see when he came in tomorrow morning. We would have to test his theory.

It took one to three hours for a body to cremate at 1500 degrees Fahrenheit, but I didn't have one to three hours. My mind replayed the sounds of Jaxon screaming as I turned the dial higher and higher until it reached 1800 degrees Fahrenheit. My hands were shaking as I switched the large knob to the off-setting while the incinerator croaked to an end. Like Jaxon, I lamented. I typically did my homework while I waited for the machine to do its thing, but this day was much different. Mr. Dennis was considering upgrading the machinery, but he never got around to it. His son Tyson also didn't keep the cleanest funeral home as I glanced around. The old security system was so outdated and not working. This might help me...

My phone lit up somewhere in the room. It was slightly dark, and it shone brightly in the crevice, even though there was no one to call right now. I mean, what would I say? Hi there, I just killed Jaxon Green. The whitest white boy—and me—the blackest Black girl. Yep, that would go over great. I knelt down and searched around the corners until I found it lit up in the room's corner. My hands were shaking as I unlocked it.

Forty-two Minutes.

That's about how long it took to annihilate Jaxon's body when I turned up the fire even hotter. And because Mr. Dennis' place was so dirty, Jaxon's body would hopefully be more debris added to the pile. A text message popped up from Malachi, my ex-boyfriend.

> **MALACHI:** Still comin' thru?

I paused and stared at the wall. I planned to meet up with Malachi and our friends, Will and Mila. The four of us have been friends since birth. Will and Mila lived a few blocks from my house, and Malachi lived in West Tunica, on the outskirts of the city. Officials section the city off by zones and

technically the four of us should have never gone to the same school, but just our luck they modge podged us together. You'd think we'd tire of each other, being attached at the hip since kindergarten and all, but it just made us closer. Today we were supposed to celebrate graduating from high school the day before. Today was supposed to be about making the most of our last summer before some of us went away to college. Today was not supposed to begin with a murder.

A deep sigh escaped me, and I placed my phone back into my pocket, not responding to Malachi. Time was ticking, and now people were looking for me. Decisions needed to be made. I gazed around the room and saw nothing that would show Jaxon had been here. There wasn't much to clean up around the room; there wasn't much to do once a body burned, but I peered around anyway. I assessed the scene of the crime — my crime. Pulling the heavy door to the studio closed behind me, I turned out the lights and walked upstairs.

Jaxon's bag sat on the visitor's bench, which was ironic as he was anything but. Should I burn that too? Maybe. I didn't want to go back down there right now; we needed some space from each other. I searched through his bag and I didn't find a cell phone. He had it in his hand when…when…that meant it burned up too…good, one less thing to worry about. Rummaging through everything, I found a black and white notebook with my initials on the front, ITL—Indigo Tina Lewis. I flipped through the pages and heat washed over me. Jaxon wrote dozens of different things he was going to blackmail me with. Not only did he reference the pictures, but he had copies of my Dad's paystubs, my sister Sidney's last report card — and even my college acceptance letter. What would he need with all that? I fumed. He was plotting against me while I was trying to keep the peace. I closed the book and slid it into my bag for safekeeping.

What led us to this point? How did this happen? How did I end up killing Jaxon, when we just graduated from high school the day before? I thought about my dad and Sidney. They needed me, and I still had so much to do for them. Jaxon had brought this on himself and that book of his proved it. My hands were shaking as I collected Jaxon's bag and anything else that looked out of place. Standing in the center of the room, I tried to remember how it looked before Jaxon Green stepped foot through the door. Maybe it was my fault, I should've never told him to meet me at work. He pushed and pushed and pushed. At first it started with doing his homework, and that was okay. A fair exchange, I believed it to be at the time. Then he changed and wanted different things...things I wasn't comfortable with. He talked to me like I was nothing—I had enough of his shit and I saw red. Maybe there had been another option? I'm not sure. But it didn't present itself, and I did what I had to do.

It was Friday morning and Tunica Rivers was still quiet. Nothing stirred outside and I cleaned up a murder inside. Who was this person I had turned into?

I was in a car accident when I was younger. Mama Jackie was t-boned by someone who missed the stop sign. It stopped traffic for miles and miles. Cars were backed up and honking at each other. I remember thinking, if people just kept driving, there wouldn't be a jam. But everyone crept by us, slowing to see the damage and revel at their luck and our misfortune. They couldn't help but stop to steal a peek. Did anybody die? Was it anyone they knew? Maybe I was the only one who had thoughts like that, I guess. Jaxon was my car accident, and this accident was *that* bad. Mr. Dennis asked me to lock up when I was finished for the day and trusted me with the keys. I cremated dozens of bodies to prepare for services, but never anyone I knew. And never by my own hands.

I killed Jaxon. I killed nothing in my life, not even a bug. But Jaxon, Jaxon was important. Somewhere in my body, I felt nervous. But not the bad nervous that makes you question yourself and everything around you — the good nervous when something happens, and you're pleased by the thought of a potential outcome. I would never say it out loud. I would dare not speak it but listening to Jaxon's cries and watching his hand bang against the small incinerator window added extra pep to my step. My heart jumped with amazement. I don't care what I allowed him to do in the past, today was a new day. My future was bright, just like the flames that illuminated Jaxon.

Girls are expected to be dainty, feminine, sugar, spice, and everything nice. Fuck that shit. Respect me or be destroyed.

I shut the lights off behind me and set the alarm. With it screaming in my ear, I inspected the room again. I really hoped Mr. Dennis noticed nothing out of order. Tyson and I alternated weekends working, and this weekend, he asked me to switch schedules with him. How do you say no to your boss's son? Plus when it was his weekend he often forgot to sanitize. It was easier for us to just switch, at least I knew with me it would be clean.

This should not have happened — I wasn't even supposed to be here. To think, maybe this could've been avoided if I said no. That was how I got in this mess anyway, not saying no...no to Tyson, no to Jaxon.

Who was I kidding? It was bound to happen; Jaxon kept trying his luck over and over again. I paced in the foyer while the alarm sounded. Locking the door behind me, I glared up at the neon Dennis & Sons Funeral Home sign. I had only been there a few months; before here I was working at the city art gallery. When I was younger, I used to throw pottery with my mom. Every week, she took Sidney and me to the studio and we sat in front of a massive piece of clay spinning on a potter's wheel. She created such beautiful pieces of pottery crafted together with different shapes and textures. I loved it; that was our thing. Mom was in the hospital now—with no foreseeable discharge date. I try to devote more time to pottery and not worry about money, but pottery didn't help pay for a prom dress or these college application fees. Money was what I needed.

Dad was a janitor at the retirement home down on Laurel Road, and he's been there for over twenty years. He did nothing else, and he didn't want to do anything else. He always told Sidney and me to do our very best and things would just fall into place. "You'll get rewarded for your brains," he mused. Jaxon Green interrupted my job, and he interrupted my life.

Once outside, I looked both ways and saw no one on the street. I took out all of the evidence in Jaxon's bag and I shoved it into the trash can next to Dennis and Sons. The trash was already rank with what smelled like dirty diapers and old milkshakes. I choked from the smell and returned the lid after I stuffed his bag under the nauseating diapers.

I headed straight for the corner store across the street. A blast of wind came and blew my braids in my face. Tugging on the door handle, I glimpsed myself in the entryway glass. When I left this morning, it was raining and overcast. My hair was in a flawless circle bun with braids and sat atop my head. You know, the kind of bun that takes you a couple tries to get right. You have to center it on your head, just perfect to stay in place all day. Sometimes I even break a sweat trying to get that baby straight. Hours later, my bun disappeared, and my braids were falling at my shoulders.

A small spackle of dust, which sat under my eye, violated my dark brown skin. Once I realized it was there, it felt like acid on my face. My stomach sank. I hoped the spackle of dust wasn't remnants of Jaxon. Glancing at my clothing, I wore jeans and a Tunica Rivers High School Newspaper Club long-sleeved shirt. That, too, had spackles of dust and was singed at the bottom from where it had burned. A lump formed in my throat.

There was no way I could go in there looking like this—people would know what I had done. Backing away from the door, I turned in the opposite direction and sat on a nearby bench. My next move, I had no idea. I couldn't call anyone. Dad would question why I was home from work so early. Sidney was only ten and couldn't drive yet. Malachi had his mom's old hooptie and might pick me up, but he would take one look at me and see my shame—plus he was currently at work at the movie theater in town. Mila would lose her shit, and Will . . . well . . . he and I are close and have been friends the longest. He would spot it on me a million miles away, better than even Malachi. There was no one to call.

All things considered, maybe turning myself in to the police was my best option. I mean, I did kill someone.

"Indigo? . . . Indigo, are you okay?"

I swung my head and looked up at Joya, a junior from school. It was May and the school year was over, so I guess she was now a senior. The sun eclipsed Joya in front of me, so I lifted a hand to block it, trying to get a better look at her. Her eyes were wide with concern, inspecting me up and down. She was at the party that night when all of this started. I remembered fragments of her dancing on the piano and a few other things. I wonder if she knew that party would start all of this and leave Jaxon dead.

"Do you need a ride?" She looked me up and down, sitting on the bench, my hair all over my head and my shirt wrinkled. Confusion lined her eyes.

Would she be safe with me? Would I be safe with her? Joya and I shared moments that no one would ever know about, but still, was she a threat? I was hypervigilant, looking at everyone sideways after what I had just done. I was editor for the Tunica Rivers High School Newspaper Club before I graduated, and she would be a part of the team next school year. I kept her secrets, even without being asked; that's what a good editor does, right? Always get your story and don't reveal your sources.

Watching her now, I felt…what was the show called? Naked and Afraid. Before my thoughts got the best of me, I stood and peered at the trash can where I stuffed Jaxon's empty bag moments earlier. I faced Joya and pulled my bag over my shoulder.

"Sure."

Joya motioned towards her white Audi. She hit her key fob, unlocking the doors with one swift motion. When she got her driver's license she shared with Mila, who shared with me, that her parents bought it for her. I knew the truth and the real reason. I shuddered thinking about what she had to do for that car, and what she gave up. It was big news in town. The rest of us were making do with old Hondas, but she copped something brand new. Walking to the driver's side with me trailing behind her, I watched her every move anticipating anything. Joya was heavyset with mocha skin. She wore a matching grey sweat suit with Jordan sneakers. She pulled her fine hair back into a tight bun and small bumps formed at her hairline from it being too tight. It was clinched with a large clip that said joy.

Joya rolled her window down and pressed, "Are you coming or not?"

Swallowing the lump forming in my throat and with no other options, I hopped into the car. Fumbling with the radio, Joya pressed a few buttons until Saweetie sounded from the speakers. She reversed the car and pulled off, glancing straight ahead as she turned. She didn't look both ways.

"8254 Trelawne Road," I managed. My voice cracked.

"Girl, I remember your address. Are you okay?" She drove with both hands on the steering wheel and glanced at me from the corner of her eyes. This was the second time we drove in the car and that question had been posed. Only that time I was asking her if she was okay. Things changed so quickly. Jaxon blackmailing me, and I thought about his hand up to the incinerator window and his last scream. Scenes from the party also replayed in my mind.

Was I okay? We would see.

"I'm good, thanks for asking." I half smiled in Joya's direction.

My hand traveled to my chest and I palmed a small locket around my neck. It was a heart, and it said Sonia and Indigo—mom and me. For the first time since the Jaxon debacle, a tear came to my eye. I wanted my mom. She was in the psych hospital; we wrote letters back and forth to each other, but Sidney and I only laid eyes on our mother, Sonia Lewis, every few months.

Each day felt like an eternity.

We were passing the Hill. I peered over Joya's shoulder and glimpsed Will's house. Mila's car was there. "Do you have any napkins?" I asked. I cracked my window while sweat formed on my head.

My breathing was still uneven, and my body was heavy, like I was underwater with weights. My underarms were drenched in sweat and the stench was threatening to run down my sides. I held them tight against my chest. Joya reached into her glove box and retrieved a stack of napkins. She handed

IX

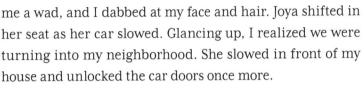

me a wad, and I dabbed at my face and hair. Joya shifted in her seat as her car slowed. Glancing up, I realized we were turning into my neighborhood. She slowed in front of my house and unlocked the car doors once more.

"Thank you," I mumbled, not looking at her.

"Indy, are you sure you're okay?" Joya unbuckled her seat belt and turned towards me in the car.

"I'm okay," I smiled as fake and bright as I could. A tear threatened to fall, and I prayed Joya accepted my lies and left them alone. I grabbed my bags from the backseat, taking in her words.

I walked the short path to my house and opened the wrought-iron gate. It creaked when I pushed. I winced and tried to close it slowly, hoping it didn't wake my dad. Walking over to his car, I placed my hand on the hood. It was cold. You can always tell when the car is cold—it's quiet; doesn't make any noise. When someone arrived home not too long ago, it tingled to sleep. Dad's car wasn't tingling, and that was a good sign. Most days he hibernated bear style, and hopefully today would be one of those days.

Our house backed up to Tunica River, and off to the side sat a small boathouse ramp and a few canoes. We lived in a tiny, two-bedroom cottage—well, maybe it was a three bedroom. There was a decent sized closet in the master bedroom, which Dad gave to me and Sidney. On the days he didn't work, he huffed and puffed, knocking down walls and making that closet into Sidney's bedroom. It only took him three months to build it, and when he finished, I saw him standing in the room doorway with his cup of coffee, taking in his work. He was so proud that day.

There was a large stone chimney, and the roof was steep but flattened out in the back to an open porch. The house has been in Mom's family for decades now, and she says when I get older, she'll turn it over to me and show me what makes it special. We have talked no more about it since she's been in the hospital, and I'm glad; I'm so over this place. I've grown up in Tunica Rivers all my life, and small-town USA is not my jam. Waking up to the sound of water nearby was a treat, but I'd trade it in for fast-paced New York City, or relaxed and sunny California. Anything but confining Tunica Rivers.

Standing on my tiptoes, I peeked in the square window at the top of the front door. I knew dad for working ten-hour days and overnight shifts. He would come home, and he would sprawl out on the couch with his uniform and work boots still on, snoring his life away.

Today he wasn't there.

"Fuck!" I whispered. Maybe he was up walking throughout the house? Or maybe he was sleeping in his room? I checked my phone. It was now 11:43 a.m. Time was flying today! Sidney would be home from her friend's house in a couple of hours. I'd shower, wash my clothes, and figure out my next move — oh shit, I have to text back Will and Mila and see what they were doing since we were supposed to hang out today. I rubbed my temples.

Yesterday there was nothing to do but be a teenager and graduate from high school. Today, a million decisions needed to be made. All I wanted to do was go to work and be with my friends. I had nothing to eat or drink since the night before, but I wasn't hungry and damn sure wasn't thirsty. I was running off fear and adrenaline today.

Walking around to the side of the house where me and Sidney's room was nestled, I glanced at my bedroom window but it was too high for me to climb through. Dad even drilled a window in Sidney's room/closet, which led outside of the house. She always kept it unlocked. Her window was pretty low, just above my knees. We giggled about Dad positioning

xi

the window where it was. Today, I was silently thanking him for its accessible placement. Lifting the window quietly, I removed the screen.

"Umph!"

I leapt through the window with as much strength as I could muster; I felt weak. My arms shook as I hoisted myself up and tumbled, hitting all four corners of the small room. I completely missed Sidney's bed, go figure. I struggled to stand and move my heavy bookbag. It busted me in the temple on the way in. Or way down. Whatever.

I opened Sidney's door and tripped into my bedroom. It sucked that she had to walk through my room to get to hers, but at least we had our own space. My area wasn't too much bigger than Sidney's, and there was just enough room for a full-size bed and my two dressers, since I didn't have a closet anymore.

A loud cough echoed from behind my door while I changed clothes in my room. Creeping into the hallway, I softly opened my dad's door. Sure enough, he was passed out in his uniform, sprawled across his bed. At least he took his work shoes off; I eyed those tossed in the corner. Dad was working overnights these days to help pay for all the things that college entailed. Although he never complained, he was gone from home a lot more, and when he was home, he was asleep like this. I was in charge at night when he was away—I was always in charge.

I exhaled and closed his door behind me. I texted my group chat with Will and Mila.

> **ME:** I can't meet today guys, I'm not feeling good. Think I ate too much last night.

Malachi was next; he went on break from work around two p.m. and I knew he would call to chit chat. I texted him the same.

> **ME:** I'm not feeling good. Think I ate too much last night.

> **MALACHI:** You good?

> **ME:** Yeah, I'm okay. I'm gonna take a nap. TTYL ok?

> **MALACHI:** Cool cool. I'll stop by later to check on you.

I powered my phone off and peeled my clothes from my body and let them fall to the floor. I stared at myself in my small mirror behind my bedroom door. What was I? A monster? Or maybe someone more like myself? His parents would be looking for him. That's for sure. There were no cameras outside of Dennis and Son's, and none on the street that I had ever seen. I wondered if my dad still had wood in the pit out back. Maybe I could burn my clothes. I didn't want to lay eyes on them ever again.

The shower was as hot as I could stand it, and the fog was thick as I pulled the curtain back and stepped in. I winced at the heat. My skin flushed, and I felt my hair curl in the front of my braids. I grabbed two washcloths and one loofah sponge. Sidney used a long hand brush in the shower, and I rummaged through the bathroom looking for that, too, but I couldn't find it. I scrubbed my skin as hard as I could—even with my nails. My dad used Old Spice men's body wash and today, that's what I pulled for, squeezing it all over me. I

XIII

lathered and fluffed, alternating between the loofahs and the rags. Next came my braids, and I squeezed the Old Spice over those too. I scratched at my scalp. Dad's soap smelled manly and powerful. Not like the flowery smells that I use. That's how I wanted to feel: powerful. Not this trembling mess before me. My face received the same intensity, and my eyebrows, eyelids, my cheeks. My hands moved in circles, rubbing everywhere on my face at the same time.

There was no room to pace, and no room to scream the way I wanted. I covered my hands over my mouth, and a deep cry escaped. I was someone I didn't know anymore; I didn't understand anymore. I clasped my hands tighter around my mouth so Dad couldn't hear. I screamed and screamed in the shower until my eyes burned and my throat was sore.

Minutes later, I turned off the water, grabbed a towel and wrapped my body. Wiping the fog from the sink mirror, I studied my face; I looked the same. My skin didn't look different, my hair didn't look different. But my eyes—my eyes, told the real story.

Back in my bedroom, I grabbed a t-shirt from my dresser drawer and pulled it over my head. The T-shirt said The Fat Cats. Before my mom got sick, she was in a band and they were a 90s R&B cover group. They toured the South and people loved it. The T-shirt was the last real thing I had of hers. If I tried hard enough, I could even smell her on it too. My hair dripped down my shoulder and I grabbed a hair tie and put it in a bun on the top of my head. I glanced down at my bag and noticed Jaxon's notebook; the one with my name written on the front. I dug it out and palmed the cover.

I paused. Let's see…

PART 1

PUZZLES

CHAPTER 1

6 MONTHS AGO...

S ITTING UP IN my bed, I peered out of the window. My dad was outside chopping wood in the backyard and the chippings shattered in different directions. He wiped his forehead and glanced around. Sidney slept soundly a few feet away from me in her room. She kept the door open again last night and I could see her from here. Studying her face, I hoped she didn't have another nightmare. No, Sonia Lewis's children didn't want the nightmares or blank stares, but that seemed to come with the territory—we just wanted wood chopped during a chilly November morning.

Mom was currently housed at Trochesse Asylum for the Criminally Insane... Great name, right? I thought so too. Why would you name a place that? They could've said for the mentally ill, for the delayed, but no—they settled on insane. Sidney stirred in her bed and her long black hair fell on top of her face; she wasn't wearing her bonnet. Yesterday we laughed because she said every time she has a nightmare about Mom, she snatches her bonnet off her head as soon as she wakes.

"Why?" I giggled.

"My face gets hot, and...I don't know!" she shrieked.

Sidney groaned while I was deep in thought. "Indy, why are you standing over me? Creep!"

"Shut up!" I grabbed her pillow from under her and slapped her with it. Her eyes were wide with surprise when her head slammed against the bed.

I ran out of the room, my feet smacking against the floor.

"Whoa, whoa," Dad says. "What's going on here?"

Sidney chased me into the hallway, and I darted around the kitchen laughing. The back of my Fat Cats T-shirt grabbed onto the handle of our frying pan in the drying rack. In one motion, it tumbled down and took a few more pots with it. The loud noise stopped Sidney and me—we both caught our breath and laughed.

"What is going on here?" Dad again questioned, his eyes darting between the two of us. Benjamin Barre stood there with wood fragments and leaves all over his face. I had on a long T-shirt with pots and pans scattered around my feet. Sidney's hair was matted to her head, and she was breathless.

The three of us surveyed the scene and stifled a laugh together.

"Are you guys hungry? I can make some eggs before you go to school?" he asked. Leaves collected on the kitchen floor as he moved about.

"I'll take some Mr. Ben," Sidney said.

Mr. Ben...I cringed.

Sidney and I shared the same mom, Sonia. I'm seven years older than Sidney. She was born when our mom was touring with the Fat Cats. Sidney's dad is King Sidney, and he and Mom were together until Mom went crazy and they had to put her away. King couldn't take care of Sidney, so my dad swooped in and saved the day. Truth be told, Dad was always down for Mom like that. I'm not sure, but I think Mom called him when they first took her away and she asked him this one last favor: please take care of Sidney Lewis, my sister. The daughter of another man, one whom she refused to give his name. She did the same with me when I was born, Indigo Lewis, her name. Mom was adamant. The Lewis children would be just that, the Lewis children.

Dad talked to King, and the next thing I knew Sidney was moving in and Dad was watching YouTube videos and teaching himself how to build a bedroom from a closet. Dad told Sidney, "You can call me Ben or Dad. Whichever you prefer."

The first time he heard her say Mr. Ben, his shoulders dropped, and his mouth fell open in surprise. I guess she had preferred to call him Mr. Ben. I think he wanted her to call him dad, and he had just realized it in that moment. It had been four months since her arrival, and she still called him Mr. Ben. Today I winced for him.

Sidney took a seat on a stool, swinging her feet at the kitchen counter. Dad sat his version of scrambled eggs in front of Sidney. I didn't know why she asked for eggs anyway; Dad's strong suit was not cooking, but he would try.

"Thank you." She nodded at him and glared at me. I smirked.

"What's wrong with my eggs? I saw those eyes," Dad grabbed at his chest, playing hurt. "Besides, you need protein for hockey."

"You didn't put cheese on them or anything," I chuckled.

Sidney pushed the eggs around on her plate before she pierced it with a fork and stuck it in my face.

"Ahhh, what are you doing?" I screeched.

"You eat the struggle eggs, that's what you get for hitting me with that pillow," Sidney teased.

3

I pushed them away from me and giggled.

"I'll eat at school." Sidney eyed the eggs and shrugged at Dad.

He put his hands on his hips and shrugged. "Don't go tell them people at school you're hungry when you have perfectly good food right here."

Sidney snorted and slinked off the stool heading back to our room, and I soon followed.

"Somebody better eat these eggs," Dad yelled down the hall. Sidney and I chuckled to each other.

Tuesday was the longest day of the week for me, Sidney, and Dad. He works at the retirement home 10 a.m.-6 a.m. the next morning. Sidney plays Field Hockey and every Tuesday she had double practice and game sessions. I'm the school editor of the Tunica Rivers High School Newspaper Club, and on Tuesdays I meet with the team and we review articles and the layout for the next edition.

My boyfriend Malachi and his friend Jaxon are planning the TRHS annual Spring Fling for the senior class in April. It was poised to be one for the books, and we were all excited to learn more information about it today.

Checking my phone, I realized how late I was. Malachi would be here in thirty minutes with his mom's car to take us to school. Malachi lives across town and has to pass by our high school to pick me up. I keep telling him how dumb that was. Why trek all the way across town for me? He doesn't have to prove to me he's some chivalrous gentleman, but he insists on making the hike every morning.

I showered and brushed my teeth. I pressed mousse into my hands, and I spread it over my braids. My hair stayed in braids. It was quick, and I knew it looked nice on me and framed my deep brown skin. I liked my braids jet black and long. My mom taught me that—always keep your hair done.

Sidney was more into press and curls these days. She was hanging out with her hockey teammates and lately, she was obsessed with straight, flat hair. I made a mental note to watch that....Today, I opted for a long, boho dress which came to my ankles with my white leggings underneath. It flowed as I walked. I paired it with my all black chucks and my Mom's locket around my neck.

"Bye Dad, love you!" I shouted.

"Love you!" he hollered back. He retired to his room where he was catching another hour or two of Z's before he went to work.

"Bye, Sid!" I screamed. She turned up her music, and I heard Tekashi 69 blaring from her room.

Kids.

Outside smelled damp. I inhaled and let the sun hit my face from over the treetops. I took a seat at the picnic table next to the boathouse. It wasn't even a boathouse. We had three canoes Ez uses. That's my mom's dad, and he lives on the other side of the lake. His name is Ezra, but we call him Grandpa Ez. He doesn't like to drive, even though he has a car. Imagine that, a grownup who doesn't like to drive. I would kill to always have transportation ready and available to me. Grandpa Ez preferred to use the canoes, and every few days, I watched him paddle in. He made his way closer and closer, and I saw his overalls and straw hat from the boat. He wore an enormous grin, and his large arms bulged when he cut through the water towards us.

"Gimme dat other paddle over there, girl," he commanded. Grandpa Ez's voice boomed and even though he stood almost seven foot and loomed over people, he was a gentle giant. My mom says he "gets a crazy check every month," whatever that meant. She had some nerve.

He was my Grandpa Ez.

The familiar hum of Malachi's mom's car makes its way down our cul-de-sac. Gathering my things from the table, I made my way to his car. He opened the door from the inside and waited for me to get in and shut the door before he placed the wettest, sloppiest kisses on my face and cheeks. I laughed, pushing him away, and we took off for school.

CHAPTER 2

MALACHI AND I were in the editor's room for the Newspaper Club and we were the first ones here. He sat in front of his computer, and he didn't even bother to even log-in. The TRHS screensaver rolled around on his screen.

I've been the Newspaper Club Editor for the past two years. I sort of fell into the job. Words have always been my favorite. Most people just see them as means to communicate, but I see them as full pictures. When I hear songs, I see the lyrics. Words, numbers, and symbols roll around in my head until they form sentences. It sounds weird, but it happens. I hated writing at first, it just seemed like a waste of time, and it was always something teachers wanted you to do. Who wants to do what teachers want them to do? I was a reader. I guess people think they are the same, but to me — they were totally separate. I could read the words and craft perfect stories in my mind, but to write it out was something different. When I was twelve, I received my first piece of mail with my name on it. It was from Black Expressions mail-in book club and the postcard read, "Send us a dollar and we'll send you six books."

Six books?

I rushed to fill out the postcard, hastily marking off my book choices before taking a dollar from Dad's dresser and sending it back. I grabbed an envelope and a stamp from Mom's purse, and I sent that baby back. A few weeks later my six books arrived, and every two weeks after that, more and more books came. I spent long days and nights combing through those books, piecing together my thoughts about the world around me. Everything seemed so open for the taking and ready to be explored.

I vowed then I would see it all and do as much as opportunity and money would let me. I wouldn't be stuck in Tunica Rivers—I would see the world. One day, a bill showed up in the mail. It was addressed to me again, and that's when Mom found out I was taking dollar bills and stamps from their room and buying books. I thought for sure Mom would lose her shit on me, but she didn't. She called up the book company and said, "Ya'll ain't got no business selling no books to a twelve-year-old girl, anyway! Don't send nothing else to this house!"

Halima was the editor before me, and last year I was sitting in homeroom when she tapped on the door, walked right in without waiting, and asked our homeroom teacher if she could speak to me. I was shocked; I had never seen a Black girl walk right into a room, address a white man, and he obliged! Maybe that was the reason I followed her out that day. She said, "I work with Mrs. Scott, the English Department Chair. I've been able to read some of your papers and poetry submissions. Have you ever thought of writing as more than a hobby? I think you're good." From then on, I took her position as Editor of the school newspaper when my senior year started. I grew up in this editor room, and I tried to build a strong team around me. We argued here. We laughed here. We tried to make sense of the world through our eyes—all here.

Putting out a once a month newspaper as teenagers was difficult. There was always a teacher or someone telling us what we could or couldn't say, but they were the same ones teaching us about censorship and how the great writers of the world did it. They described them as fearless, visionaries. However, they wanted us to idly listen and be inspired but not act. I'm not sure how those two went together, if they even did. I tried to inform the school of current events but not enough to keep administration on my back about it. It was a delicate dance of keeping two sides happy and one I knew well.

Tunica Rivers High School sat on the edge of town where the big houses were. Our cottage house somehow made it just past the county line touching the border, otherwise, I would've gone to the neighborhood high school, which wasn't the best. Mila walked in with her small car keys swinging in her hand.

"Ya'll kissing again?" she rolled her eyes.

Mila was my favorite white girl. She had long brown hair, and she's played softball ever since she was a kid, so she has those super toned legs. I told her she was the thickest white girl I've ever seen, but she never sees that as a compliment. Funny, what one thinks is a compliment another sees as their sore spot.

Mila sat her bag next to me and leaned closer. "I need your help with something, Indy."

"What, you pregnant!?" My eyes widened.

She snatched my arm and said, "Shut up!"

We giggled.

"I filled out the application for City College, but they need a $50 fee. Can you help me?"

I froze. When I joined the Newspaper Club, she joined, too, even though she preferred the photography editorials and excelled at those. When Mila told her mom, Ms. Janet, she wanted to go to college and maybe even take up photography, Ms. Janet flat out told her they couldn't afford it, and

9

she should get a job down in the factory with her and their family. Mila never asked her again about anything college related, but we helped each other as best as we could. That was our secret we shared.

"Of course, girl. I thought you had something serious to say," I nodded.

She shrugged her shoulders. She never wanted to talk long about the important things. Mila and I were probably an odd pair. Admittedly, she was my only close white friend, and I loved her, nonetheless. When she and I were in elementary school, I was on the playground and my fake ponytail and bang combo flew off my head while I was mid cartwheel. The ribbons and butterfly clips Mom added in remained, but the white teachers who knew nothing about a pony-and-bang combo stood around with my hair in their hands discussing what to do. Eventually they sent me to the main office with my hair labeled in a zip lock bag. The secretaries in the front office were the only Black staff in the building, and I guess they thought it smart to let us handle us.

When I moped into the office, I met the prettiest white girl with the bluest eyes I had ever seen. Mila.

I heard her pleading to one of the secretaries, "Please Mrs. Johnson, I'll pay it back. My mom didn't have the money this week."

"I'm sorry, Mila, but those are the rules. You can't keep borrowing lunch money from the school and not paying it back. Tell your mom to send us a check to make your account current. You'll have to eat the brown bag lunch today." Mrs. Johnson closed and locked her big book of negative lunch accounts.

I had a few extra bucks that day Dad had stuffed in my pocket, and I bought Mila a bag of chips during lunch. We were best friends from then on.

Loud crunching sounds escaped Malachi while he ate his chips and flipped through articles, still with no computer turned on. Mila and I peeked at his greasy fingers from here and we rolled our eyes. I handed him a napkin and with no words, he took it from me and grinned.

I peeked my head outside of the room when Will, and all six foot five inches of him, came barreling through the door so fast he almost ran me down.

"What the hell, Will! Damn!" I yelped.

"Ugh, Indy! My fault, I didn't even see you there." His height made him tower over people. Will steadied me as I fell into him. Out of the corner of my eye, I watched Malachi not flinch or make a move. He was too busy eating his chips—now with headphones on.

I rolled my eyes. He never paid attention.

Malachi works at the movie theater, and I loved the cinema. Watching movies was the equivalent to reading books; I saw the words on paper and now I got to see them translated onto the big screen. Every Tuesday during the summer, they had a buy one movie and get one free deal in town. I was first in line for the matinee every Tuesday. Although the four of us had always been friends, Malachi and I grew close that summer—through the movies. We began dating. Not long after, Will and Mila tried their hand at dating. I'm not sure what happened, because each of them don't speak on it often, but Will said they were better off as friends and nothing more. Even Mila was tight-lipped about it, and she was never tight-lipped about anything. I glimpsed something in Mila's eye when Will walked into the room. I wondered what that was about. My calendar alert on my phone went off, reminding me that our meeting started in fifteen minutes. We were still waiting for a few people to arrive.

"Indy, I picked this up for you the other day at the flea market." Will handed me a small clay piece. Lifting it up, I

11

examined the imperfect cracks and examined its glaze. It was clay molded in the shape of a letter I.

"Thanks, Will, this is so cool," I whispered. Will knew my mom and I used to throw pottery together. I mentioned it one day while we were sitting by the water out back at my house.

"Mila, look at this," I waved her over.

She sashayed towards us and examined the piece. "Cute." Looking up at Will, she punched him in the arm. "Awww, he's Drakin' again."

Will's face flushed as he shushed Mila. They walked away together, laughing.

After their breakup, Mila decided Will was emotional, and because he was considered high yellow with his tan skin, he reminded her of Drake. Every time he did something that Mila deemed soft, she called it 'Drakin.' I thought it was sweet, but Mila put him on blast about it now and then.

Sometimes they could be weird.

When I thought I figured out their friendship or relationship, they both threw me off in some way. I was just glad we were still the foursome, at least for the rest of this year before we graduated and things changed.

The rest of the team arrived, and I stood at the front of the room, glancing everyone over. Shantiel was here. She was always first. Nico and Trish Ann. Good. Everyone was here.

"I think we should jump right into the Spring Fling; that's the first thing we have to cover." Trish Ann blurted from her seat. Her gum snapped loudly.

I peeped at Shantiel. She shook her head and pursed her lips at Trish Ann. These two.

Shantiel was a junior, but she was about her business. If she played her cards right, she could be the next editor in her senior year; she was the only one who was serious enough to take the helm.

"We still have another three months before we need to cover that," Shantiel reminded. "What else will we write about until then?"

Trish Ann slumped in her seat.

"We could do a countdown. Something like, all the events that take place beforehand and the preparation that goes into planning something like Spring Fling?" Malachi suggested.

Malachi's assessment was partially correct. We could cover the preparation beforehand, but he described the event as little Coachella. Spring Fling was always a one last-hoorah party chaperoned by staff members in a rented hall. How wild could things get?

"Plus, this year Jaxon Green said his parents will pay for everything," Malachi added.

I stopped talking. "Pay for everything?"

A portion of the Newspaper Club stipend was always used to help pay for Spring Fling. This year we wanted it to be nice and go out with a bang. With Jaxon Green footing the bill, maybe that was possible.

"I was going to tell you later, he wants to meet with you to go over the details. I invited him to the meeting today, but I guess he couldn't make it," Malachi reported.

"But why would he want to do that?" Mila questioned.

Exactly, I thought. Jaxon Green was one of the rich kids in town. He and Malachi played on the football team together and now he was offering to foot the bill? Didn't make sense. And why does he want to meet with me?

Malachi must've read my mind. He said, "He wants to meet with you because he said he has some project he wants you to help him with for college. Said his mom follows your newspaper column and thinks you can help. I guess she's a fan."

Wow…I mused. Besides the school newspaper, I wrote a monthly teen blog for our *Tunica Rivers Times*. I didn't know

the newspaper had that kind of reach. Jaxon Green and his parents were loaded, and somehow, they found my small articles.

"Okay," I finally nodded. Maybe we could use Jaxon Green as an option.

I turned back to the whiteboard and began writing. "I like all of those ideas, but we still need more."

"We always have our old faithful," Nico suggested. "We could rent the banquet hall in town."

"Nahhh," we all groaned.

We have held events for so long at the old banquet hall in town that my mom told me that when she was in high school at TRHS, she wrote her phone number in the third stall from the right, in the men's bathroom. One night we were there for a school event, and I couldn't help myself. I was with Will and he said he would go look for the number since it was the men's bathroom, but I had to see for myself. While Will held watch at the door, I entered the men's bathroom third stall. Sure enough, I found my Mom's name and handwriting. I traced it with my finger, pretending I was her that long ago.

"Did you find it?" Will asked with wide eyes.

I grinned and nodded. Memories of my mom were everywhere and in everything.

I snapped out of my thoughts. "Shantiel, how is it looking for the college corner for the football team?"

Shantiel shuffled through her notebook before landing on a full page of words. "It looks like we're interviewing one of them so far, Eric Lagares."

"Just one?"

"No one else signed up," she lifted an eyebrow.

Shantiel and Will were interviewing incoming senior football players who were interviewing the outgoing senior football players. School do's and don'ts. This piece was one of the school's most popular, and I put Mila in charge of the flyer and interviews.

"How can we only have one sign up? The flyer has been out for over two weeks, right, Mila?" I turned towards her. And why didn't Malachi sign up? He was on the team too.

"Uhhh…Malachi and I swapped assignments." Mila looked down and said nothing else.

"Why would y'all make that change and not tell me?"

"I meant to tell you," Mila said. "It was my fault. I forgot. I got sidetracked and I figured since Malachi was on the team, he could just ask them."

My eye twitched.

She swapped tasks with Malachi, and now, we had one person signed up for the event when this time last year we had at least a dozen.

"Malachi? Anything?" I turned towards him, and he was chugging down juice. He gulped and wiped his mouth with the back of his hand.

"I forgot, Indy. I'm sorry. I'll talk to the guys today and have some of them sign up."

Malachi tried hard, but he was definitely our weakest link. Sometimes if I gave him an assignment, he would return it with large parts of the story missing. He had names and dates wrong. We had to issue a retraction once based on him dishing out incorrect information. This was our senior year, and I just couldn't bring myself to fire my boyfriend in the fourth quarter, so I let him stay. But like Santa, I made a list and had to check it twice with Malachi.

"I mean, do we have to do that article?" Will asked.

My fist gripped the computer chair as I swung my head around. "Seriously, Will?"

"Hear me out, I'm just saying. They've done that same article in the exact same way for years. Why not switch it up?"

15

"And what do you suggest? Trish-Ann quizzed.

"This has always been the final senior piece. It's always been that way," I scoffed.

"I don't know, Indy. I have no ideas. I'm just saying, let's do something different."

I rolled my eyes at Will. "Yes, we have to do it. It's tradition and administration loves this one."

Will leaned back in his chair and shrugged.

"Is there anything we're missing from any of the other pieces? So, everyone knows what they're supposed to do?" This question was really for Malachi since we already established at our last meeting the articles we would write. I glanced around the room. "Malachi?"

Everyone shook their heads no, and Malachi choked a little on his sunflower seeds when I said his name.

"Yes, I'm on it, Indy." He gave me a nod and a salute.

"Okay, good meeting guys, let's get started with our assignments." I closed my book.

The team gathered their bags and shuffled out of the room.

"Anyone want to grab burgers?" Will raised an eyebrow.

"I'm always down for that," Malachi rubbed his stomach. He never paid attention to anything unless it involved food.

I placed my things in my bag without saying a word.

"C'mon, babe. I'm sorry," Malachi said. "Let's fight it out over burgers."

"I'll drive," Mila offered, flashing a smile now. She said little during the meeting, and even though she smiled, her eyes looked far away.

"Fine, let's go."

Mila and I walked out together with the boys in front of us.

"I'm sorry girl, I've had a lot on my mind."

"You good?" I stopped her in the hallway. "For real?"

"Yes, I'm fine," she nodded. "It's just this college thing."

"You know I got you. We'll figure that out."

Mila gave a pensive smile.

"Y'all still back there having your catfight? Let's roll." Malachi danced. Will towered next to him, waiting for us.

I loved my crew. Flaws and all.

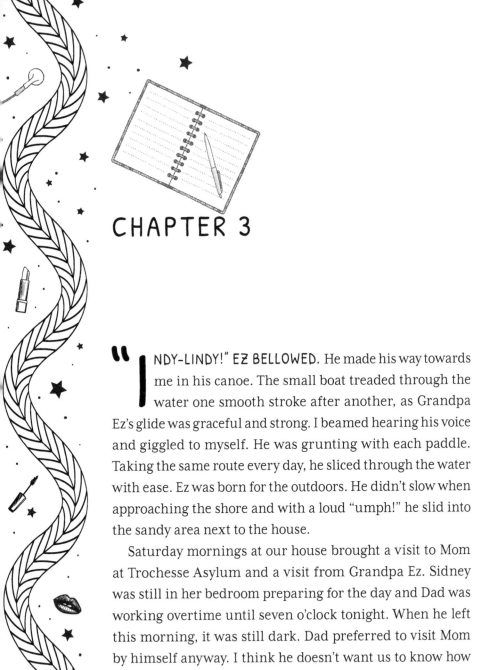

CHAPTER 3

"**I**NDY-LINDY!" **EZ BELLOWED.** He made his way towards me in his canoe. The small boat treaded through the water one smooth stroke after another, as Grandpa Ez's glide was graceful and strong. I beamed hearing his voice and giggled to myself. He was grunting with each paddle. Taking the same route every day, he sliced through the water with ease. Ez was born for the outdoors. He didn't slow when approaching the shore and with a loud "umph!" he slid into the sandy area next to the house.

Saturday mornings at our house brought a visit to Mom at Trochesse Asylum and a visit from Grandpa Ez. Sidney was still in her bedroom preparing for the day and Dad was working overtime until seven o'clock tonight. When he left this morning, it was still dark. Dad preferred to visit Mom by himself anyway. I think he doesn't want us to know how often he makes his way up there. Every two weeks Sidney, Ez, and I made the trip to see mom. I enjoy the scenery because it's the only time I get out of Tunica Rivers. Watching the seasons change and checking out car bumper stickers was a welcomed change of pace. When we drove, I thought about the other people on the highway. Were they good folk? What kind of secrets did they hold?

"Where is SidRock?" Ez demands. His eye twinkles and his lips curled. Grandpa Ez's voice boomed loudly, and to people who didn't know him, he was probably scary. I knew him better though. That boom was laced with love for us. He called Sidney, SidRock. He explained, "She's a kid, and she's my little kid rock—that's my SidRock." Just stuck, I guess.

"She's still getting ready," I told Grandpa Ez. He pulled me towards him in a big bear hug and lifted me off my feet. My sneakers slid across the dampened sand and Ez squeezed the wind out of my chest.

"Grandpa Ez, how long did it take you to cut across the lake today?"

Today Ez wore a stained white t-shirt and khaki pants cuffed at his ankles. He pulled a pocket watch from his pants and it creaked open. "Oh, about twenty minutes."

"Oh, about twenty minutes," he says. He spent more time on the water than anyone in Tunica Rivers—and we were water people. It took thirty minutes by car to get to Ez's house from ours, but he preferred the water. His muscular arms told on him, and his dark brown skin looked almost black when he came gliding through the water at night. Mama Jackie passed away a few years ago, and Dad says Ez ain't been right since he lost her. I don't think any of us are.

"Ez, are you wearing that?" I glanced at his t-shirt.

Ez looked down at himself and back at me. "What's wrong with this, girl?"

"Nothing."

I patted my pockets and realized I didn't have my cell phone. I ran back in the house and grabbed it and saw a missed call from an unsaved number. It also texted me.

19

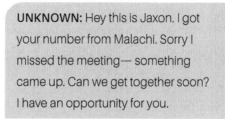

UNKNOWN: Hey this is Jaxon. I got your number from Malachi. Sorry I missed the meeting— something came up. Can we get together soon? I have an opportunity for you.

An opportunity? I paused. What could he have that was an opportunity for me? I was busting my ass to make it through high school and then college, and then to watch Sidney do the same. Jaxon came from money, had money, and he would probably make even more money without trying. I envied people like him. They never seemed to worry about the hard things because it didn't seem hard to them. No roadblocks—just opportunities.

I peered at Sidney in her room. She was pacing in the small area and the way she moved halted me to a stop. She was folding and refolding the same blanket. Two and three times she did this. Picking it up and placing it back down.

"Sid?" My voice cracked. I cleared my throat.

She jumped in place.

"What are you doing?"

"Nothing, I-I was folding my blanket." She touched the fabric one last time before shutting her light off behind her. "Ez here?"

"Yes, he just pulled up." I eyed her, "You okay?"

"I'm fine, just worried about the visit."

"It'll be fine. She knows we're coming this time," My voice was soft and I tried to shield Sidney from the hurt that parents sometimes caused in the ways only a big sister could understand.

"You're right, Ez is with us." Sidney whispered.

The last time we visited Mom, we took a bus and Sidney and I went alone. Mom cursed us. She was loud and showing off her musical chops as she rapped through the room. Sidney cried, and I didn't know what to do, so I called Dad from work and asked him to pick us up. He took the highway and was there in less than thirty minutes. After that, Dad made us vow we would never go there alone anymore.

"Oh wait, I have to grab Ez's shirt." Sid dashed to the dryer in the pantry and returned with a checkered button-up shirt.

"His?" I pointed.

"I figured he would need one, you know, like last time."

Sid was right. Our last visit almost didn't happen. Ez wore a wife-beater white T-shirt, and they refused to let him into Trochesse. We had to leave, run to a store, and buy him a shirt so we could see Mom that day. Ez fussed the entire time and said he didn't like the way the material felt on his skin. He picked at it the whole time we were there and practically ripped it off himself when we left the visit. Ez could be funny about stuff like that.

"Good thinking, I think he has on dirty clothes" I admitted. Sidney shook her head and seemed so much older than her ten years.

"I figured," she nodded and walked out of the room.

I heard the back-door creak as Sidney walked out and Ez screamed, "Siddrocckkk!"

Sitting on my bed, I chuckled to myself and grabbed my phone. Malachi picked up my video call after one ring.

"Don't be giving my phone number to strangers; they could sweep me off my feet." I batted my eyes.

"Huh?" He chewed. He was eating a bowl of cereal.

"Jaxon Green?"

"Oh yeah. He asked for your number after flaking on the meeting. Just see what he has to say—could be good for both of you. He mentioned something about your blog with the Tunica Rivers Times."

"Oh? I thought he wanted something school related?"

21

"I don't know, just repeating what he said," Malachi shoved a large spoon into his mouth.

"Did you pour the entire box of cereal?" I asked with wide eyes. Malachi was eating from a large serving bowl and spoon.

"Mom just went food shopping."

I snorted, "that's not an answer."

He shrugged.

"What time are you leaving?" His head was crouched in the bowl as he asked.

"In about twenty minutes. Ez just got here."

"Ol' Smoky Jo made his way across the great Mississippi River?"

"Shut up!" I giggled.

"The first time I saw him racing through the water on that little tugboat, I said, now there is a man whose granddaughter I'd like to date."

Malachi and I fell into a fit of cackles. Hearing wood being chopped, I squinted from my window and saw Ez using Dad's ax to finish hacking at a tree. His shirt was now off, and he was bare-chested and sweating.

"I got to go," I rushed.

"I love you; look at me. Don't be too hard on her. Okay?"

"Love you too." I pressed end and Malachi's face disappeared. I wasn't too hard on my mom. At least I didn't think so.

Outside, Sid slid into the front seat of Ez's car while he stopped to tinker with the tires. Grandpa Ez's car was as old as he was. It was a goldish brown color with sunspots splattered across the top and roof. It was funny, his yard was filled with junk cars but the car that actually worked he kept at our house. "We'll make it today. Not a coola in sight." He nodded at us.

"When have we not made it?" Sid giggled.

Ez has these random one liners. It's like he thinks about something, but he just has to say it out loud. Just has to. 'Coola' is code for problem. Mom told me when she was younger, Mama Jackie and Ez couldn't afford a refrigerator, so they used large coolers. When the ice inside the cooler melted, Ez would groan, 'The coola is gone, the coola is gone.' Now, if anything was a coola, it's his version of a problem.

Sliding in the backseat, I popped in my headphones. My phone buzzed again. It was a text from Will.

WILL: Have a good visit

ME: Thanx

Chris Brown sang in my ear, and I closed my eyes. Grandpa Ez pumped the brakes and his old Cutlass roared to life. The car was old and loud — I called it The Bus whenever we drove; it was just as noisy. Sid fumbled with the radio and turned the dial louder.

"Jackie!" Grandpa Ez yelped. When he was angry, we became Jackie to Ez. "Turn that noise down, you trying to scramble the rest of my brains?" He covered his ears. He didn't like loud noises either. I think this was partly the reason he kept his car at our house and used the canoe. When the bus and its missing muffler clamored down the road, the noise couldn't be missed. He said the water was quiet and everything else seemed to scream at him. Sidney lowered the music and Grandpa Ez slowly pulled from the driveway. He used his blinker to reverse. Why, I don't know.

The trip to see Mom usually takes forty-five minutes, but Ez drives below the speed limit. People beeped around us, honked their horns, and a few even gave the middle finger. A few tense visits back we discovered driving on the highway was not his favorite, and he jumped and screeched at cars honking and large semi-trucks. It was a sight to see; my grandfather

23

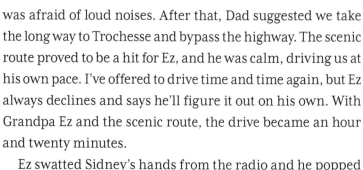

was afraid of loud noises. After that, Dad suggested we take the long way to Trochesse and bypass the highway. The scenic route proved to be a hit for Ez, and he was calm, driving us at his own pace. I've offered to drive time and time again, but Ez always declines and says he'll figure it out on his own. With Grandpa Ez and the scenic route, the drive became an hour and twenty minutes.

Ez swatted Sidney's hands from the radio and he popped in a cassette tape. "Ya'll don't know nothing about this," he crooned.

Ez's loud baritone voice echoed through the car, and he sang at the top of his lungs. Ez could carry a note! It surprised me even though it shouldn't since Mom could sing too. Ez's voice was so full of life. Sidney and I shared a glance and grinned.

About an hour later, we arrived at Trochesse Asylum. Wiping sleep from the corner of my eyes, I adjusted to my surroundings. Scores of people lined up to get inside. I saw children and families, some appeared happy to be here and others looked guilted; their presence required by their needy, inpatient families. Some days I understood that feeling. Trochesse brought me sunshine and happiness when I needed to see my mom. To touch her and reach out, look into her eyes and see my own staring back at me. I was the highlight of her week and for that reason—I had to go. It was a cycle I hated.

Sidney was out of the car first and slammed the door behind her. She wore a black baseball cap, red checkered flannel shirt, and jeans. I opted for a TRHS hoodie, sneakers, and jeans. My braids hung down my back to my waistline. Ez moaned, exited the car, and placed his gigantic hands on the hood to steady himself. The car sank under his weight. Ez adjusted his pants, pulling them even higher around his broad waist. He straightened his new shirt that Sidney gave him, and he fumbled with the buttons under his neck. He was sweating at his brow line as he fussed with the collar, tugging it from his neck. "Ya'll ladies reckon' you ready, Freddy?" he said.

I shook my head at him and walked towards the end of the line. "Insane asylum for the colored." That's what the sign read. I hated this part. Sometimes when we got in line, we made it early enough to the front and I didn't have to see it. Sometimes we got here late and stood at the end where the large cinder block glimmered back at us and got larger and larger as we made our way closer.

Back in the day, Trochesse Asylum had two wings; the right wing was the white side, and the left side was the colored side. I eyed this sign whenever we got in line. I wondered what it meant to be a Black woman in an "insane asylum," during a time when no one cared you were actually insane; they categorized you by your skin. As if your skin was the crime, not the act which got you there. The asylum integrated sometime in the 70s, but the sign remained. You think the first thing they'd remove is the symbols reminding people they were not the same and not equal. But no—they kept them up. Every two weeks I stood in line and bore witness to this sign. And to make matters worse, my mom—a Black woman with medium skin and maximum character was housed on the left side. Poetic justice.

Ez placed his hand on my head. He stared at me. "Don't be taking on nothin' that ain't yours." He motioned to the sign. The line moved and Ez and I brandished our IDs to the security guards, while Sidney flashed her school ID. They checked us for weapons and drugs but did a poor job. The female guards brushed over my clothes while talking amongst themselves. They never glanced in my direction or made eye contact. The male security stood with hands on their wide hips, showing us how much they loved the sweets in the break room. A few visits ago, a family next to our table had a full feast complete

with rice, beans, and biscuits. How and where they snuck food in; I don't want to know. Clearly security was lax.

The inside of Trochesse Asylum opened into a large foyer area with cathedral ceilings and a second-floor balcony overlooking the entrance. The floor was checkered with black-and-white tiles, and on the walls were erect, naked white people. Strange décor I thought, for an insane asylum. Built-in wall book-shelves and carved wood balusters lined the great room. A wide, spiral staircase spilled into the room at the foot of the nurses' station in the center of it all. There were three nurses, all of them standing on their feet in their bubble fielding questions, phone calls, med requests, or general cuss-outs. This morning my mom was the one giving the cuss out.

"Whherreee is my phone call? This ain't no damn jail and I need to call my peoples." Mom glared, slammed her hands on the nurse's station and pointed at the nurse. "Is you gon' let me use the phone? I got to call my man. It's Saturday morning and he better be home from getting his haircut. It's 11:10! He's late again. I know where he at…Ohhh yeah, I know where he at." Mom's shrill voice echoed through the room.

I swallowed.

Looking up at Ez, he watched Mom. His face was hard, and he didn't move.

"Ma?" Sidney's soft voice cut through us.

Mom's eyes widened, turning towards Sidney. She glanced at her, then me and Ez.

"I'll be back, Hoe," she pointed to the nurse.

"Bye, Ms. Lewis." The nurse shooed Mom away from the station and nodded at me.

"My children, my lifelines, hellooo hellooo," Mom sang. She now talked in an English accent. Mom wore a long blue housecoat, tights, and white crocs. Her hair was short and tapered to one side. The last time we saw her it was long, but this shorter cut framed her chubby face better and elongated her neck. Mom was heavy set with soft brown skin.

Sidney latched onto Mom and hugged her. Mom stopped moving and held Sidney's head to her chest. "Come here Indy-Lindy." Mom pulled me in, and I held on to her and Sidney. Mom's hair smelled like soap. Not the good kind of soap Malachi's mom keeps in her shower. The kind of soap that's free and you can ask for extras. Whenever I saw her she gained weight, and today I used two hands to hug her large waist. Her skin was still the smoothest I ever felt; almost like silk. Or like Ez's. Hugging Mom felt like climbing out of a nice, long shower into clean sheets and rubbing your legs together. For a second, everything is still and peaceful.

Shoving us, Mom eyed Ez and sang, "Who loves you like ya Daddy girl, who loves you like your Pappy girl, never leave your side, you're his worlddd..." She bellowed her last note into Ez's face as he stood in front of her. Soon, he cracked a smile.

Everyone else sat with their families while Mom stood singing in front of Ez. The room was cold, and all the families sat close together at long metal tables attached to the floors, savoring every moment. Her voice was beautiful and obnoxious, all at the same time. Mom's nurse cleared her throat in our direction and motioned with her eyes for Mom to quiet down. Mom sauntered to the last empty table off to the corner of the room. When we settled, she said, "So would anyone like any tea, darlings?" in her English voice.

"Cut it out." Ez was curt. He was never fond of Mom's voice changes and the dramatics of it all.

"Why my loving Dadddyyy?" She pouted in her English voice. Mom pronounced every syllable.

Ez's jaw tightened.

Dad said Mom began saying she was a different person in her teens, and Ez and Mama Jackie didn't understand it. They

27

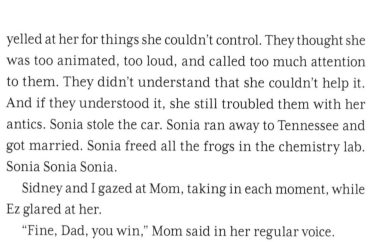

yelled at her for things she couldn't control. They thought she was too animated, too loud, and called too much attention to them. They didn't understand that she couldn't help it. And if they understood it, she still troubled them with her antics. Sonia stole the car. Sonia ran away to Tennessee and got married. Sonia freed all the frogs in the chemistry lab. Sonia Sonia Sonia.

Sidney and I gazed at Mom, taking in each moment, while Ez glared at her.

"Fine, Dad, you win," Mom said in her regular voice.

"I don't like all that nonsense." Ez's voice was gruff.

"Sidney, how is your Father?" Mom's eyes remained on Ez.

"He's okay. The boys keep him running around." Sidney has two older brothers: Prince and Trent. They're both excellent dancers and last I heard; they were touring with Mary J. Blige. The musical gene was in their family, and King traveled the world with them, managing their careers. When he realized Sidney didn't have any musical talents and she required a full-time dad, King didn't hesitate and may have breathed a sigh of relief when Dad offered our home. He sent money once in a blue moon, but Dad held it down for us girls. Mom never asked about Dad. Only King.

"I dreamt of Mama Jackie last night... She was sitting by the lake and she said, 'Sunnie, what's that you got over there?' I had a cigarette I was hiding from Mama. She came down there and found me puffing from it. I knew for sure she'd kick my ass. But she came to me and took the cigarette out of my mouth. She puffed it two times and said, "These things will kill ya," and she stomped it out before sending me back upstairs...did she ever tell you that, Dad?"

Grandpa Ez took his cap off and palmed his face in his hand.

"The memories too much for you, Daddy?" Mom sneered.

"Enough, Mom," I warned.

She turned to me and her eyes softened.

"My firstttt loveeee," she sang louder this time.

Mom's nurse eyed us again above her glasses.

"I know you just love coming to see your Dear Mother in Versailles," Mom rose from her chair and danced around us.

Ez remained silent in his chair, arms folded.

Sidney followed Mom around the room and her eyes danced with wonder. She held onto Mom's every word. She was nervous earlier, but now she was in awe.

"I'm okay. This is senior year," I reminded her.

"Senior year, huh; I hope ain't no one seen ya' cooty cat," she tee-heed and slapped her knees.

Ez pushed his chair back on the linoleum, and it made a loud screech. He unbuttoned the top of his shirt from his neck. "I'm going for a walk," he scowled.

"Cooty cat," Sidney repeated. She placed her hands to her mouth, stifling a giggle.

"My Bellas, come close, let's have girl talk." Mom shimmied in her seat. Sidney and I moved closer and closed the gap between us.

"I have a secret to tell you." She shrugged her shoulders. "I don't know if I can tell you though."

"You can tell me, Mom," Sidney promised. Her eyes were wide.

Please don't say something crazy in front of Sidney, my eyes pleaded.

Mom's eyes didn't catch mine. Or maybe they did. She leaned in close, and said, "I had another dream too." She smiled crazily, her mouth open.

"You kill someone, Indigo…you did what you had to do…I liked that dream." She threw her head back and cackled to herself.

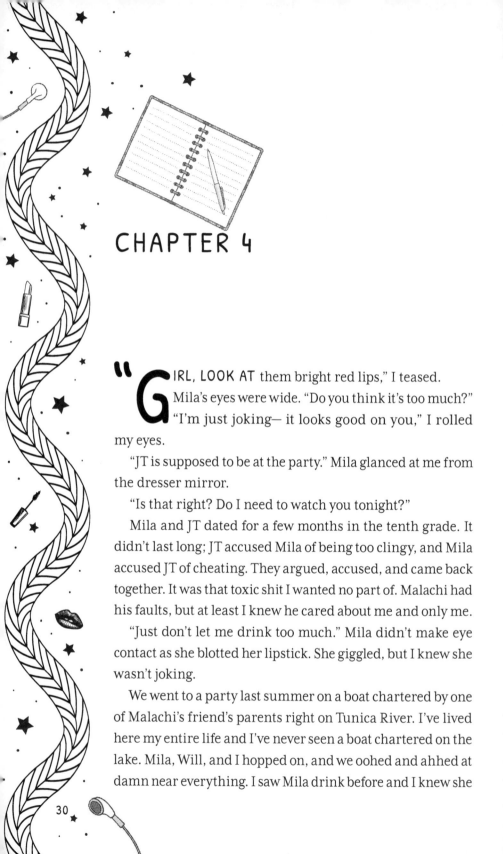

CHAPTER 4

"**G**IRL, LOOK AT them bright red lips," I teased.

Mila's eyes were wide. "Do you think it's too much?"

"I'm just joking— it looks good on you," I rolled my eyes.

"JT is supposed to be at the party." Mila glanced at me from the dresser mirror.

"Is that right? Do I need to watch you tonight?"

Mila and JT dated for a few months in the tenth grade. It didn't last long; JT accused Mila of being too clingy, and Mila accused JT of cheating. They argued, accused, and came back together. It was that toxic shit I wanted no part of. Malachi had his faults, but at least I knew he cared about me and only me.

"Just don't let me drink too much." Mila didn't make eye contact as she blotted her lipstick. She giggled, but I knew she wasn't joking.

We went to a party last summer on a boat chartered by one of Malachi's friend's parents right on Tunica River. I've lived here my entire life and I've never seen a boat chartered on the lake. Mila, Will, and I hopped on, and we oohed and ahhed at damn near everything. I saw Mila drink before and I knew she could throw them back, but this night was different. Drinking wasn't really my thing; I hated the way it tasted going down. Maybe I did it wrong because it sat in the base of my throat, threatening to come back up. You know, now that I think about it, I don't think that I've ever been drunk. I don't think I've ever drunk enough alcohol to consider myself drunk. But Mila—Mila couldn't stop. She took in more and more. It was one thing to drink for senior year with your friends, but Mila liked to get blackout drunk. Especially when she wasn't the one footing the bill.

My phone buzzed in my pocket, and I took it out. Another message from Jaxon Green.

JAXON: ???

ME: We can talk tonight.

I saved Jaxon Green's phone number as a new contact and placed it back in my pocket.

Dad was working another double, and Sidney was with her brothers this weekend. The unofficial senior class Christmas celebration was underway tonight. It's unofficial because if any school staff find out, my name is Bennett, 'cuz I ain't in it. We all took that stance. Rumor has it a couple years ago someone was drinking after the party and was found sprawled out naked on the principal's front lawn. Since then, the school has been extra vigilant about shutting down senior class parties.

Mila was in my mirror applying lip gloss over her red lipstick and I had all my drawers open, trying to figure out what to wear. Malachi told me he was going to wear his jean jacket and I should wear mine too. I wanted to do my own thing today, and so I pulled for my black leather jacket instead. It stopped just above my waist and if I turned at just the right

moment, on just the right hip, it looked like I had some behind. I paired it with black sneakers and gold hoop earrings. I put my braids in a half bun at the top and let some hang down in the back. Standing next to Mila, I picked out the darkest shade of brown lipstick I had. I was in a dark mood tonight. Earlier in the day, storms poured so hard I thought they were going to call it quits on the bonfire tonight, but the skies opened up and dry clouds peeked through.

Arriving at the party, I smelled the heavy scent of burning wood and hay. A large barn was lit with twinkling Christmas lights. Teens littered the barn with red cups. JT settled under a tree, bobbing to the music; his hood was over his head. His boys draped around him like he was the prize. I swear I saw Mila inhale when she saw him. We walked in the barn side by side, but when she saw him, she sprinted in front of me and darted in his direction. He spotted her coming and turned the other way, avoiding her eyes.

"Hey, JT," she waved.

"What's poppin,' M?"

"M." She beamed at that.

"Have you been here long?" Mila licked her lips.

JT leaned further back, putting space between the two. "Na, me and my boy just got here a couple minutes ago. But we're not going to stay long." JT was tall—towering over Mila. She looked up at him the way a girl likes looking up at a guy.

Mila stamped her foot in place, like a child, and poked her lip. I can't believe I just saw that. I was going to tell her about her ass later, but for right now I stayed quiet in front of the bonfire, watching the embers smolder, and feeling the heat against my face, waiting for her to finish making a fool of us while she ogled JT. We stood there a full thirty seconds until the silent daggers I was throwing finally caught up with her.

"Text me when you leave. maybe I can slide too." Mila's arms were open, and she leaned in closer to JT.

JT didn't return her body language and stayed frozen.

"Indigo?"

I turned around and spotted Jaxon Green.

"Hey, Jaxon." I gave a wave. His blond hair stood out against a sea of dreadlocks and weaves.

He wore a small stud in his ear that sparkled when the fire caught it. He held his car keys. I could make out the JEEP symbol from here. Jaxon stood like he belonged.

"Mila, I'll be right over here." I pointed to a tree, but Mila was too focused on JT's face to notice. She was dancing to the music, but everyone else watched and cut their eyes at her. I kept an eye out while walking the short distance with Jaxon. He started first. "I'm not sure if Malachi talked to you. But your blog. It's good, I guess."

He guessed? Something in me countered.

Jaxon's hair moved every time he shook his head. He brushed it out of his face as he talked. My teen blog wasn't a big deal—at least not to me, but enough people said to me, "Ain't you that brown girl in the paper?" That made Dad puff his chest out a little further each time. I just shook my head and said yes. Now that Mom is gone, she and I write to each other. Every week one letter arrives from her. She tells stories when she writes; she can set a scene with characters and an entire act. I just reported the facts, but what I did learn came from her. When her letters come, it's our time.

What could he want with my blog? I wondered. I mostly wrote about girl stuff and the occasional 'I am Black, please don't ignore me' rant. Old people seemed to love those the most, I noticed. They loved to read them and share with their friends, but never enough to actually make a change. And the most important item of business—only once a month. I

33

tried to write two articles back to back, and the paper rejected them back and said, "Only one BLM piece every thirty days." BLM? I never mentioned that. My article that month was about Historically Black Colleges and Universities. Anything associated with being Black in America was only tolerable once per month, so it seemed.

"Thanks," I replied.

"My mom is on the school board. Our family goes to UGA— my uncles and dad. We're legacy members."

"Okay?" I eyed him.

"She really likes your blog, and well, she was the one who said, 'get that writer girl from your school to help.'"

"Help what?"

"Instead of an essay for the admission application, I was thinking I could send a video — nothing big. Maybe a few pictures and voice overs to tie it all together."

"But I write. I'm not a videographer or anything," I shook my head.

"You still take your notes and whatever you do, but you make it into a video blog. If you can write it, I'm sure you could probably speak it, right? Sort of like a 'Day in the Life of Jaxon Green.' That would make me stand out." His eyes studied mine.

I glimpsed JT talking to Trina, another girl in our class. Mila stood beside him, but behind him — playing on her cell phone.

"I'm not sure if the school would approve that. I'd have to run it by them."

"Well," Jaxon cleared his throat. "We weren't thinking about the school newspaper; we were thinking about your blog through *Tunica Rivers Times*, since it's semi well known. My dad knows the editor there. Sheila, right? He knows her. She said it was okay."

"We? Who is we?"

"My mom and me. Well, more her than me. She really thinks this will be a good opportunity to get our name out there."

"And what's in this for me?" I crossed my arms.

Kneeling in front of me, Jaxon said, "I, too, have a heart. One, my mom has agreed to write you a letter of recommendation to any college of your choice. And two, my parents have agreed to rent us the Bordeaux Mansion for Spring Fling—if you do this article for me. Also, I can pay you, that's not a problem."

"Really?" Now my eyes were wide. A letter of recommendation from Jaxon's mom would really make my application stand out. Not that I needed a boost, but shit, it couldn't hurt. I also quickly ran the numbers in my mind about all the things I wouldn't have to pay for that month if I had money from Jaxon.

"Uh-huh." He shook his head. He brushed the hair from his face once more. I glanced down and noticed his man flops.

"They think it's a good idea to do the video. It's kind of my last option or else I have to —"

"My Lady, what it do!" Malachi grabbed my waist from behind and placed a wine cooler in my hand. "Ya'll talking business?"

Will walked over with a beer in his hand, and I noticed Trina noticing him.

"Finally here," I kissed Malachi on the cheek.

"What you trying to do, girl?" He closed the space between us and nuzzled my face.

I giggled and pushed him back.

"Come on!" He punched his chest.

Looking for Mila, I found her standing in a circle around the bonfire. It was hazy through the smoke, but I saw JT inside the circle, freestyling. "JT wanna be the one ya need, she won't leave me be, can I get a 1, 2, 3!" he yelled. Mila danced too hard to his mediocre flow and beats.

35

His shit was trash. If he could rap, I could rap—and I cannot rap. And she was drinking.

"I was telling Indigo that my parents have agreed to pay for the Bordeaux Mansion if she helps me with a project for college." Jaxon said.

He didn't mention the money.

"Bordeaux Mansion?" Will blurted.

"Uh-huh," Jaxon repeated. This time with a sly grin. The boys slapped and congratulated Jaxon like he accomplished something. No one thought to ask me anything. I've been writing this blog for two years now, and Jaxon and his family came in and volun-told me what I needed to do. He clearly came up with this whole thing first and told me last. I didn't like that, but I said nothing. I still fixed my eyes on Mila. She took another sip of her wine cooler, and she was tapping on JT's shoulder. JT and his friends were pointing at her and laughing.

"I'll be back." I left the guys and marched towards her.

"Let's go," I grabbed Mila's arm. My eyes burned from being so close to the bonfire. Leaning in, I sniffed Mila. Not only was she buzzed, but her deodorant clearly wore off because she smelled like an Italian sub. No wonder JT and his friends were laughing at her.

"Where we going?" Mila stumbled. "No, me and JT going to the Waffle House in a lil bit right, JT?"

JT and his friends giggled at Mila and imitated her dancing. Thinking they were laughing with her and not at her, Mila laughed too, her white cheeks now rosy red. They chuckled even harder at that. A vein in my temple tapped at my head and I balled my fists. Pulling my arm back, I was ready to attack. I fantasized about knocking JT's head into the tree over where Malachi and Jaxon stood talking. I could push him into the fire.

Just do it... a voice somewhere far inside of me said....*You know you want to.*

The anger came from somewhere in me, so foreign but so familiar. I hushed away the thought even though my anger got the best of me anyway and I swung at JT. I missed, and embarrassment had me in its clutches as my right arm reared back to try it again. This time I aimed directly for his nose. I lined those Jay-Z nostrils up right between my knuckles and a hard glare. Before I could make the connection, Will grabbed me.

"Indigo!" Will screamed. He grabbed me by the shoulders and had to duck as my fist whizzed by his head.

"Oh, um, yeah-yeah?" I blinked back to reality. I dropped my aggressive stance and immediately relaxed under Will's gaze.

"It's not that serious. I got her," he fussed. He released his grip on my shoulders and he took hold of Mila, hoisting her up before she collapsed in his arms. He walked her towards her car before shooting daggers at JT and his friends. I glanced at my phone; we had been at the party two hours, but it seemed like we just got there. Breath escaped my body and the little voice telling me to end JT went away. Blinking back the red, I unballed my fists and my body trembled as I tried to calm down. Now three steps back, JT and his friends stood gawking at me.

"Do you have her keys?" Will said it like he was tired of asking. Mila was slumped in his arms talking about going to Waffle House. Her eyes were low. My chest felt like someone or something was sitting on it; I felt the pressure right in the center and heat found my face. We just discussed this earlier, and it was like she purposely tried to get tipsy. As if she was more comfortable this way—being cared for and gawked at. It did something for her, but what did it do, and why?

I dug in my pocket and retrieved Mila's key. Thank God she didn't carry a purse and needed me to carry them. I didn't want to argue with her tonight about driving.

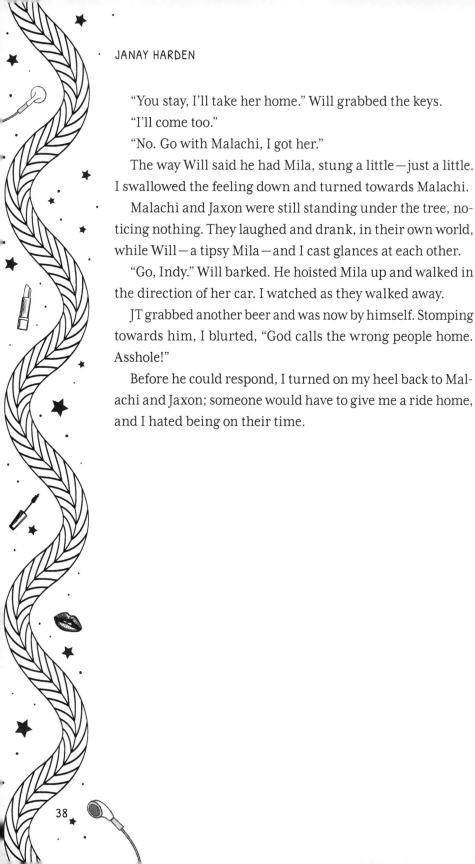

"You stay, I'll take her home." Will grabbed the keys.

"I'll come too."

"No. Go with Malachi, I got her."

The way Will said he had Mila, stung a little—just a little. I swallowed the feeling down and turned towards Malachi.

Malachi and Jaxon were still standing under the tree, noticing nothing. They laughed and drank, in their own world, while Will—a tipsy Mila—and I cast glances at each other.

"Go, Indy." Will barked. He hoisted Mila up and walked in the direction of her car. I watched as they walked away.

JT grabbed another beer and was now by himself. Stomping towards him, I blurted, "God calls the wrong people home. Asshole!"

Before he could respond, I turned on my heel back to Malachi and Jaxon; someone would have to give me a ride home, and I hated being on their time.

CHAPTER 5

January 2nd.

My Indy-Lindy. Happy New Year! I pray this letter reaches you well, my oldest girl. We are halfway through your senior year of high school! Has Daddy taken you prom dress shopping yet? When he came to see me in the summer he fussed at me and said, "Don't worry Sun, we have time to worry about all that." Him fussing at me about prom, but he makes you learn to fix a car at ten. Imagine that? I remember my prom. I wore this white, slinky, lace dress. The split was high up my left leg and I made sure to kick it out whenever a camera snapped. It looked like a wedding dress, but I didn't care. I had these hips that almost look like yours—yours are better than mine, but you hide yours. But I was killing them bitches. They didn't stand a chance. I bet Ez even has the dress still at the house. How are the birds outside? I think of them often. Do you think birds come and go from Trochesse? Or do they stay in the trees, never making their escape?

Anyway, I need a favor, honey. Remember Ms. Montague from the pottery studio? She's holding an art auction, and she is displaying some of my pieces—I read about it in the newspaper. Can you go down there and check it out for me? Take some pictures, actually take brain pictures and real pictures so you can come back and describe it to me at our visits, and we can act it out. I'm rubbing my hands together like Birdman, hahaha Indy. Now I'm going to give you pottery, insider tips. I want you to check out the person who buys it too. What do they look like? Why would they want this piece out of the rest? How will it fit into their life? Ask yourself those questions and then take the brain picture and report back to me. Okay? Break!

Make sure you go see Mama Jackie's grave. It's her birthday, January 17th.

Did I tell you I started a singing group? Ruth-Ann, Cordelia, Minister, and Gordy. We call ourselves the Band-Aids. It was the only name we could agree on and the only thing we have tons of in here. Minister wanted us to be Minister and the Minnies, but Ruth-Ann shut that shit down baby! She was in here screaming and she told him, "Ain't nobody bout to be your flunkie bitch Minister," and she grabbed his ice cup and tossed it in his face, and honey, we got that good ice here! That shit you get straight from the hospital. So, he had to go ask Nurse Blister, with the glasses, for more (that's what we call her because she always has a blister by her lip. You know one of THOSE blisters), and he had to wait and wait because she was busy. He dropped the Minnies after that. Cordelia told her she didn't have to go off on him, but Ruth-Ann just shook her head. She said, "You let em' slide once and next thing you know they think they ice skating!" Gordy said nothing, Indy. He doesn't talk much anyway — he just sings and can hold a note like that heavy-set boy from Dru Hill? Did I mention I'm the group manager? I figured my singing days is over. It's time I raise some young pups. I think you and your sister turned out pretty good. A singing group can't hurt.

Speaking of your sister, make sure she is spending time with her daddy and brothers. She has to spend time with them, so she learns she can't depend on them. You're her big sister, and I'm counting on you to teach her the ropes. She still has hope, which is a good thing. Sheeitt, maybe even it's a noble thing. She needs to know though, don't be depending on no man.

Tell your Dad I said Hi and why he ain't come to see me in a couple months? It's almost my birthday? But I bet he's at work all the time ain't he? Indy, if there's a woman there sweet on him, go down there and take brain pictures of her, too, for me, okay? Don't ask me how I know, I just do. I feel things and see it in my dreams. You'll see it in your dreams too. It's a family trait.

Love you lots and can't wait to see you guys,
Mommy Dearest (Not like the movie though)

I HATE WHEN SHE did this. She was bat shit crazy when we visited her. Shouting and dancing, putting on performances for us. After our last visit, Ez said he wasn't coming anymore. He claimed it was because his car couldn't make the trek any longer, but I knew it was because he couldn't stand to see Mom this way. Ez didn't have words for Mom's behavior. He just knew she could be better and wanted her to stop. If anyone read her letters, they would think she was the best mom. They didn't know the mom who saw things that weren't there or heard things that weren't there. Who sang to no one and everyone all at once?

I read Mom's letter three times, and I lingered on the spots where the ink from her pen pooled on the paper. What made her pause there? What was on her mind?

Writing letters to her became my homework. I tried writing to her every two weeks, but she outnumbered me and wrote at least three to my one. She had a list of things for me to do or people to go talk to on her behalf. I told her about Dad, Sid, and Ez, although she never asked.

This was our new normal. I was her sometimes daughter, sometimes friend, all the time secretary.

41

The Pottery Palace was Mom's favorite place when she was home. When she got out of the hospital the first few times, they told her she needed a hobby. One day she came home with a mound of hardened red clay, and soon she began taking me to the studio where I watched her make art. Sometimes Sidney even came too if she wasn't with her dad. Mom, with her hair tied in a black jersey knot bun and silver stud earrings, sat with her legs slightly opened — making room for the sculpting wheel perched in front of her. Her arms were bent at the elbow and red clay splattered over her hands and wrists. Sidney and I parked atop the counters and watched Mom sing Nina Simone and throw clay pots. Ms. Montague screamed, "no eating in the studio!" but she gave Sid and me potato chips. She handed them to us on the sly and eyed the room in case someone saw, but no one ever did. Days in the studio with Mom and Sid felt normal. Those days felt real. Later, Ms. Montague let me pick up a few hours here and there and she hired me for events or parties. She didn't call often, and I realized right away she saw me as a ticket girl and nothing more. But my Mom loved her, so I went. I could learn to love her too.

I pulled my phone from my pocket and went to Ms. Montague's social media page, and sure enough, I saw a flyer with an upcoming date. I sent her a message and told her I would be there in my mom's place.

Bursting into the room, Sidney plopped on the bed. "What does yours say?" She grabbed the letter from my hands.

"Give it back!" I shouted.

Before Sidney could roll off the bed, I pushed her down to the ground and tickled her.

"Stoppp! she screamed, dropping the letter.

"Give me my shit!" I snatched Mom's heavy thoughts displayed on dingy notebook paper. "What did yours say?"

"She said she wants me to go to the pottery studio. And then I have to tell Daddy I'm going to live with him when Mommy comes home."

When she comes home. Mom gets Sidney's hopes up and tells her stories about when she was coming home and the fun things they would do together. Once, Mom wrote Sidney a letter and told her not to celebrate Thanksgiving because it was a Capitalist holiday. It had Sidney in a frenzy, trying to justify not eating fried Turkey with us on the big day. Her ten-year-old mind didn't get it. Dad shut down communication between Mom and Sidney after that. Her letter today was the first one in a few months.

"Siddd. You are not going to live with your dad. You're staying here. With us."

"But Mom said —"

"I know what Mom said, but it's not happening. Mom is sick."

Sidney sank into my bed and laid her head on my pillow. Lying beside her, our heads touched, and we were quiet.

A knock tapped at the door.

"Come in," I yelled.

Dad walked in and smiled at Sid and I lying down. "What's my girls doing today?"

"Dad, I feel like I haven't seen you in days — let me look you over," I glanced at him up and down.

"Work calls, I have to keep all of this going," he waved his hands and looked around. Dad joked it off, but I didn't think it was funny. I thought back to the last time I saw him. Numbers and dates flashed through my mind and I realized it had been three days. I last saw my Dad three days ago. He was working all that time? He made jokes about paying for senior year and Sidney's field hockey, but now I was concerned. Was he really working that much to support us?

"That's too much, Mr. Ben. Even I know that," Sidney crinkled her eyebrows.

Stunned, I glanced at Sidney. Her saying his schedule was too much was big, even for her. She would put herself on grueling schedules for field hockey, waking up at 6 a.m. breakfast, school, practice, more practice, game. It was never-ending for her and what I considered fun for a ten-year-old, but she managed it all.

Dad's face softened.

"Prom season, graduation. These things cost money."

"I'm helping Ms. Montague at the pottery studio. I can see if she'll give me more hours. I can get a better job," I assured. That wasn't true. Ms. Montague could be a pain in my ass, and I preferred not to deal with her. She only wanted the "right" girls upfront. She never said it but whenever we had an event, she made the lighter skinned girls work the front room. Ms. Montague put me in the back, taking bids. I never told Mom that part. Ms. Montague was a high yellow woman. Small moles peppered her face, and her hair was pulled back in a tight, low bun. She was always nice to me, but I had a feeling she helped me because of Mom and nothing else.

Dad's cell phone rang, and he held one ear so he could hear better. I'm not sure why he did that. I guess habit; he could hear perfectly fine. "Yes Sir, I can be there. No, Sir. Uh…about an hour? Okay, Sir. No, thank you." Dad fumbled over his words. He didn't look towards us as he yessed through the phone. He hung up and scratched his head, then he peered around the room like we weren't there. "Girls," he began. "I have to go into the center. A pipe burst in the basement. Will you guys be okay for the day?"

I thought about everything I had to do today. Christmas Break from school came to a close tonight, and tomorrow, we would return for the second half of my senior year of high

school. I had my college applications saved online; I only had to hit send. I wasn't sure how I would pay for my entrance fees, let alone Mila's. The money I saved from Ms. Montague's came and went, and the pennies that *Tunica Rivers Times* paid me was just as meager.

Dad was absentminded and didn't keep up with the bills. Sometimes he had the money, and he forgot to pay. Sometimes, he didn't have the money to pay. Sometimes, I used my money for the electric bill. When Mom lived with us, it was the same way. She never held a job down long enough to help with anything in the house. She mainly stuck to what she knew, and that was performing and music. Mom, King, and Dad went back and forth many times with Mom torn between her want for King, creativity, and passion—and her need for Dad, stability, and us.

We always had what we needed; we never went without food or clothing or anything like that. I wasn't greedy, and I tried to keep that in perspective. But the things that I wanted, damn, I really wanted. I don't know whether these college applications fees were a want or a need. I wondered if they would stay saved somewhere in internet land, unsent because of money. I hoped not.

Sidney and I took Ez's car to visit him. I got my license a few months ago when I turned seventeen, but getting a car was the last thing I could afford right now. Besides, I was only applying to colleges with decent campus transportation. The good thing about being an editor was the access I had to information. I researched everything after Mom went away. I always thought there was something I could learn or do to help her. For now, these letters would have to be enough.

45

On the more remote end of Tunica River where Ez lived felt heavy. The woods here were thicker, and the sun wasn't always visible. Deer ran throughout the dense forest marking their territory and with so many creatures and things that made you go bump in the night, Ez's house fit right in. He lived in a small two-bedroom bungalow. The tall trees crouched overtop and the back of the house opened to his side of Tunica River. He didn't have a driveway, only a small boat ramp.

Ez got hurt in one of those old wars where they promised you the world if you fought for them, and became a patriot for their country, but reminded you constantly that they didn't respect you. That didn't last long because Ez hurt his back and was soon discharged from the Army. Mama Jackie got this house and our house with his benefits. She was the brains behind the operation. If it wasn't for her, Ez and our family wouldn't have anywhere to live.

Ez doesn't always shower, and he doesn't eat every day. Sometimes he eats too much. He burns great enormous bonfires in his yard, and he had a large shotgun laying in the attic that he says he used to shoot deer, but I've never seen him shoot not one deer. I asked Sidney, and she said she's never seen it either. He did everything every day at the same time. He woke up at the same time without an alarm. He ate breakfast and milled around the house at the same time. Minutes, sometimes even seconds — if out of place — seemed to throw off his schedule.

Grandpa Ez was a hoarder, and he was straight off the show. Piles of newspapers were shoved to the ceilings and stacked. Mama Jackie had two cats before she passed away. Ez kept the cats around and they got fatter and fatter. They trotted the land with glee. Soon, more and more cats came, and it seemed like they went and told their friends there was a new spot to post up with a crazy old man. Grandpa Ez welcomed them as he stood outside throwing crumpled Ritz crackers and chunks of ham he ate for dinner the night before. In the summer he left the windows ajar, and the back door cracked to "let the air flow come and go," as he said it. The cats had free range, coming and going as they pleased. Not long after, Animal Control came to the house. And then once more, and then once more, threatening to condemn the home if things didn't improve. Dad, Sidney, and I suited up once a month and visited Ez to clean the house. Dad had to work again, so Sidney and I went at it alone today.

"You driving my car again, girl?" Ez pointed a chicken bone at me. "Hey Sidrock!" He sneered at Sidney. "Want some chicken?"

"No thank you, Ez," Sidney giggled.

Ez gnawed at his hunk of meat. His overalls were black at the knees and his white undershirt was torn at the neck. Sweat peppered his forehead.

"Ya'll ain't coming in here." Ez barricaded himself in the doorway and shook his head when he saw us walking up.

"This is my stuff, SidRock. Tell her," he pointed to me. My giant of a grandfather stomped his foot to his youngest granddaughter in frustration.

"Come on, Ez, you know we have to do this now and then. Dad couldn't come, but we're here."

"I said no." His voice was snappy. "Your Dad said he would not throw out my bikes, and he did. He lied. I had brand new Huffy bikes, and he tossed them away. I was going to use them."

"You were not!" I screeched. The anger flowed through me and within seconds I felt hot. "I don't have time for this today, I have to go to the gallery, and I have a project!" My voice was gruff too.

Sidney and Ez shot wide eyes in my direction. Sidney got up and stood next to Ez, and together they glared at me.

"Ez," I tried again. I eyed the time on my phone. I was meeting Jaxon later to go over the details for his "Day in the Life" bullshit. "Is there anything you don't want us to touch?" I lowered my voice above a whisper. The plastic gloves on my hands started to sweat, and they felt clammy inside.

Ez lowered his arms, and tears formed in his eyes. "Just don't be moving my pictures of Jackie," he whispered.

"I won't. I promise I won't,"

Sidney looked up at Ez and held his hand tighter.

"Indy never moves the pictures of Mama Jackie; I think that's Mr. Ben. But we'll talk to him," Sidney promised. She nodded her head at me. She looked so small standing next to Ez, like David and Goliath.

Ez hesitated in the doorway before dropping his arm and letting me through. Entering the kitchen, a stench hit my nostrils and my eyes watered. Ez was collecting bottles of old oil he used to fry food. Pots and kitty litter cluttered the room. I couldn't see through to the living room. Peeking around, I noticed Ez nailed white sheets to the ceiling and used them as dividers.

"Ez...what are the sheets for?"

"I reckon I make me some rooms," he answered.

"You have rooms. What's wrong with your bedroom?"

"Ain't nothing wrong with it nosy girl, I got everything I need right here."

Sidney stood in the corner of the living room, dry heaving and covering her mouth. Dead flies covered the fly traps above her head and new flies whizzed by mine.

"You sick or something, girl? I got some Ginger Ale," Ez boomed.

Cats were purring throughout the house, jumping in and out of the windows. The noise from dozens of felines sounding at the same time was deafening, and I found myself yelling to Ez and Sidney and they were right across the room.

Sidney and I grabbed trash bags, glancing at each other. I paused and checked the time on my phone. I would be cutting it close, cleaning Ez's house, meeting up with Jaxon, and then going to the gallery. Sidney and I moved around the room as quickly as we could, trying not to pause too long. If we paused too long, the smell would hit our nostrils again and we didn't want that. We moved in sync around each other, and I was glad Dad didn't come today; he would have just slowed us down. Once a month was too much for us and we hated doing it, but clearly not enough for what he needed.

Grandpa Ez was not okay.

CHAPTER 6

JAXON GREEN WAS late. This was his project, and he was late to our meeting. Glancing at my watch, I sighed. People have been playing with my time lately, and I didn't like it. My phone buzzed, and it was Dad.

"Hello?"

"Indy, where are you?"

"I'm waiting at the park for a friend."

"Waiting at the park for a friend — now that doesn't sound suspicious."

I giggled. "Remember I told you I was hired to create a video blog for *Tunica Rivers Times*? For Jaxon Green? You know the Greens' dad! The rich ones."

"Him?"

"Yes. Him, Dad," I chuckled.

"I remember you mentioning something or the other. They used to buy your Mom's pottery if I remember correctly. They have a few of her larger pieces. Do you need me to come down there?"

"What, Dad? I didn't know that." I wonder if Jaxon knew he possibly had my Mom's art in his house. Maybe I could get some shots of it on filming day! My mind was moving fast now.

"What time will you be home? I'm done with work for the day, and I thought the three of us could do something together. They got that new skating rink down on Lexington, and I thought we could bust some moves." Dad steamrolled my question about Mom's art, and picturing my Dad, "busting moves," made me chortle out loud, and soon, he was laughing too.

"I still got it!" Dad yelled into the phone.

"What's Sid doing?"

"She's napping. Said something about Ez's house being worse than ever." He huffed in exasperation.

I nodded into the phone, agreeing with Sidney's assessment. "Go wake her up, Dad, you guys have to spend time together."

When Sidney, Dad, and I were together, things were fine. We became our own little family and meshed well together. I was nervous when she first came to live with us. It had become me and Dad; and Mom, occasionally—when she decided she wanted to be with us over King.

"I'm going to college next year and won't be here every day..." my voice trailed off. "Not to bridge the gap."

Dad was quiet, then said, "I know, Indy, I know."

I didn't know what else to say. "Love you, Dad."

"Love you too, Indy," he replied and hung up.

I held my phone to my lips. I wanted so badly to call Dad back and say, "Hold tight, I'll be home soon. It'll be the three of us." But I couldn't today—I was waiting for Jaxon. With Mom, we had no stability. We didn't know which house she would choose or if she chose us at all. Sometimes she chose the things her mind chose, and we had to battle that for time too. When Sidney was a baby, Mom tried taking her to Mexico because she believed something possessed Sidney when she wouldn't stop crying. On the way there, Mom turned around in Texas because Sidney had settled down. When she got home with Sidney she said, "It's the house—the baby doesn't like

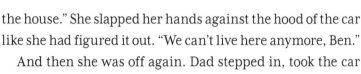

the house." She slapped her hands against the hood of the car like she had figured it out. "We can't live here anymore, Ben."

And then she was off again. Dad stepped in, took the car keys, and told her she couldn't take Sidney anywhere else. He called King but couldn't get ahold of him. Dad faced off with Mom that day about me and Sidney. A child who was more his than King's, but she wouldn't call him Dad.

Dad put his foot down and made Mom leave the house. I was in my room listening with my ear to the door. I didn't want to come out and see them like that. Mom marched back to her room and grabbed a bunch of clothes and left that night. She didn't even say bye to me—she just left, and she took Ez's car.

That was the last night she stepped foot in our house—her house. The family home. We were a family no more.

After that, she raced down Lenape Avenue, the main street in Tunica Rivers. Our city was an average one; I didn't think there was much to write home about. Mom and Dad went to high school together. Tunica Rivers was the type of small town that had one main road which housed all of the arts, shops, and restaurants. Wealth was proudly on display with American flags lining the flagpoles and a thin blue line was painted down the middle of the traffic lines, letting us know which line they preferred. If someone moved one street over on the outlier blocks, they would find the real city and us; the everyday prison guard, schoolteacher, construction worker. I was thankful to attend the school near the big houses where they had way more clubs and activities. I could write at this school. The other school didn't have a newspaper club or even writing club.

Mom felt like Tunica Rivers held her back. She set her sights on the big cities of New York and Chicago—places I only read about in my books I loved so much. So, when she came barreling down Lenape Avenue, with an old man in her sightlines, he reminded her of what she didn't want. A slow, mundane life in Tunica Rivers. The old man paused in front of the pedestrian walkway, his head and neck hunched outwards, his shoulders slumped. If he were a tree, the man had many rings around his trunk. Mom came flying towards him and when she laid eyes on him, she picked up steam and pressed her foot to the gas. The car roared louder down the road and Mom narrowed her eyes at him and the car speedometer, which jumped higher and higher. She struck him hard, and the man flew in the air.

Bystanders say he hit the ground with a loud thud, and then there was silence. He didn't say a word.

There was no blood—there was no anything.

It was silent.

Mom collapsed from the car, laughing. "Punch buggy! He was worth fifty points—easy" she giggled. "Where can I find some ice cream guys? Anyone?" Mom sealed her fate, and she didn't even know it. We didn't know it. When it happened, Dad told Sidney and I that she accidentally ran into someone. Sidney accepted that story, but I knew better. Mom was off the hook...but she was still my mom, so I guess I accepted it too. After that, Mom was convicted and sent to Trochesse for the rest of her days. She wasn't found competent to stand trial, and she was so outlandish at times it would've been embarrassing to watch.

My heart beat out my chest sometimes late at night when I couldn't sleep around 3 a.m. or so. I would still replay that scene in my mind...how does it feel to floor the gas pedal? To lower your eyes at someone and know this was it? Her foot on the gas and picking up speed. I bet her heart was racing. I wonder if it felt the same as being at the top of a roller coaster. The thoughts, especially that late at night scared me, but somewhere else it also excited me. I pushed those thoughts

53

away just as I hung up with Dad and Jaxon whipped around the corner in his blacked-out JEEP. He had the doors off, and I spotted his man flops and blonde hair whipping through the wind. His music was loud, and curse words from NBA YoungBoy drowned out the park.

I sat at a picnic table by the water and watched Jaxon pull up next to Ez's car and glance it over.

I cringed.

My bag and notepad were on the seat next to me. Jaxon flopped down beside me and moved the bag.

"I'll take that," I grabbed my bag from him.

The fuck? He just move my shit?

"Sorry I'm late, got held up." He looked past me and used his key fob to lock his car.

I swallowed.

"I just wanted more information about what you're looking for. Everything is set. I've blocked the entire day to follow and film you. I thought we could title it, 'Jax Gives High School the Ax.'"

"'Jax gives High School the Ax'" he repeats. He scrolls through his phone and pauses for a second. "Yeah, yeah, that could work."

"Is there anything you would like me to focus on? Or should I just capture everything as it happens?"

"Yeah, I guess you can get all of it as it happens."

I needed more direction, and he scrolled through his phone. Curiosity got the best of me and I asked, "Tell me again what you want from this? I just want to make sure I'm understanding your expectations. I can write something, but I'm a little unclear about the video portion."

Jaxon was silent, his finger still swiping up. An awkward silence fell between us—or maybe it was awkward on my end. Jaxon didn't seem to notice it.

He finally looked up as he clicked his phone screen locked.
"My mom says she likes your writing, and a lot of her friends read
your column in the newspaper. I told her you don't do videos.
She said everyone has to start somewhere and to give you some
money. So, I'm here." I swallowed when he mentioned money.
I didn't tell anyone that part of the agreement; I wasn't sure
exactly how it worked. I had no idea how to talk about money
with the likes of the Green family, so I googled what was considered fair payment. I was three pages deep into Google and
I never found anything that felt appropriate. All the numbers
seemed so high, and I could never ask for those types of large
sums. Jaxon's mom would laugh me out of the building!

I was grateful she even offered.

Still, it didn't make it an easier topic to talk about, and I
waited with bated breath for him to bring it up.

"Since you brought it up…" I started. I held my breath and
studied his face. My hand gripped my ink pen. "What were
you guys thinking…for payment?"

"I don't know, one hundred? Maybe?"

I exhaled, and my fingertips were now cold. One hundred?
Gulps. Dollars?

I made more than that at the *Tunica Rivers Times*. I was thinking at least double, according to what Google said and what
I thought was fair. I had to rent video equipment from the
technology department down at the library, and since I was a
teenager, I had to carry something called liability insurance,
but because I'm a minor, they made me get it in Dad's name. I
had to watch endless YouTube videos to teach myself to design
a video, and I had to be available all day long, and wouldn't be
able to go to work at Ms. Montague's. It was costing me money
and time to create the video, but he offered one hundred dollars? Maybe we could negotiate it later. I didn't want to lose
this opportunity sparring off about money.

I swallowed. "Sure, that's fine."

And with three words, I gave up my power.

Jaxon gave a half smile, like he expected nothing less.

"And this will be in place of your entrance essay for the University of Georgia, is that right?" I copied in my notebook. My voice cracked, and I coughed into my fist.

Jaxon clicked on his phone again, and he was back to scrolling. He didn't seem to look for anything in particular, but more so, scrolling out of habit. I was a mindless scroller myself when there was nothing better to do—but not when the topic of conversation was about me. He told me about his mom and what she wanted, with no mention about what he really wanted. And if she was so interested in my reading, why didn't she reach out? Clearly, they had some pull if they could call the newspaper and request that I do the assignment.

Weird. The Greens were weird.

"My family are legacy graduates. They've all gone to Georgia and I will too. My grades…they aren't the best…" Jaxon looked away again before continuing. "My dad called someone at UGA, and they granted us special permission to create this video instead of a…written essay."

"Why did you need that?"

Jaxon's cheek turned red, and he leaned away from me. "I hate reading."

"Reading, what's that have to do with the essay?"

"They go hand in hand, don't they?"

Confusion flashed across my face, and I paused. I hated math myself. It sickened my stomach to think about algebra and geometry—literally sickened my stomach. I worked hard and earned my C fair and square. But was that reason to get 'special permission?'

Unless…

Did Jaxon have trouble reading and writing? How did he make it this far in school? Not to mention, at Tunica Rivers High School—at that. It's a gifted and talented high school. I'm sure he had other talents. But how did he make it this far with no one knowing?

"Jaxon, is it reading?"

He peered over my shoulders at nothing. Anything to avoid my eyes. His phone buzzed again, and he glanced at it before responding to me. Jaxon was tethered to his phone.

"No, I can read," he stuttered. His eyes were worried. "I can't write pages and pages like you can, I guess. I never had to."

I never had to, he said. He was right. Words became my diary when no one was there and my communication with my mom. Words would take me to college, and later I could make a career out of it. What meant so much to me and my well-being he never had to do.

"What will you do when you get into UGA?" I leaned in. I was intrigued.

Jaxon shrugged. "My parents handle that stuff. I just have to make the video. I've made it this far," he smiled.

He made it this far with no one making a big deal about his inabilities. People that looked like me didn't have someone to place a phone call to a college. This interview for Jaxon may improve my chances of getting into college, with the help of his mom's letter of recommendation, of course. I could make it part of my media kit portfolio. It could be life changing for me if I played my cards right. Looking up at Jaxon, I would do just that.

People were living vastly different lives in this city, clearly.

"Are we good here? I have to get back to weightlifting," Jaxon questioned. He didn't wait for my response. He stood and pressed his phone to his ear.

"Yea, we're good," I muttered behind him. He waved at me over his shoulder and started his big car and pulled away.

Gathering my things, I heard another car door close. Over my shoulder, I glimpsed at our track coach Mr. Chestnut. Mr. Chestnut was an older white man, and rumor has it, he was sweet on the younger girls. He was at the school since my mom was a student there. In fact, it was mom who told me about the rumors surrounding Mr. Chestnut. I never ran track and wasn't interested. If I had to run somewhere to get there, then it just wasn't meant for me to go. Running seems like a mindless sport to me, and I really had no contact with Mr. Chestnut as a result.

Mr. Chestnut walked around to the passenger side of the door and opened it. Joya Ranks stepped out of the car, still wearing her book bag over her back. She tilted her head back and laughed at something Mr. Chestnut said, and I could see her perfect white teeth shining from here. Now back inside of Ez's car, I couldn't take my eyes away. If they really were paying attention, they could see me beyond the large patch of oak trees that separated us. They were far enough out of sight not to see, and the way Joya was laughing, and the way Mr. Chestnut extended his hand to her, I doubted they were looking for anyone anyway.

A few minutes later, I arrived at the pottery studio buzzing with activity and a flurry of people milled around the room. I stood a little straighter when I saw Mom's pieces scattered throughout. She was so talented, and she made bowls, paintings, and even custom planters. These days she was drawing in Trochesse and mailing large portraits back to Ms. Montague. All proceeds and purchases went to Mom and she depended on the money in there. It had been less than two years since she went away, and Mom seemed to make more consistent money in Trochesse than she did while she was home. She had a knack for placing colors together that didn't seem to match but they somehow always looked beautiful. I didn't get to look at them long before Ms. Montague asked me to work the coat room in the back.

Casey and Lauren sauntered throughout the room wearing all black and their hands were behind their back just like Ms. Montague always taught us. "Hands down and out of the way. We want them to come to us and ask about the pieces. Be welcoming." I knew the script well, although I rarely got to practice it. Ms. Montague had who she wanted up front, the girls she thought had more appeal to the safe, mostly white crowd.

I watched from the back room leaned up against the doorway. My arms were folded, not open or welcoming.

Ms. Montague's heels clacked as she came around the corner. Seeing me in the door frame she rubbed my shoulder and with a concerned eye said, "Don't worry, the sickness skips a generation. You shouldn't worry, my dear."

What? The sickness? She and Mom were friends but why say that now? Out of all other times? I had more questions than answers. Ms. Montague said that I could work at the studio as long as I wanted. She never seemed to call with work. I always had to ask her for events, just like this one even though it was my Mom's work being displayed. The last few times I called and she said, "there are no hours this week, Indy," and I would show up anyway because I can't help myself, and there would be more of her favorite girls serving and smiling at patrons during exhibitions. I never mentioned it to Ms. Montague directly and neither did she. A job was a job and I tried not to complain.

Mom loved her and I dare not mention it to her. Besides, we all need something to hold on to and love, right? Mom held on to her and the studio like it was her fountain of youth, and who was I to take that?

I tried to catch as many glimpses of Mom's piece as I could. One piece was in the shape of a heart and daggers shot through it from all different angles. The gallery was slammed tonight and before I knew it, a SOLD sign was tagged on Mom's art.

"Casey, Casey," I said, motioning to her from the coat box. Coats were piling all around me, and I had to lean over them to whisper to her.

"Who bought the big heart?"

"I'm not sure—that one went fast. It was one of our first sales tonight."

"What's going on?" Lauren walked into the coat box guzzling a bottle of water. "It's a madhouse out there tonight; be lucky you get to stay back here, Indy."

"I want to be out there with you guys. We can switch at any point in time." The studio was usually filled with lots of middle-aged people looking for something to waste their money on, and tonight was no different. The catering company sauntered around carrying Hors d'oeuvres. The men wore open collared jackets that showed the top of their chest hair.

"I didn't think it was break time, ladies," Ms. Montague interrupted, walking by with large manila envelopes. I wondered if she had any information about Mom's piece.

"Ms. Montague, who bought the heart?"

"I can't remember her name. Find me tonight, and I'll let you know," she winked. "Places everyone! For the second time."

I resumed checking coats and Casey and Lauren walked back to the gallery floor. Before long, hours went by and my feet hurt so bad the last thing on my mind was who bought what.

I hobbled out, walking slow on my throbbing toes.

All in a day's work.

CHAPTER 7

DENNIS AND SONS Funeral Home loomed in front of me. It was overcast and had rained all morning as I pressed the wet buzzer. Mr. Dennis said they were looking for a funeral attendant to set up and assist with viewings, funeral services, and transfer remains to the funeral home when I called earlier. We needed money, and the little money Ms. Montague was paying me wasn't enough to hold me over after high school. The funeral home was right in town and I didn't need transportation. Mr. Dennis asked how old I was and without thinking I said, "Eighteen."

I had to get this job; we needed it.

I knocked on the door again and checked my location. It said I was at the right spot; I looked around, and a large door opened in front of me. A short Black man poked his head out. "Ms. Lewis?"

"Yes," I extended my hand.

"I am Mr. Dennis, please come inside. The dead alerted me you were here. I didn't even hear the bell!"

The dead altered him?

I gulped.

"I'd like to walk you around so you can get a tour of the place. Do you have any certifications?"

"Uh…no." I admitted. He wore suspenders and creased pants, and his loud dress shoes clicked and clacked everywhere he walked.

"Okay. We may be able to work around that. If you think this is a good fit for you before you see the end, then we can move forward."

"Before I see the end?" I repeated.

Mr. Dennis chuckled, and his round stomach jiggled. "Sorry, Ms. Lewis. Most people take the tour and before we even make it to the end, sadly they say this isn't the place for them."

I said nothing.

He gazed at me and extended his hand. "Let's get started."

"When a body comes in, the first thing I do is bathe and disinfect it. Using soap and water, I bathe as you would the living and that includes the legs and trunk. Now, many people don't like that step because secretions may drain from all orifices. Remember, you will wear a mask and face shield the entire time so as not to expose you to any DNA or splatter."

A rock was lodged in my throat..

"There will be times when you may need help to move the bodies. They get settled into their weight when they transition, and their bodies can be so much heavier. My son, Tyson, works here too. He will assist you with any help you need moving the bodies. He has a license, so we'll make sure he's always here to help with these steps."

"Tyson? Tyson, boy?" Mr. Dennis yelled down the hallway.

Someone barreled down the steps, and a tall and skinny brown boy peeked his head in the room. His eyes were bloodshot red, and a fog of smoke followed him.

"Hi," he waved.

"This is my Tyson," Mr. Dennis beamed. Funny, even with the stench of dense Marijuana smoke lingering around us, Mr. Dennis grinned at his son, either none the wiser or picking his battles to leave alone.

"I'm heading out, Dad, see ya."

Tyson didn't look like a Tyson to me. Mr. Dennis watched his son walk and waved him out.

"Moving on," he nodded.

"When you bathe the body, you add some fragrance or essential oils to the water. This step is not required however; here at Dennis and Sons, it is. It sets us above the other places in the area."

Mr. Dennis spoke with a twinkle in his eye. "A clean body to the dead can be the difference between the dead telling their family to use our business again or sending them down the road to them other jacks who don't take the time to freshen the water." He stopped walking. "Did you catch all that?"

"Yes, I did." I stood next to him. "Will I have to do all of this?"

"My heavens, no, dear. Tyson and I will always be here to assist you. Very rarely will you be here alone, but things happen, and you should know how each and every part works around here at Dennis and Son's. Next, inject the arterial system with embalming fluid after you clean the body. Now some people don't like this step either because you have to get real close up on the body now," he showed with his hands. "We tend to use the right artery because it's a major one and easier to spot to the trained eye. You make a small incision with this precision knife. Real careful now," he whispered. "Then you feel for the vein and once you find it, you inject the fluid."

"How do you know you found it?" I asked wide-eyed.

63

Mr. Dennis smiled. "It will feel like a fat piece of Ramen noodle. You'll know it when you see it."

My stomach churned.

"Are you still with me?"

I nodded.

"After you do that, the fluid disperses throughout the body. Here's another part that people don't like. The only place the embalming fluid doesn't reach is the abdomen." Mr. Dennis touched his stomach with animation.

"For these areas, we have to stick the body with a larger syringe, and we attach the syringe to a pump which pushes embalming fluid directly into the belly. And that's how it gets to the places that can't be reached," he explained.

"And the organs?"

"You don't have to take them out. I defer to the family on that one. The fluid is strong enough to preserve the abdomen and chest for some time. What you have to watch for is fumes. Some common symptoms are runny nose, watery eyes and your throat may burn. Make sure you're always wearing your dressing, which is a full gown and mask at all times when working with the bodies. Oh, and another thing. After you make the first incision in the neck, stop for a second. And check again to make sure there are no signs of life. This is important. It doesn't happen too often, but sometimes you might still have a live one," he said with wide eyes.

"Have you ever had a live one?" I asked with bated breath.

Mr. Dennis cleared his throat and said, "enough of all that," changing the subject. He opened a set of double doors to another room and welcomed me in with a grin. "I call this room The Stage because this is where all the magic happens."

The space was filled with long sinks around the perimeter. Three rectangular counters were in the middle of the room where the bodies lie. The room had no windows and reminded me more of a torture room than a stage.

Walking throughout the space, Mr. Dennis led me to a large chamber built into the wall and banged on the side. "Now this, this here is Shelby. Shelby has been humming along with us for the last ten years. She's an older model incinerator. The places down the street have the nicest, newest model, but old Shelby here just keeps ticking along. No need to replace her when there's nothing wrong. Sure, she takes a little longer to burn, but the bodies don't like to transition too fast, anyway. Here at Dennis and Son's we give them all the time they need."

Mr. Dennis opened another door, and this one led us up a flight of stairs back to the front room.

Something came over me and I blurted everything I was thinking. I told Mr. Dennis I was looking for a new job — a better job that helped pay the bills and helped my dad keep food on the table. Putting up with Tyson and the cold, dead bodies was a job I would do with honor. I welcomed the quietness.

"So, Ms. Lewis, what say you? Fifteen dollars per hour?"

"Fifteen dollars per hour? The listing said $12.50?"

"You've made it to the end of the tour. Few people do. I have a good feeling about you," he gave a sheepish grin.

"One last thing, Ms. Lewis. The state law says you have to be eighteen to work as a funeral assistant and you have to be licensed. I have a buddy who can make you an ID and a license. Is that an issue for you?"

I paused. I knew where he was getting. A few students at school had been working part-time jobs since they were fourteen because they knew a guy who knew a guy, who could make a legal identification card. This was a creepy ass place. Goosebumps raised on my arms as we moved from the room. But it piqued my interest and so did that $15.00.

65

"You have a deal," I said to Mr. Dennis, returning his handshake.

"Yes, ma'am! Meet me here next Saturday at 6 a. m., and we'll get started."

CHAPTER 8

I WAS STARVING. I shoved two honey buns in my mouth, putting them together to make a sandwich. There was no breakfast this morning; I woke up early to take Dad to work. His car stalled, and we had to take Ez's. As much as I drove The Bus and Ez used the canoe, maybe I should just ask him for it; it would help so much.

"Look at that ass," I heard from a table across the cafeteria. I watched Jaxon with his friends holding up his phone watching a video, and their laughs echoed through the room. Groaning to myself, my thoughts turned to me shadowing him in a few days and I was not looking forward to it. I searched through college admissions books and the only thing that even sounded like me was the communications major. They required a press kit with their application, and last night I was up late putting mine together. I included articles I wrote the past two years, some of my best features in the *Tunica Rivers Times*, and even a poetry contest I won freshman year. Poetry wasn't my favorite, but it was the first thing I wrote after Mom went away. A letter of recommendation from Mrs. Green would really send my application over the top.

Mila slammed her lunch tray next to mine and squinted at me eating.

"Have you seen Will?"

I took a long swig of my iced tea and wiped my mouth with the back of my hand. "He texted and said he was skipping lunch; something about a project with Trina."

"Trina?"

I stopped chewing and glanced up. "Yes...Trina."

Mila sighed and pushed the corn around on her plate with her plastic fork.

"What's up with you?" I bit into my chicken sandwich.

Mila had been quiet since the party with JT. I thought about the rage I felt towards him. Mila was acting crazy for JT while he peacocked himself and poked fun at her.

It drove me crazy.

"I don't know, girl. JT won't talk to me; he says you went all Carrie on him."

I almost choked on my bread.

"Fuck him!"

"No—not like that," she shook her head. "He wasn't serious. We got together that night and I just don't feel right about it."

Mila wanted me to like whomever she dated, but I rarely found things in them to like.

"But you were drunk that night? And when did y'all hook up? After Will dropped you off at home?"

Mila shrank into her seat and looked away.

"I kissed Will too."

"When? I thought you were done with that!" I slapped my hands together.

"I was drinking, and he was driving me home, and he was ranting about you and Malachi, and I leaned over and tried to kiss him. I put my hand on him."

"He was ranting about me and Malachi? You put your hands on him?"

"Are you a recorder—yes, that's what I said." Mila rolled her eyes.

"And then what happened?" I stopped chewing.

"He doesn't want me. He...he pulled away. I went home and texted JT."

"And?"

"I snuck JT in. He was gone before my mom woke up."

My stomach turned. Mila's shapely body got her a lot of attention, but she used it to throw herself at guys. The fact that she snuck JT into her house said a lot.

Mila lives with her mom in an older double-wide widow trailer. That's what Mila calls it. A widow trailer.

"A widow?" I had pressed.

"There's no happiness there," she scoffed. She left it at that and so did I.

I had no issues with her house; Ms. Janet had it hooked up inside but no matter how nice it was, Mila always sorely said, "but it's still a trailer." She didn't like for people to visit, she preferred going to their house. If she snuck JT into her house, she was surely desperate.

"Hey, guys." Will interrupted.

He and Malachi stood there with their lunch trays.

Mila said nothing.

Will and Malachi sat down, and Malachi went right to work on his lunch like he always did. He carefully set out his napkin and used the salt and pepper packets to season his food. Next, he pulled a small bottle of hot sauce out of his pocket that he brought from home and dabbed some onto his sandwich. Malachi had a special love affair with food, and each bite was an experience.

Will eyed me and then Mila as Malachi shoveled food into his mouth. No one spoke for a while, but the four of us shared eyes around the table. Mila had kissed Will, and he did not tell me. Not that he had to—but still. He could've at least mentioned it, as a friend.

"Ugh!" Mila exclaimed as the silence around the table deepened. She grabbed her bag, snatched her tray off the table, and stormed out of the cafeteria.

I turned back to Will and searched his face. It was blank, and I couldn't read him.

Malachi continued eating, "What's up with her?" he asked. He never looked up from his food.

My phone buzzed and my calendar reminder popped up. Dennis and Sons 1 p.m., it said.

"I have to go," I gathered my things at the table and wiped my mouth.

Malachi stopped chewing, "Where are you going?"

"Today is my training day at the funeral home."

"But you've already been there for two weeks. And we're still in school, Indy?" Will probed.

I sighed. "I know, but today was the only day Mr. Dennis's son could squeeze me in for the actual body cavity training. He's going away for the weekend, and if we don't do it today, I have to wait until next week when he comes back." Truth be told, I couldn't wait. Two weeks already lapsed between now and my last day at the pottery studio. Dad signed off on the work release paperwork, and I could leave early to head to work. Although I had picked up a few hours here and there working the front desk at the funeral home, I needed the extra hours that the body preparation would give me. Next month I had to submit those college applications, and I needed the money for application fees—and Mila's fee too.

Shoving the last piece of sandwich in my mouth, I took one last swig of my tea and tossed it in the trash.

"Talk to you later?" I leaned into Malachi's face.

He grabbed my cheeks hard and said, "Love you, woman."

I giggled.

"See ya!" I screamed over my shoulder to Will.

Heading out of the cafeteria, I passed Joya in the hallway. I raised an eyebrow when I saw she was heading in the direction of the Track and Field office.

I had called Will that night after meeting with Jaxon and told him what I saw. "It's probably nothing, Indy. You know the track team practices there sometimes."

The team did practice there, but something didn't feel right to me.

Glancing over my shoulder, Joya and my eyes connected. She smoothed her hair before she knocked on the Track and Field office door. I couldn't see who was behind the door from the distance, but I had a feeling.

Searching for my cell phone in my bag, I realized I left it on the lunch table. "Shit," I thought. My hands were roaming my stuff when I turned in the hallway to head back.

"Ouch!" I shrieked. I ran straight into someone tall, soft, and smelling good.

Will.

He held on to me as we fell against the wall. He grabbed my shoulders to steady me, and I bounced against him, pulling myself away slowly. I inhaled and stole one more scent. Damn...when did he start smelling like this? His arms bulged through his shirt, I felt them up against the wall. When did Will get muscular?

"You okay?" he gasped.

I could feel his breath on my face and in a flash, something registered in his eyes. Something. The something was fast—had

71

I blinked I would've missed it. Did he see something in my face too? Was there something to see?

"You left your phone." he handed it to me.

We were still pressed against each other on the wall. He towered over me and I peered up at him. "Th-thank you," I stammered.

Will took a step back, and I was no longer sandwiched between him and the wall behind me. I turned and walked away but not before I peeked over my shoulder, where Will was already peeking over his.

He was watching me — watching him.

My breathing was ragged as I relived Will's scent. I smoothed my braids and fixed my shirt. I was still feeling some type of way about Mila and the kiss — but why? One day Will and I were best friends and the next day he was…attractive. Very attractive.

I turned back around and folded my arms at my chest. I had to get to work.

"Generally, more conservative states tend to embalm instead of cremate. You can put an embalmed body in a cooling container, and it should look okay a couple days after death," Tyson explained.

This was the most boring shit ever, but I listened anyway. We had an older, deceased white man on the table covered with a white sheet. His eyes were a glassy blue color when Tyson wheeled him in. I shut his eyes when Tyson turned his back, so he wasn't staring at me.

Tyson walked me around, pointing out various trinkets and fluids we would need. Downstairs where the body lay and upstairs where the funerals were held were drastically different. Upstairs was stuffy, and full of pained, crying people. Downstairs smelled of mothballs, and there were no windows. The halls were dank, and the lights jumped when you walked through the space.

Tyson blasted J. Cole through the speakers.

He showed me how to attach the large hose to a body's abdomen and I slid over the floor as liquids dripped out. I struggled to lift the large hose while it pumped solution out at the same time.

Tyson announced, "You might want to get some non-slip sneakers," as I slammed my knee into the cadaver table for the third time that afternoon. It was starting to swell.

"After we clean the body and let the fluids drain, the rest is easy. The process has been the same for decades."

"So, what makes you guys different from the next funeral home?" I scoffed, looking at my soaked shoes. My wrists were also wet, and I hoped it was just the water.

"This place is my dad's lifeline. He prides himself on low prices and taking care of his community. He really believes the bodies talk to us if we're open to listening. He honors them in a way."

"And you? Is this your lifeline?" I wiped sweat from my brow.

Tyson said nothing but shook his head no. I didn't press.

After we got cleaned up, Tyson led me to another smaller room attached to The Stage. I crouched my head as we walked under the cinder block arch and the mothball smell were more intense back here.

"This is Shelby, the Incinerator. That's my mom's name. Dad named it after her because it was her idea to have it installed. She told Dad we had to 'keep up with the times.' She convinced him to have it installed, and she took business to the next level." Tyson tapped on the side of Shelby. Tyson beamed, talking about his mom the same way his dad beamed talking about him a few weeks ago.

"It can take up to three hours for a body to fully burn and become ashes on the low setting. The incinerator can get up to 1800 degrees, but Dad likes to send the bodies off at 1500 degrees. He says it's more comfortable for them. After the timer goes off, you wait for it to cool. This part doesn't take long and then you can begin to scoop the ashes for urn collection. After that, the rest is gravy. There's only dressing and refrigeration," Tyson smiled. "Dad comes in Monday through Friday. He's an early riser and usually gets here at 5 a. m. The weekends will be yours and mine. He would like you here at 6 a. m., but really, just make sure doors and phones are on at 7:30 a.m. — that's when people start to call."

"Do you enjoy working here?" I had to ask.

The smile left his face, and he frowned. "I don't dislike it. But it's the family business, and it's getting me where I need to go. But once I show you the ropes, it'll be all yours."

"And where do you want to go?"

"Anywhere outside of this town. I'll start there."

Me too, I thought. Me too.

CHAPTER 9

JANUARY 26TH

Indigo,

Girl, did you go see Ms. Montague like I asked? I know you're busy, but I need to know who bought my things. The newspaper says the art show is coming up. By the way, I bought me a newspaper subscription, and I read your last article in the Tunica Rivers Times. Great work, honey! The rest of these people's kids don't even come see them, but mine comes every month, and she's an artist. Writing is an art too, and you got it my dear. Any who, when I called King, he said Sidney was starting Softball this Spring. Make sure he goes to the games and is there for Sidney. He ain't shit.

Can you believe Nurse MeanFace made us break up The Band-Aids? You know she's a square. She let me slide that one time and told me I didn't have to shower one night, but Ruth-Ann's funky ass cussed her out for making her take her meds and that was the end of The Band-Aids. We'll see though—I think we might put on something for Valentine's Day. Hopefully, she's over it by then and I'm trying to convince Ruth-Ann to apologize. You know, Ruth-Ann can be a Celine Dion in here. She can hit those notes that leave you scrunching up your face and saying "wheewww." She's that good. But she likes to cuss everyone out, and she has a nasty attitude sometimes. A group can't function like that. We'll see. We will see.

I called Ez. He was out of breath when he answered the phone. He said he tripped over a motor he found on the side of a road. A motor, Indy? What is going on? Can you please check on him?

How was Mama Jackie's grave when you went? I had a dream about her. Have you had any dreams? You know your dreams are an extension of real life. I've been reading about dream interpretation and I found this old, dusty book in the library in here.

I remembered one day, when I was away at camp, I called mama and she said, "Sonia, the sky is a beautiful shade of indigo tonight, you should see it." I peeked out of the mess hall where everyone ate. The phone was attached to the wall, and the screen door slammed behind me when I stretched the cord to stand outside. I stood there, watching the indigo sky with Mama. I felt close to her. She was home, and I was at camp, but we were gazing at the same thing together.

How are you, honey? How is Malachi and that cutie Will? Malachi still eating everything but the kitchen sink? I swear that boy got a tapeworm.

Love,
Mommy is the Bomby and I'm eating Pastrami. Not really, only white people eat Pastrami. Hahahaha I crack myself up in here, up in here…I've been practicing my rap skills and I think if I get good enough, I can replace Ruth-Ann. I mean, eventually we still must get another singer, but I can rap some of her parts. Ugh, there's so much to do.

PS: Please tell your Dad hello and did you see about that woman? Is she light skinned? And your Dad still hasn't come to see me.

I READ MOM'S LETTER with Malachi by my side on the couch. Her words were a bright spot in my day. Coming home from school and knowing there may be one waiting for me in the mailbox was enough to make me race home and Sidney to squeal with excitement. Other people had their mom every day, but Sidney and I had these letters. Malachi watched TV, and I rewrote a few articles. Dad was in his room and Sidney was sleeping. Shantiel penned an article about what teachers did on the weekends, and it had potential. I made a mental note to talk to her after the club met this week about the editor position next year. I mulled over my mom's words about Will...Mila's words too...she said Will was ranting about Malachi and me. What was that about? Work was endless these days. I left school early a couple more times to get to the funeral home, but I didn't tell Dad, and Mr. Dennis didn't ask. I made the money I needed for Mila's and my application fees, but was I missing something? In my absence, had Will's and my friendship changed, and I was the last to know it?

Nah, we were still best friends, I concluded.

"Do you want some Skittles?" Malachi interrupted my thoughts. He shot them into his mouth a handful at a time.

"No, thank you," I feigned disgust. He was truly always eating. "Do you have to work tomorrow?"

"What you need baby—I can be off?" He leaned close to me.

Giggling, I said, "No, I'm serious. We have to work on your applications."

Malachi backed away from me and straightened his face. "What's wrong?"

"I don't think I want to go to college."

"Since when? Did something happen?"

"Nothing happened. We've been in school the past twelve years, I'm ready for a break."

I searched Malachi's eyes. "How long have you felt like this?"

77

"Not long; don't act like that. I just don't think college is for me. I don't know what is for me, but I know I won't find it sitting in class again. At least not right now."

"Okay...Okay..." I mumbled. I tried to wrap my mind around this, but it made little sense.

Malachi and I always discussed going to school together. If we didn't go to the same school, we would at least stay within two hours of each other. A two-hour, long distance relationship was manageable, but three hours was a recipe for disaster. Now, he was potentially putting much more than hours between us.

"When were you going to tell me?"

"Tonight actually, you just brought it up before I did." He popped another Skittle in his mouth and I wanted to snatch them out of his hand and mush him in his head.

Stunned, I stared at the TV, letting it watch me as my thoughts ran wild. Were we breaking up? Was this the end? For over a year we had been comfortable. I thought we agreed, but here he was — rewriting the chapter. I didn't want a long-distance relationship, and I didn't want to be persuaded into one either.

The window was ajar, and I heard splashing sounds moving closer. I rose and peered to the lake. Illuminated by the moon, Ez was treading through the water, and I saw the gleam of his shotgun. He was paddling fast and hard. Glancing at my phone, it was 11 p. m.

"Dad!" I yelped. I charged down the hallway and burst into his bedroom. He was on his cellphone and I noticed the look on his face; he was grinning and laying on top of his bed rubbing his feet together. The stench from his work boots wafted through the room and I scrunched my nose and almost coughed. Who was making him grin like that on the phone? Even I knew the answer to that.

A woman. Had to be.

"Ez is on the water with a gun," I screeched.

In a flash, Dad jumped out of his bed and slid into his housecoat and his man flops. Jaxon's man flops looked expensive; shiny, with tight leather. Dad's man flops were dogged, shaped to his feet from years of wear and tear.

Malachi jumped up, and his Skittles spilled. He and I ran behind Dad out of the house and to the water's edge.

"Now what are you doing, Ez?" Dad approached him from the boat ramp outside.

"Be nice to him, Mr. Ben!" Sidney called out, watching from her window. I guess she was up now. I stood behind Dad as he inched forward to Ez. Malachi stood behind me.

"Nothing is wrong with me!" Ez roared back. "Y'all made me go to that doctor this morning, and I didn't get a chance to paddle the lake, so I'm doing it now, Nosy-like-his-daughter, Man."

Dad's jaw tightened at that last comment. Sidney and I took Ez to a neurologist this morning per a request from the city. They sent a letter and asked that he be evaluated due to the condition of his home. It was scheduled for months and it took that long to convince him to go. We had to be there at 7 a.m., and the appointment lasted three hours! I dropped Sidney off at school and thanked her for coming.

"Anything for Ez," she shrugged.

Ez sat in the backseat and patted her head.

"Go on to school, girl. Big Ez will be fine."

Sidney had made him wear a cotton sweater, which he complained about the entire time. He took it off and scratched his neck until it was red and as soon as the appointment was over, the sweater was in a crumpled mess next to him in the car. Sidney got out of the car and hesitated in the doorway.

"Love you guys," she blurted. She had slammed the door shut before we could respond and walked towards her school.

"Now why she go and do that? When someone says I love you, you can't leave them hanging, you have to say it back. How will we say it back?" He sucked his teeth.

He rolled down his window, "Love you too, SidRock!" he screamed. His loud voice echoed outside. That was hours ago and a different Ez.

"Why do you need a gun, Ez?" Dad asked.

"Because I thought it might like to come out and play. It's been cooped up in the attic for two weeks now. Is that Eat a Lot? Heyyy Eat a Lot!"

"Hi Mr. Ez," Malachi yelled back with a wave.

"Don't mister me boy—only make the white man call you mister."

My shoulders softened.

I glanced at Sidney peering from her tiny window. She and Ez were partners in crime. If Dad wanted a better relationship with Sidney, he would have to go through Ez. I don't think Dad realized it yet.

"Ez, do you need anything?" Dad yelled.

He paddled fast and cut through the water at lightning speed. His large gun gleamed under his arm against the moonlight. Dad stood in his housecoat, watching Ez.

"I said I'm fine, boy; don't have soft knees."

Dad flinched under Ez's barrage of word assaults. This was our routine: Ez insulted Dad with every word he could think of. Trying to talk to Ez about his voice and his tone was pointless; he didn't understand it, nor did he try. He didn't try to purposely hurt anyone, but he truly had no filter. Sidney and I knew how he was, and we didn't take it personally.

Dad took it all personally.

Dad put up with him because of his love for Mom, but Ez made it difficult. He blasted Dad for working too much, not chopping down wood fast enough. He even told him he should go find a "candy girl," when Mom got sick and went away. That was the only time I saw Dad raise his voice towards Ez. He slammed his hands on the table that day and said, "Dammit Ezra! Don't tell me to get a new woman when you haven't let Mama Jackie go this whole time!" Ez said nothing to Dad that day. He started up The Bus hard and peeled out of our driveway kicking up dust home. Not canoed home—he hopped in his car and drove home.

A roar escaped Ez's body, and he guffawed with laughter. "I'm going home now—my stories is about to come on." Ez paddled toward his home and as he cut through water, he laughed the entire way.

The four of us sighed and watched Ez paddle in the opposite direction.

"What stories come on at this time of night?" Malachi asked.

"Who knows," I whispered, watching Ez paddle away as he disappeared into the night.

When he got out of view, Dad flopped back towards the house, a scowl in tow.

"Go home Malachi," Dad slammed the door shut.

PART 2

MIND-*FUL*

CHAPTER 10

GLANCING MRS. GREEN up and down, I repeated, "Excuse me?"

"Oh, honey, it's just that the cleaning ladies will come, and they must pull up right out front. It's not a big deal, we have plenty of parking in the back."

Giving Jaxon's mom, a blank stare — I retreated the way I came.

I arrived at the Greens' residence this morning at seven o'clock, per Jaxon's instructions. He was still asleep, and when I turned into their long driveway, the house loomed in front of me. It was like one of those houses you saw on HGTV. The grass was green, and baskets of flowers sat on the front porch. Mrs. Green asked me to move The Bus. Ez let me use his car, and it clambered down the street, the timing belt squealing along the way. Mrs. Green wanted me to park it in the back. I called bullshit already.

"Sure, Mrs. Green," I lied. "Not a problem."

The car fired back to life with thunderous noise, and it backfired as I pulled out. Mrs. Green's eyes widened while she squinted around the neighborhood.

"Come on in here, chile," a Hispanic woman ushered me from the back door. She wore a maid's outfit, and she waved me inside.

"You the girl making that video for Mr. Jaxon?" Her eyes were roaming me.

"Yes." My camera bag dug into my shoulder and I switched arms, carrying the load. I was careful with it, the library acted as if it were a bomb they were loaning me. "When will you return it? What are you doing again? Are you planning for personal use?" The tech department's questions were endless. It would be safe with me — I did not want to lug it around either.

"You know what you doing?" she gave me quizzical eyes. Her Spanish accent was heavy, and her gaze held mine.

I nodded.

"Okay Mrs. Green wake up early, but she know you coming so you see her already. Mr. Green wake up next, and Jaxon last. Maybe Mr. Dylan here, I go see."

Dylan was Jaxon's older brother. I hoped they were all up so I could get shots of them together. "Is there somewhere for me to set up my camera?"

"Come with me," she pointed.

"I didn't catch your name?"

"I'm Ivette, and I cook three times a week."

"Three times a week," I repeated. "And what is that like, cooking for the family?"

Ivette shrugged her shoulders and pursed her lips together.

"It's a job, and it puts my daughter through school...don't put that in your little video," she muttered, her accent becoming more pronounced.

A tall, heavyset man with bright blue eyes walked in and he looked exactly like Jaxon except his hair was salt and pepper and he had deep laugh lines all over his face. "Are you the new housekeeper? Hold on, I have my dry cleaning," he disappeared into another room.

"No, Mr. Green," Ivette interrupted. "She no housekeeper. She write the article for Mr. Jaxon."

I nervously smiled at Mr. Green and turned slightly to show the bulky camera on my shoulder.

"Oh, I'm so sorry." He gave a sheepish simper.

Ivette squinted at me and stood in the kitchen's corner.

"Is there anything you need from us?" Mrs. Green walked into the kitchen at the perfect opportunity. Too perfect. Maybe she heard him accuse me of being the help.

"N-no," I sputtered. "Is Jaxon awake?"

"I don't believe so. You can go in his room—it's time for him to get up. You can see how he really lives in that cave of his he calls a room. It's the third door on the left at the end of the hallway," Mrs. Green pointed. Mrs. Green didn't say hello and didn't mention making me move my car. It was already forgotten in her eyes.

"I'm up, Mom," Jaxon strolled into the kitchen. He greeted me with a hug and looked me in my eyes for the first time. His smile was natural, and his hair was tossed and disheveled. He wore a crumpled T-shirt and basketball shorts. He still wore his man flops.

"This is Indigo, Dad, she's writing my piece for the *Tunica Rivers Times* like we discussed."

"Indigo, what an *interesting* name," he commented. He scrolled through his phone and he said interesting, like it was a curse word. I didn't like the way it rolled off his tongue. I gave another pensive smile. "I hope you don't mind. I contacted your supervisor at the *Times* about the project. She and I used to golf together, and it seemed like the obvious thing to do."

The obvious thing to do, I mulled.

"It's fine," I nodded. What else could I say?

"You know I just love that blog of yours, it's so refreshing to read from someone your age. When UGA wouldn't admit Jaxon without an essay, and his SAT scores were so poor, we knew we had to pull some strings. Since he's majoring in broadcast journalism we thought instead of an essay, we could do a video blog. Who wants to read a stuffy essay anyway? You were my first choice to help put something like this together. Right, Jaxon? Our boy wants to be an ESPN reporter!" Mrs. Green babbled and exposed her son in more ways than one.

When Jaxon and I met the week prior, I asked him if there was anything I needed to know about his article and video, and he had said no. Meeting his mom for the first time, she told it all. UGA declined to admit him? Why? Majoring in broadcast journalism? That was news to me. It made more sense now, why they chose me for the piece. I was the hometown, around the way girl. If they ever needed to pull their 'I have Black friends spiel,' they could point to this moment and detail how they hired a Black girl to help their dear son. And did Jaxon's parents really like my writing? Or did they think it was good enough for a Black girl?

"That's our boy," Mr. Green beamed.

"There's your boy late already," Mrs. Green scolded. "Do you want breakfast?"

"No, I'm going to grab something at school," Jaxon said.

My hands felt clammy watching the dynamics within Jaxon's family. I stood off to the side next to Ivette, invisible.

I need to keep my hands busy or else they would shake. "Do you guys mind if I get some family shots for the video?" I suggested.

Mr. Green perused the newspaper, still in his pajamas. Mrs. Green wore a long black business suit with high heels that clicked and clacked with every step.

"I guess that's okay," Mrs. Green never glanced up from her phone.

"Mr. Green, what do you do?"

"I'm a Construction Inspector,"

"And I'm the lead attending doctor at Ochsner in NOLA." Mrs. Green added.

Wow, a doctor.

"And what school are you attending in the fall?" Mrs. Green skimmed me up and down.

"I will be applying to a few schools, but I haven't finalized my plans just yet." I had at least four colleges I narrowed it down to. I hated to admit it, but it seemed like it may come down to price and location for me. I wanted to stay within three hours of home, for Sidney and Dad, but I also didn't want to spend an arm and a leg—we just didn't have it like that.

"You won't have any issues getting in as the schools are big on cultural diversity this year." She nodded her head and leaned in as if she shared an insider tip with me.

"Woman!" Mr. Green proclaimed and shook his head.

My stomach churned, and heat rushed to my body. Instinct told me to ball up my fist, and I did.

Did she just say what I think she said?

"Ma, come on, we have to get to school," Jaxon cut his mom short in mid-sentence.

"Well, you let Jaxon know what school you're interested in so I can write your letter of recommendation. If you need anything else, please let me know—I love to see another girl taking on the world," she smiled.

"Thank you, I will keep that in mind," I pursed my lips together and waited for Jaxon. This was going to be a long day.

"I can drive myself," I said, walking towards The Bus.

"No, you'll drive with me," Jaxon ordered.

He glanced at The Bus just like his mom did.

I gritted my teeth.

"Jaxon, will you be able to bring me back tonight to pick up my car?" I clenched my teeth.

"Of course, why would I leave you?"

Not saying anything, I walked to the passenger side and hopped in. I would've preferred to meet him at the school anyway, but I thought it would look more authentic if we opened the video with shots from his house and family. The inside of Jaxon's JEEP looked different from when I peered at it zooming down the street. Under my feet, his floor mats were embroidered with "JG." The letters were bright red with orange flames shooting from the bottom. This symbol was also in the headrests. His massive dashboard resembled a motherboard of some sort with social media icons on the touch screen. The inside had that new car smell. Jaxon hopped in, touching a few of the icons on the screen, and pulled off. He didn't buckle up.

CHAPTER 11

DRIVING IN THE car with Jaxon was a crash course in why safety belts were invented. He didn't use blinkers—like, at all. He took the four-way stops first, regardless if it was his turn.

I remember Dad teaching me to drive. He said, "Let the other car go first. Even if it's your turn. You'll wish you waited a second longer when everyone else wants to go first too."

Jaxon didn't stop. He always went first.

We stopped to grab breakfast from a corner store and Jaxon gave a homeless man three dollars. He turned to me and said, "did you get that?" I got it. Oh, I got it Jaxon.

Jaxon's Advanced History class was a fucking joke. First of all, they held the advanced classes in a separate wing of the school. I've had no reason to enter this wing of the school, so today with Jaxon I was mind blown by the difference. My side of the school ran out of paper for the printers, and our walls were littered with "Join the Army" and "Save a Life, Be a Nurse" posters. I stopped in front of a sign-up sheet for engineering camp. Engineering! I don't know any engineers, and I don't even know what they do. That wasn't a word I heard too often

unless I went looking for it for a story I was writing. I wrote about engineers from what I had read—but for this side of the school, it was a real option.

With one word they segregated us—advanced. What was an Advanced History class, anyway? Did someone know more history than others, and that made them advanced? Made no sense to me. I saw a poster encouraged girls to consider chemistry as a career choice. Chemistry! Another flyer called for tryouts for a poetry slam! That one stung the most. At seventeen, they weren't told to join the army or become a nurse. They could explore their creativity, while the other side of the school had to hit the ground running with vocations and skills that ultimately still benefited them.

The bell rang and students took their seats. "You can sit right here, Ms. Lewis. I'm Mrs. Fagoli. I think it's so nice you're taking the time to do this for Jaxon. You know he has some struggles," she nodded her head at me and raised one eyebrow.

"What does that mean?"

"Oh nothing," she hesitated. "Is there anything we can do for you while you're here?"

"I'm not even here," I waved my hands at her. I didn't want to be noticed—I just wanted to get the information I needed, and then my letter of recommendation from Jaxon, and be done with it. Mrs. Fagoli sat me in the back corner of the room, and although I wasn't a part of the classroom, I had a bird's-eye view of everyone.

The class was comprised of juniors and a few seniors who needed the extra credits. Jaxon was one of those seniors. I wasn't familiar with many juniors; hell, I wasn't familiar with this wing of the school. Everyone's privilege was on display in this class. iPhones, car keys, and varsity jackets lined the student desks. Speaking of the desks, theirs were larger, and they had more space to place their expensive water bottles.

Jaxon sat at his desk and laughed with a female student. His hand landed on the small of her back while she stood next to him. One of the girls wore jeans with slits at the knee, and I remembered when Mila and I were on our side of school, they often sent her to the vice principal's office for knee slits. Mila got sent home and one day of in school suspension. These girls got a warning. There was even a whole separate entrance for these students to enter, one that we never noticed. Wait until I told Mila about this. Crazy thing was when I looked around the room, Mila resembled some of these girls, and she would probably fit right in—if given the chance. And even though we did attend TRHS and not the other high school in town, Mila still lived on the rough end of our town in a double wide widow trailer. I guess home really is where the heart is. Or it could be your quicksand.

"Settle down, class, let's get started," Mrs. Fagoli said from the front. "There's a lot going on in the world right now. Can we agree on that? I found this article, which gave an interesting editorial piece on current events. Let's read together and then discuss," Mrs. Fagoli passed a copy of the article around the classroom.

"I'll take one too," I said as she passed me by.

I skimmed the article.

To the man in the red brick house:

Every day, I take the same route to work, and every day, I pass the police station. Then further up the road is the fire station. Half a mile later, I hit an intersection, and I make a left at this corner. On the right-hand corner sits a red brick house. A man lived in this red brick house, and some days when I drove to work, I caught glimpses of a large, red, Republican flag. It wasn't there every day; some days he

took it down. I always pondered his reasons for taking it down. Did a neighbor oppose it? Was someone messing with it through the night? The questions remained as time went on because the flag always re-emerged, brighter than ever. So did my curiosity.

Now — let's talk about this flag for a second. The man had the type of flag post that needed to be mounted into the wall. Yeah, he had that one.

He meant business.

That told me he was the real deal and about that flag life. Along with the flag proudly perched on his stoop, sat a Veteran's yard sign. Deducing that he was probably a Vet, I was curious. I rode by this house every day for two years. The weather changed and transitioned from fall, winter and then spring. His red, white, and blue stars stayed in place. What made him put it up or take it down? Did kids come by and think it was funny to torment him by ripping it from the post? Did he have to buy new ones often? I made up wild stories in my mind trying to put logic to his actions — all based on a flag. Does anyone remember seeing the flag displayed this much? Unpopular opinion: I don't know about you guys, but I've never seen a more proud American, until another movement decided to ask for basic human rights. But I digress . . .

Election day came and went and we're aware of what happened. Justice prevailed and Blue took care of business. We jumped for joy — it felt like a new day! If this had been the 1940s, we'd be kissing in the streets, celebrating the end of World War II with our feet kicked up. In my happiness, the man in the red brick house ran briefly across my mind. I wondered when he would remove his flag and how he would feel. Was that the humanity in me? Or the crazy? I figured his mood was in dark contrast to my happiness

and excitement. A few days later, I drove past his house once more and the flag was still there and again the next day. The next day, yep, you betcha — it was there again. Finally, one Friday morning, there was no flag. Is it wrong of me to say I was excited? I had so many thoughts and had pictured this moment in my mind. What had been the tipping point? Did someone come and take the flag down — angrily snatching it away from his house? Or did he come to his senses and realize his dashing dreams for a red nation were over? Did he even care, or did he want all this nonsense to be over? Did he indeed believe that Black lives mattered? Finally?

I questioned myself during this time. I kept asking why do you look for his house every day? What makes you pause? I wondered about the man in the red brick house. I had tons of questions, but I knew one thing for sure. No matter which side of the coin we fell, we needed healing. Most of us needed to heal from that red flag. The world had been operating at 50% and ready to boil over at any moment. The bandage was ripped off, and it forced the country to tackle racism head on. How can we do that when people still deny that it even exists, and they fly their flag proud?

To the man in the red brick house... I'd love to sit down and talk? My stoop or yours?

"Thoughts, anyone?" Mrs. Fagoli gave a sly smile, glancing up from the article.

"Whatttt?" A girl said from the front of the class. She shook her head and tossed the article back on the desk. Her friend next to her slapped her arm and snickered.

"The man in the red brick house removing his flag means he now believes that Black lives matter?" A student questioned.

95

His face was turned up like he just heard the most ridiculous thing ever.

"So, let's talk about the Black lives and why they matter," Mrs. Fagoli urged.

Sitting up straighter, I was keenly aware of my melanin today. I crossed my feet under the desk and rested my hands under my chin. They held their conversation and didn't notice the one melanated person in the back of the room. Unseen and unheard. I was still subservient, and they didn't notice. Just like at Jaxon's house.

"I get it man, I really do, but why do you have to take down the statues? What did they do to anybody?" A boy said aloud. A few students snickered.

"Yea, like they want us to like, kiss their ass because of slavery? Dude, I didn't do that shit," the boy said.

"Language!" Mrs. Fagoli warned.

You let me say 'shit' out loud. Off to the VP's office I would go, I huffed.

"I just don't get it." A soft-spoken girl from the front added. Her voice was so low I could hardly hear her. "I mean, if you break the law, shouldn't you be held accountable?"

Jaxon remained quiet throughout the conversation, and a few times his eyes connected with mine. Something inside told me had I not been in class that day, he would engage with his friends and tee-hee about the article. He briefly cut his eyes at me and because my presence was a service to him, he remained quiet. He needed me, and at this moment, we both knew. That thought settled me, but I still crossed my arms and exhaled slowly.

"It's like you can't say anything nowadays without being called racist," someone said. The class grumbled and nodded their heads in agreement.

Another girl said from the left side of the room, "My parents raised me to not see color. I don't care if you're Black, white, purple, or blue; if you treat me good, I treat you good."

The class clapped for her, and even Ms. Fagoli applauded.

I gritted my teeth so hard my neck hurt, and my body twitched. I relaxed my shoulders, but the heat flushed over my body. What was I even doing here? I was used to being the only Black girl in class. These were things that were a given and I knew to expect at some juncture in life. Being the minority. But sitting here through this conversation and knowing that I was just a tool to help them get to where they wanted, hurt. I steadied myself on the chair and locked my ankles tighter. I fought for everything I had all my life and they mocked it. Their half-assed stories about why the statues depicting slave masters and rapists who brutalized my ancestors were important. They were angry that their families paid money on their summer vacations to visit a slave plantation and when the tour guides wore costumes and actually discussed slavery, they were aghast. They just wanted to 'see the land,' and not be burdened with the truths of history they claimed they wanted to experience. Experiencing it real time was almost too much as I listened to their half-ass stories. The reasons to help them justify the dumb things they did. And what was my justification for sitting there and listening? Was it because I needed them like Jaxon needed me at this moment? We were using each other, that was for sure. But this, this felt different.

If Ez was here, he'd slam his hands on the desk and get up there and tell them about the time when he was a young boy and two white boys kidnapped and waterboarded him.

When he first told me that story, I said, "Why do you stay on the water so much then, Ez?"

"I got to stay on the water so it don't stay on me," he replied.

I was a kid then, but now I understood.

If my dad was here, he'd quietly rise and leave the room. Never one to make a scene, he would exercise his right to choose, and he would choose to walk away.

My mom, she'd be up there raising holy hell—this I know for sure. Out of those three, I sided with Mom right now; but, I did nothing. I cringed and listened to it all.

My hands were still clenched, and I glanced around, fantasizing different ways to hurt any student who found humor in what was said. That one over there had long hair…it could be chopped off in her sleep…him over there…he palmed his varsity jacket like it was his lifeline. What if it mysteriously disappeared? And Mrs. Fagoli, never choosing a side and preferring to play the grey area. Yeah, her too…I seethed with rage at her for not checking her students. Checking them for what though? They didn't think they said anything wrong.

Stop Indigo, what are you even thinking? My breath quickened. Don't even joke like that.

Before I let the rage take over my thoughts again, Mrs. Fagoli asked, "and how can we make ourselves better?"

The class hushed, and Jaxon finally spoke. He cleared his throat. "We fight, for our right, to paarrtayyy," he sang and played an air guitar with his hands.

The class erupted into laughter, and Mrs. Fagoli chuckled.

Hot tears sprang to my eyes as I brushed them away. My heart pounded, and I hoped they didn't see me wipe my face. I didn't want to give them the satisfaction of seeing my eyes red. Jaxon and I weren't close by any means, but even with me sitting here at his request, battle lines were clearly drawn, and he chose his side. Race existed in my world because I had to exist in theirs. I was not okay.

CHAPTER 12

AFTER JAXON'S HISTORY class, my stomach was in knots. I never even filmed anything I was taken aback by the assignment. Stopping in the girl's bathroom before lunch, I burst through the door and glimpsed myself in the mirror. What was the purpose of this? Why was I doing this? It helped Jaxon get into college, but how was it helping me? The newspaper loved the idea of following 'one of their own' before his college journey. Funny, I worked there part time for two years and they never considered me one of their own. But Jaxon—his status came without thought. Everyone knew where he stood and what he could attain, just because of his skin color and gender.

Jaxon didn't remind me of any man I knew, not that I had too many men to look up to. Ez was Ez. And Dad, I tried not to give him any trouble, so he didn't have to worry about me. Going to college was his greatest wish for me, and I wanted to give him that. I wanted to be the first to go to college and get a degree. Mom was in the army for a short time before she got sick. She said she always regretted attending the army and not college, if only for the experience. I didn't want any of those regrets, and I looked forward to the sleepless nights and endless schoolwork. College would get me where I needed to go, and I was ready.

This morning before I left for Jaxon's, I couldn't sleep and woke up early, staring at my computer. I reread my essays and glossed over the applications once more. I filled them out and agonized over every word. Now it was real. The date was here, and I couldn't force myself to press send. Dad inquired about the application fees and when I told him how much they were, he didn't fuss and didn't even suck his teeth. He said he'd work on it. I told him not to worry, and that they had waived the fee. I didn't tell him how many hours I spent at the funeral home and writing extra articles for the *Tunica Rivers Times*. Working two part-time jobs and holding down an editor position at school was still not enough, but I made it work.

"Let's talk Spring Fling!" Jaxon sat on his lunch table next to his latest fling, McKenzie. "It's going to be so lit. My mom got The Bordeaux Mansion as planned. And guys, my parents won't be there," he grinned. McKenzie grinned too.

I'm sure this would excite Will and Mila. Hell, I wanted to check out a mansion too.

I gawked at Will, Malachi, and Mila from across the cafeteria. Will was shooting chicken nuggets into Malachi's mouth as they laughed.

I swallowed. We sat together every day. The four of us. They were having fun without me and not even concerned that I was over here with Jaxon. And Jaxon. He only noticed my presence while we were alone. When his friends came around or a girl he flirted with, I soon became invisible.

I stayed by myself in another corner of the table. They sat with their backs to me. I nibbled at my sandwich and ate a few potato chips at the same time. When the anger built up, I wasn't hungry, and when it settled, I was ravenous.

"Have I introduced you to Indigo?" Jaxon interrupted the laughter. He made his way towards me while I was in mid-chew. I gulped and a lump of sandwich stuck in my throat. This was not happening.

"H-h, hi-," I stammered, reaching for a drink of my iced tea.

"Indigo, that's an interesting name," Jaxon's friend said.

"Indigo. Is it like, Indian or something?" Another one of Jaxon's friends teased.

"I don't think so," I said. What was so interesting about my name that made people say it twice now?

"You sit over there, right?" The same girl asked. She pointed to the table with Will, Mila, and Malachi. Now the three of them were taking selfies without me.

I nodded.

"You and Will are dating?"

"No, Malachi and I are dating. Will and I are just best friends," I corrected.

"Humph," she grunted.

"Do you have classes with them?" I asked.

"Yes, Technology class with Will. He's a nice guy," she nodded.

"He is."

"Do you listen to Lil' Baby?" a boy asked, standing next to Jaxon.

"Umm, sometimes," I said. *What the fuck?*

"He's my man," the boy nodded his head in approval.

"And?" I pressed, with major attitude.

The boy crinkled his nose and said, "Chill, I just wanted to know what kind of music you listen to. I listen to everything."

My breathing was shallow, and I blinked back tears for the second time that day. Dammit. I was madder at myself for letting them get to me. I had to be on point with these people; their racism showed back up whenever I let my guard down.

"But why would you come out and ask me if I listen to that one rapper? Because I'm Black, so I listen to all rap music?" The words flew from my mouth and the more I talked, the more I heard my Mom's voice.

"*Take them out,*" she whispered. "*Run them down, they want you to.*"

The thought brought goosebumps to my arms.

"Indigo, chill," Jaxon squinted.

"I'm cool," I said. "*Back in your place they want you to go,*" I heard a voice within me murmur. I shot a look at Jaxon before turning my head. I hadn't taken my camera or my recorder out during lunch. There was nothing here to see, folks.

My phone buzzed.

> **WILL:** You okay?

I glanced up and spotted him across the room, looking at his phone. I smiled.

> **ME:** Where do I begin?

> **WILL:** Last class of the day! What's he got?

I wasn't sure which class was the last one of the day at this point. I just needed it to be over. I checked out Jaxon's schedule.

> **ME:** English.

> **WILL:** 1.5 hours, how bad could it be?

We would see.

"Hi Jaxon, how are you? We are reading and working in pairs today. Will that be okay?" his English teacher asked. "You can pair with Mitchell."

She said nothing to me.

"Hi," I said, stepping forward. "My name is Indigo, and I'm shadowing Jaxon. Where can I sit?" My arms were open and I plastered a fake smile on my face, but I didn't feel like smiling. My mask spoke for me.

"Oh hello," she glanced at me. "I'm Mrs. McGill. You're doing the article, right?"

It was interesting. Jaxon told his teachers about the article for the *Times*, but not about the video for college. "Yes." I took a long breath. "I'm not here though; I'll take a chair in the back." I waved my hands again. How many times would I wave away people who didn't acknowledge my presence anyway?

She shifted her weight from one foot to another and gave a short chuckle. "When he said someone was shadowing him, I just thought...nevermind, you can sit here, India."

"Indigo."

Mrs. McGill paused. "...Indigo," she repeated. The way she sounded it out made me question how long she had been an English teacher.

Jaxon was sitting with his partner, Mitchell, off to the side of the room. He had walked off and left me to introduce myself to all of his teachers. Jaxon had disappearing acts like Malachi did. Malachi went wherever things were fun and full of food. Jaxon disappeared fast so he never had to answer questions.

"Okay class, we have our passages on our desks. Let's read through them together and answer the attached questions."

I sat up in my chair and spied Jaxon. If my suspicions were correct and he couldn't read, English should be his most difficult subject, right? I wanted to talk to him alone about the video, anyway. Maybe get some on-air commentary, in his own words, about why we were doing an alternative video/article combo. I wondered if I could get Jaxon to a comfortable place and he could discuss some of his reading issues, maybe it would help his submission to college. Everyone loves a sap story, and a rich white boy who couldn't read did the trick. I shared my suspicions about Jaxon's lack of reading with no one though, but I already knew the real deal. The way his mom dropped his business on the kitchen table this morning told me more than I needed to know. No more words were necessary. It was time for Jaxon to put up or shut up, and I needed to *see* it.

The class descended into a sea of murmured voices as they read the passage in pairs. Mitchell began reading for Jaxon. This went on for a few minutes until Mrs. McGill said, "switch." One by one, each pair changed readers, only Jaxon did not read. Mitchell continued reading for Jaxon, and not only was he reading—but Jaxon took out his cell phone and began texting through the lesson.

"And don't forget the questions," Mrs. McGill sat at her desk. She took a sip of her own large Yeti water bottle and cut her eyes at Jaxon and Mitchell. She didn't look surprised or upset.

He would at least pull his weight and complete the questions. No ... no, he didn't. I watched Mitchell take the worksheet and begin completing those too. Mitchell and Jaxon engaged in this symbiotic dance of reading and writing. They made no eye contact, nor did they share a laugh. It seemed so formal and business-like. This wasn't their first time behaving like this in English class; this was their norm. Mitchell did the work and Jaxon put his name on it, rendering it his. No wonder Jaxon struggled. People made it easy for him to skate through life doing the bare minimum. It had gotten him this far, why change it now? I was complicit too—doing what he wanted me to do to help him get along. When would someone help me get along? I slumped in my seat and placed my bookbag in my lap. There was nothing to see here either, I griped.

The last bell rang, and I jumped in my seat. Drool sat in the corner of my mouth and I wiped it, realizing I fell asleep. When I woke, Jaxon's friend, the same one from the cafeteria who told me to chill, and asked if I listened to Lil Baby, was holding my camera and eyeing it. "This is so cool," he held it up and placed it on his shoulder.

"I'll take that," I said, rising from my seat.

He snatched away from me and palmed the lenses. "This thing is huge."

My hands shook as I watched him clumsily fumble with getting the camera back into its bag. I hesitated and extended my arms forward to help with the bag, but he snatched away again and this time, the side of the camera struck the wall corner and a piece of black plastic popped off and the lens cracked.

The boy's eyes widened.

I searched the room for Jaxon, but he was up front flirting and not paying attention. I exhaled and balled my fists again.

"I told you to put it down!" I screeched. "This isn't even mine!" I thought about the third degree the library ran down on me about the camera, and if I was in a cartoon, surely steam would be fuming from my ears.

"Uh, my bad. I just wanted to see it." The boy's face resembled a tomato. He hastily shoved it back into the camera bag he removed it from while I fell asleep in the back of the class. I snatched it back from him and picked up the broken piece off the floor. This was not happening.

"Take care of him Indy, you already know how!" something in me whispered.

"Uh, Indigo." Jaxon walked towards me. By his side stood a leggy blonde — not Mckenzie.

"I'm going take Marissa out, can you find a ride home?"

My ears fumed. Was I hearing him correctly? No sooner had Jaxon walked up that the boy scurried out the door. "You told me not to take my car because you would bring me back. And your friend broke my camera."

"I know, I know, I'm an asshole, and so is he" His blonde hair moved at every head nod.

His leggy blonde said, "Just call her an Uber, she'll be fine."

The one thing I asked Jaxon was if he could take me home, and now he was ditching me for some girl. "You know what," I said, putting my hands up. "It's fine, I'll figure it out."

"Okay, thanks, I owe you big." he didn't look at me. Jaxon walked away with his leggy blonde and I faintly heard her mutter the word "angry." I grabbed my cell phone and texted Will for a ride to Jaxon's house to retrieve The Bus. In one moment, they made me an angry Black woman. And this time, they got it right.

A few nights ago, I started having a recurring dream about Mom. We were both in the car and she was driving about to hit that man, only in this dream, it was Jaxon's friend who broke my camera, walking across the street—not the old man. I wanted to rush the boy like Mom had rushed the old man. I felt her foot slam the floor as she sped up. She giggled as she picked up speed and I sat in the passenger side. At first, I was scared, and I hung on to the grab handles, but Mom and I giggled together as we closed in on him. His eyes were wide, and he turned his back to the car, bracing for impact. In the dream, that made Mom and I laugh even harder. It scared me, but it didn't at the same time.

When I woke up after that dream, I smirked. It felt so real, and when my thoughts turned to hurting others, it didn't seem like such a bad thing. Don't get me wrong, I didn't fantasize about hurting other people all of the time. But while I shadowed Jaxon, I felt like something shadowed me. There were different versions of myself coming out today while with him. His world brought out different sides of me. The anger threatened to boil over, and I didn't know where or why. The dream ended the same way, Mom and I beamed at each other as we ran the man over. I was equally complicit and wanted to see how he bounced in the air—if he hit the ground with as much force as people said. I've been doing the right thing for so long that when the opportunity presented itself, albeit a dream—wrong tasted so good. And that thought, indeed, was scary. I was fighting myself for myself.

The classroom was empty now, even Mrs. McGill was gone. I glanced down at my camera that I'd tossed into the bag, while squeezing the broken off piece into my hand, and made my way to the front to wait for Will. He had senior release too and would sometimes leave school early to get to work. Today was just my luck that he was already gone when I needed a ride. I hated to be a burden and hated even more that he had to leave work to come pick me up.

All because of Jaxon.

While sitting on the curb, Joya walked next to me and plopped down. She breathed and looked as if something heavy was on her heart.

"Are you okay?" I asked.

She said nothing but one tear fell from her eye. "Have you ever felt like things are falling apart, and you know what needs to be done to fix it, but you know in your heart you won't do it?"

Joya's honesty jarred me. I wondered what she knew, and how she knew it. Things were falling apart and the voices in my head told me to resort to violence, but my heart wouldn't let me do it. I couldn't explain that to her though. I'm pretty sure we were not talking about the same thing.

"Yes-yes, I have."

"You can't trust men. You just can't. They'll say anything to shut you up in the moment," she sulked.

I was sullen. "Yes, yes they will."

Joya wiped her tears and sat up straighter. "Anyway, while you're here, I want to submit a couple poetry pieces. I've been writing them myself," she smiled.

Even I knew that changing the subject, would not make it go away—whatever it was. But I played along anyway. "That's great; we always need poetry. Can you email it to me?"

Joya nodded. Her eyes were red and puffy.

Silence fell between us, and before I could think about what I was saying, I blurted, "I saw you, at the park…with Mr. Chestnut."

Joya sighed and closed her eyes for a few seconds. Fat tears squeezed from her eyes. Again.

"Is it him you can't trust?"

She nodded.

"Joya…are you okay?" I asked earnestly.

"I'm fine. My parents are buying me a new car, and I won't have to wait for rides like this. Senior year is coming up. I'm fine!" She sniffed.

I became very aware of sitting on the curb waiting for a ride. I, too, knew the feeling of not being able to trust a man, I sulked.

"I'm pregnant…" she whispered.

I think she was waiting for me to freak out. For me to say, Joya, are you crazy? What are you thinking?

I didn't.

I exhaled and took in her words. High schoolers got pregnant all the time but not by a school staff member—that was an entirely different story. "So, what are you going to do about it? Does anyone know?"

Joya was quiet and pulled her legs to her chest. She rested her face on her knee and closed her red eyes. They were swollen, and more tears squeezed their way out.

"I-I'm getting the procedure done next week."

"Are your parents taking you? Is it his? Do your parents know it's his?" The questions rapidly fired out of me.

"My mom said she was coming, and Dad offered to drive and sit in the car. I told them I'd rather be alone; besides, I don't want them to have to take any time off from work. I'd never hear the end of it. They have to use a PTO day to take me to have an abortion. I just don't want to be around that energy, you know? So, it'll be just me. They haven't directly asked about it since, and we don't really talk about it like it's real. Like it's here, and it's happening in real time. We talk about it like it's already a thing of the past. It's the one stain on their parenthood certificate they had to overcome and sweep under the rug. I told my parents it was someone from school. I didn't want him to get into trouble."

"Joya…this isn't your fault." My heart ached for her, and I wanted to grab and hug her for dear life. The sky thundered as we sat on the curb and I hoped it wouldn't rain on us. I placed my hand on her shoulder and rubbed it, trying to console her in some way. Black girl to Black girl. Sister to sister. We didn't need to be close for me to be there for her. Joya closed her eyes and more tears fell from her eyes.

"I know it's not but still. I learned a lot from him. It's just easier this way, to not rock the boat. He's there for me, he listens and cares. I know what people say. That he's done this before, and he just hasn't gotten caught. I hear all of it."

"Joya, you love him," I said. It was a statement, not a question.

She was quiet while she hugged herself. She couldn't get an abortion and go by herself. I didn't know her that well, but no girl should have to go through that alone. Funny how Mr. Chestnut wasn't even in the running for who was accompanying Joya on that emotional day.

"What about your other friends?"

"I never told them anything. I wanted to, a few times I wanted to." Joya picked at the frayed ends of her jeans. "But I know the way we talk about people, and I know the way they'll talk about me. Again, I don't want that energy."

Then why tell me? Why share with me while we're sitting on a curb with clouds lightly spitting over our heads? Why would Joya lay this on me when she hasn't even shared it with her friends? Before I asked myself any more questions, I blurted out, "I'll go with you."

"What do you mean?" Joya lifted her head and cocked an eye at me.

"To the procedure. I'll go with you."

Joya and I were quiet for a few moments before the same silver car from the park pulled up in front of the school. The window rolled down and this time I was sure what I saw. Mr. Chestnut, our track coach, was picking up Joya. There were three other juniors in the car, and they all wore their Track and Field suits. Joya didn't wear hers today, but he was still here to pick her up from school. He pulled up right out front, not even afraid.

"Okay..." Joya nodded. "Okay."

She stood, wiped her tears and hopped into the car. Her eyes locked with mine and I could see them behind the tint. They were sad.

Hot tears sprang to my eyes. I opened my bag and retrieved my broken camera; I needed something to occupy my mind. It made a whirring sound and the lens was jammed halfway shut. I screamed out loud in frustration and shoved the camera back into the bag. Jaxon Green's video had officially cost me money; the library would have my head for this one, I was sure of it.

When Will arrived fifteen minutes later, I watched the white kids whizz by me in their muscle cars while the kids who looked like me took the after-school bus. I fumbled with the door handle trying to get in. Mad that I had to wait and mad about Joya, for Joya.

"What's up with you?" Will's eyes were wide.

I said nothing, but the tears in my eyes wouldn't stop pooling as Will exited the school parking lot. He pulled over on the side of the road and put on his flashers and he rummaged through his dashboard until he found tissues. He handed me a large wad as rain started pouring around us. Loud splatters of water hit his car, and I couldn't hear the radio anymore. Thunder cracked over us, and it raged outside like I raged inside. I heaved and cried, sitting in the car with my palms in my face. I didn't know what to do; I didn't know why I was crying, but at the same time, I knew perfectly well why. Favor was not fair.

Will said nothing and handed me more tissues. He'd never seen me cry. Not like this. Once, when we were in middle school, I caught myself being a bully. I was teasing another student outside during recess, and he ran down a small hill to get away from me. Chasing him, I tripped over a loose branch and fell down the hill. Rolling all the way down, I landed on my back with a loud "umph." Students circled around me and laughed while I struggled to stand. The sun was blinding. Will came over; and he stood in front of me blocking the sun. As I lay on the ground, he extended a hand to help me rise. That was the last time Will saw me cry. Today, I was sitting in his car, hysterical in a thunderstorm.

Will looks like he wants to hold me, to comfort me, but I wasn't ready. I held myself and grabbed at my arms and rocked myself in the car. Will's presence was enough, but I didn't need him to touch me.

111

CHAPTER 13

Hey Mom,

It's me — sorry I didn't get a chance to write last week, a lot of things have been happening. Mom, I hope you're okay and I can talk to you. I have some questions and I don't know what's going on with me right now. Sometimes I'm happy, and sometimes I feel so heavy. The feelings come out of nowhere. They're just so quick. My mood shifts and I think about hurting someone the same way they've hurt me. What happened to the man that you hit? We never talked about it, but I want to hear it, from you. I know it's hard to talk about things in person, and maybe that's why our visits don't get deep. I mean, there are a bunch of people around, but I'd still love to talk about these things. Anyway, what happened to him? Did you do it on purpose? And why? How did it feel? I know this sounds weird, but I don't know. I think I need to know.

How are Minister, Ruth-Ann and Nurse MeanFace? Are they still not letting you guys perform? I'd love to see you all in action when I come up there the next time. I'll try to get Ez to come, but you have to promise to be on your best behavior and not be so loud. You know he's funny about stuff like that.

Sidney is doing so good; you should see her playing Softball now. She tries to keep up with everyone else, but her legs are so short, haha, it's funny to see—but she keeps up. And she's good Ma, really good. Maybe she'll even keep up with it and get a scholarship for college or something. That would be great. She wouldn't have to worry about money and fees; she could just be who she wanted to be with nothing standing in her way. Crazy thoughts, I know.

Anyway, love you. Hope to see you soon.

Love,
Indy

DAYS AFTER THE Jaxon fiasco, Mr. Koffman, my guidance counselor, called me down to his office. I wasn't sure what he wanted. I only saw him one a year when it came time to pick my classes. I don't know what guidance he gave—but it wasn't to me.

"Indigo Lewis, take a seat," he smiled. He said my full name like he knew me, but he didn't.

"They call me Indy," I said.

I plopped down, sinking into the chair. I glanced up at a lopsided framed picture on the wall. It was a still shot of a waterfall and one word was lettered across it.

OPTIMISM

"Indy, yes." he scribbled in his notebook at his tiny desk. I peered around his office; I guess you could call it an office. It was the size of a small closet, even Sidney's room was bigger than this, and it was filled with large file cabinets and smaller notepads everywhere.

"Have we thought about college? After graduation plans?"

113

I cleared my throat. "Yes, I have applications to a few colleges ready to submit."

"Oh?"

"Yes, Titus University and Virginia State University," I said proudly. I had narrowed my choices down to these two. One was close and one was far.

"Virginia…Isn't that an HBCU?"

"Yes."

Mr. Koffman searched through his sea of notebooks, and when he didn't find what he was looking for, he stood and opened his large file cabinet. He pulled a small manila envelope with my name on it. Indigo Lewis.

"It looks here like your dad, Benjamin Barre, is above the poverty limits."

My heart skipped a beat. "What does that mean?"

"It means in all likelihood; you may not receive a good amount of financial aid. He makes too much money, and you may only qualify for loans."

Makes too much money? Did this man want to see our house? Or Sidney's closet? How in the world did Dad make too much money?

"No, he didn't!" a voice in me cried.

"Excuse me?"

Mr. Koffman glanced at me over his glasses. "You may want to take Virginia State off the list. Typically,, HBCU's don't provide a lot of financial aid."

What? I mulled over his words.

"Have you thought about cosmetology school? Or data entry? Those are low-cost programs, and you could have a certificate in one year." He smiled as if he had done what his name implied and provided guidance.

"I saw a sign in the advanced wing, about Engineering camp. What's that about?"

He chuckled and said, "It's a little late for that young lady. We have to get you out into the workforce now. Besides, you have to have a certain GPA and I think…" Mr. Koffman trailed off, his eyes shifted to the manila folder with my name on it in his lap. His ankle was folded over his leg exposing his checkered socks. Why did teachers always wear those types of socks?

"Ah yes, just like I thought. You missed the GPA minimum by a smidge, so you wouldn't have been eligible anyway."

"Oh," I said, sinking into the chair. I wasn't eligible for something I didn't even know existed. Had I known; would I have been interested? Probably not, but I didn't have the choice; it was decided for me when the information wasn't available.

"Mr. Koffman, thank you. I will look into that." I don't know why I said that. I don't know why I lied. My hands shook as I avoided his eyes and I slid them under my butt, so Mr. Koffman didn't see how jittery I was. I had to use the bathroom, and now my palms were clammy.

"Are you cold?" he asked.

"No, no, I'm fine."

"Well, here is some information about the technical school in town. Please let them know I sent you," he beamed.

I took the pamphlet Mr. Koffman handed me with only Black people on the cover wearing nursing scrubs, construction hard hats, and salon aprons.

"Good luck, Indy, please let me know if you need anything else." He extended a handshake. I didn't even need this pamphlet, but I shook his hand anyway.

This was the good high school. The school I was proud to attend. The high school I felt lucky to be a part of. The school that told me to go be a hairdresser.

Sitting in the editor's room a few minutes later, I glanced outside; the trees blew wild against the large windows. Tunica

Rivers in February was not brisk but not warm. One thing I loved about this town was the same thing I hated.

Creating Jaxon's video invaded my afternoon. I had a lot of Jaxon footage from that fateful day, but it proved hard for me to watch. Certain parts made my blood boil, and I had to fast forward. The camera I borrowed from the library was still busted and I still hadn't told anyone what happened, not even Will after I broke down crying in his car. People would think I was careless and irresponsible. I mean, I did fall asleep in class. Maybe I was careless. Dad would have a fit if we had to pay to get it fixed. I didn't know what to say just yet, so I said nothing. My phone chimed.

> **JAXON:** How's the video looking?

> **ME:** It's fine

I couldn't even ruminate in peace; he occupied my phone as well. Jaxon sent back a thumbs up text and I slammed my phone onto the editing table. The word that came to mind for me was triggered. Yeah, that's it—triggered—that's what I would call the article and video. It showed me exactly how we were different and so not the same.

Why did I have to work three times harder for everything? Why did things come so easily to Jaxon and his family? His parents didn't want my car in their driveway, so they made me move it. Jaxon's dad could easily call my job and create a project for me to complete. I had no say in it. Jaxon could fuck up one hundred times and still be deemed successful, but I planned and curated my entire life to even have a seat at the table with him. It just wasn't fair. I spent an entire day in white privilege world, and it was too much for me. It made me bitter and angry.

Sidney, I didn't want her to go through this. To live in this world where she was only judged by her talents or abilities, not by how much money she had, or the color of her skin. None of it made sense to me. When it was her turn to attend Tunica Rivers High School, would there still be two separate sides of the school? Would there be a side where we all took the regular classes and a different side where the honors kids went? And why was that?

When Mom and Dad went here, was it the same way? They were high school sweethearts. He was studious and read books; she was popular and sang in school performances. And now she was at Trochesse Asylum, performing for them. I bet Mom and Dad never thought their life would end up this way.

I would have to make it different and I would have to change it. But how? I was a senior in high school getting ready to go to college; I still wasn't sure which college yet, but I knew I was going somewhere. Somewhere wasn't soon enough. But how could I go to college with these feelings?

The rage inside was tearing through me. I had dreams about hurting other people, but since my time with Jaxon, they just got worse and worse. My fantasies about driving with my mom to hit that man ramped up but now included us riding over the curb and hitting more people. We still laughed, she and I. I wonder if she had those feelings too? Or maybe she was insane like people all said. I wasn't so sure. Mom wasn't the easiest person to talk to. When I went to see her, I never knew when we were getting the truth or another performance. Maybe I should ask her? Did she think about slitting someone's wrist vertically? Had she ever thought about slamming someone's head into a wall? Did it excite her, like it did me? Goosebumps ran up my arms at the thought. I hushed it away.

"Indigo, are you okay? Indigo?" Shantiel's voice snapped me out of my mind.

"Oh-oh, I'm good." I jumped in my seat at her voice. She stared at me with quizzical eyes.

Nico and Trish-Ann walked in behind Shantiel.

"Let's get started," I stood. "Anyone have anything they need to say?"

Nico and Trish-Ann glanced at each other and Shantiel slowly spoke. "Um, are we going to edit the articles?"

Shit.

"Oh, right, right," I rubbed my temples.

Shantiel shot me another look.

Nico turned up his music and Meg Thee Stallion screamed from his computer. "Ayyeee, ayyeee," Nico bounced in his seat.

"Will you turn that down!" I snapped.

Nico looked at me and rolled his eyes. "What's the problem? You don't like Meg?" he swiveled in his rolling chair.

In a flash I was on my feet and I thought about punching him in his face. I bolted in his direction and I was two steps from him when Will intercepted us.

"Whoa, whoa, whoa—come with me," he took my arm.

My heart was beating so fast, but I had a one-track mind: lay hands on Nico. Shantiel spied me and Nico turned his music all the way down. I heard nothing. The three of them stared at me with confusion.

Leading me to the hallway, Will asked, "What the hell is wrong with you?"

"N-nothing," I stammered. I wasn't sure what was wrong with me. These days I wanted to cry, but not in front of Will, not again. I wanted to hide. Hide from myself and everyone else. Why did I take on this dumbass editor job, anyway? I wanted to live the good life, like Jaxon, that's why.

"I'm fine," I replied with a glare, pulling my arm back from him. "Don't grab me like that."

"Are we serious right now? Indy, you know I'd never hurt you. I'm trying to figure you out; you're so hot and cold."

"I know nothing. You know nothing." I stared back. I turned on my heel and walked back into the editor's room, and by the time I got there, Malachi was there chomping on peanuts.

"Hey, Bae, everything okay?"

The Three Stooges sat together at a computer desk, avoiding my eyes. I guess they filled him in.

"I had a rough morning, that's all. Nico, my bad, I was tripping."

"No worries," Nico said, "not everybody likes Meg."

The Three Stooges laughed and returned to their computers.

"Can I talk to you for a second?" Malachi stared. He was seated, chomping on peanuts.

I huffed, "Sure."

Walking back into the hallway now with Malachi, Will was still standing there with his cell phone in hand, texting someone. I looked past him. They both pulled me into the hallway with questions.

"Hey man," Malachi said to Will.

Will said nothing but eyed me.

"We'll be right back," Malachi nodded. He paid no attention to Will's silence. He never paid attention to anything.

The empty classroom next to the editor's room was dark, and I flipped on the lights as we walked in. I plopped down into a desk and Malachi stood in front of me. I peered up at him, ready for his bullshit too.

"Is this about what I said the other night? About me not going to college?"

I said nothing. Did I care? Yes, part of me did. Malachi and I were a team, so I thought. Did I think that we would be high school sweethearts, get married, have kids, then live happily

119

ever after? No, but anything was possible. Malachi was my comfort for the past year now, but we were clearly on two different paths. I'm not sure how I felt anymore.

"Well, I guess it is about college," I started. "Listen, I have a lot going on right now with me. It's not you, it's me. Maybe we should take some time apart."

Malachi's eyes widened. "You're going to hit me with the 'it's not you, it's me' cliché? Really, Indy?" He leaned in and squinted his eyes at me in disbelief.

I didn't blink and repeated what I said. It sounded dumb, that I knew. But too many thoughts and too many emotions that I could not explain were running through me I had no explanation for right now. One minute I wanted to hug him and kiss him; the next minute I was having visions of hurting him and others. Maybe I needed some time to myself.

"I'm sorry, Malachi. It's not just about the college thing. I have a lot going on right now."

"So, what about prom? And Spring Fling?"

"We can still go if you want." If he still wanted to? No, Indigo. Something in me bubbled up again, and I knew that wasn't true either. I didn't want to go. I wanted the choice, and my choice was to not go. There were too many men in my life telling me what to do, and I had enough.

"No. I changed my mind about that too. I don't want to go to Spring Fling with anyone." My head ached and splotches of black clouded my vision. I felt nauseous, and I held onto the small desk to sturdy myself.

"Are you okay? Where is all of this coming from?" His eyes searched mine for answers and he leaned down toward me in the desk.

"I can decide for myself."

"But this just seems so out of the blue."

"So was you not wanting to go to college anymore."

"Again. Is that what this is about?"

"I just don't want to do this anymore!" I screamed. I leaned in close and grimaced until we were almost nose to nose. He stood and stared down at me, so many questions running through his mind. I slammed my hands on the desk glaring up at him. He searched my eyes for something. For what, I didn't know because whatever it was, it wasn't there anymore.

CHAPTER 14

MILA'S CAR SPUTTERED down the street, and I sat over a hole in the floor. She laid down a brown floorboard to cover the hole with duct tape holding it in place. I sat carefully with my legs open on either side. We were on our way to Bordeaux Mansion for Spring Fling, with no adults. The day was finally here, and people were more excited about it than prom. The text message went out about an hour ago from a fake phone number, telling us what to bring. Mila and I were bringing lemonade, and the jug of juice sat in my lap, so it didn't fall in the hole on the floor.

I had put rollers in my long braids the night before, and the curls framed my face. I wore my leather jacket, and I opted for my silver hoop earrings and the locket of my mom. Mila wore a bodysuit, skirt, stockings, and boots. We both pulled for the lip gloss tonight.

"Is Will going to be there?" I looked at Mila.

"You still haven't talked to them?"

"No…" I trailed off. And Mila said them. The "them" had to mean Malachi too.

"You guys have to talk—and soon."

"What has he told you?" I quizzed Mila. I didn't want to admit my anger got the best of me the last time Malachi and I were together at school.

"He said you broke up with him for no reason. And Will I haven't heard from. We've texted, but that's it."

The tone in Mila's voice made my heart flutter. We both weren't talking to Will but for different reasons. Well tonight we would talk—all of us. I would apologize to Malachi and explain that I just needed some time to myself to figure things out. I would also talk to Will because we've been best friends since we were kids, and nothing came between us; we always stuck it out.

Will and I met in daycare. Even though we both don't remember being that young, his mom chuckled recalling how Will carefully helped me down the slide when we were toddlers. "He was so careful with you. He didn't let anyone get too close to his Indy." It was Will who first called me Indy. Not my parents, not Sidney. It was Will.

When we were in middle school, he went away for the summer to his uncle's house in Chicago. I didn't call him because I didn't think he wanted to be bothered. When someone goes on vacation, they don't want to be disturbed, right? I've never been on vacation and wasn't sure. Not wanting to be a bother—I didn't reach out. Will called about two weeks into his visit and said, "If you want this friendship to work we have to treat it like a relationship. We have to put in the time and effort to talk to each other. You don't go two weeks without talking to me and I don't go two weeks without talking to you, okay?"

"Okay," I said to him, my heart full.

Two weeks was our limit, and here we were at ten days. Tonight, tonight would be the night we would talk. I can't remember a time when we weren't able to fix us. Why was I thinking about this now, all of a sudden? Will was my best friend—and nothing more. Will made our friendship complete; our circle became a square—all sides equal. He knew me in a way that I couldn't deny. Something even beyond Malachi. But what was beyond Malachi?

Mila turned down a gravel road and the house sat back on the property blocked by woods. Cars were parked up and down the long driveway, and a short distance away, we made it to the front of the house. Every room was lit up through the windows and music pulsated the air.

"You ready?" Mila gave a devilish smile.

"Let's do it," I grinned.

Mila and I entered the house, and I spotted him immediately.

"Hey, there are my girls," Jaxon made his way towards us.

I gritted my teeth. "Hey, Jaxon."

"Are you finished yet?" His dumbbells he called friends chuckled behind him with their red cups already filled. Some-one came out of nowhere and handed me a red cup filled with red juice. Mila was already sucking hers down, and I followed suit. The taste burned my throat, and I needed something to wash it down, or it would be akin to nasty food I would send back in a restaurant after one bite.

"Oh no chasers tonight," Jaxon teased. His friends giggled again before he spoke once more. "But seriously, are you done with the video?"

I took another swig from my cup. "Jaxon give me a minute, damn. We just got here."

"My bad, my bad, I just thought you would take this seri-ously; you know it's probably the opportunity of a lifetime for you." Opportunity of a lifetime, he said. Opportunity of a lifetime…was it the alcohol making me hot? Couldn't be—it didn't work that fast. I was not in the mood for Jaxon's bull-shit tonight.

"And what does that mean?"

"Hey, I don't want any problems," Jaxon put his hands up. "Don't shoot, don't shoot," he teased.

I winced. I didn't like when anyone said that phrase these days. But it sounded especially vile coming from Jaxon. I wrung my hands. Why did Jaxon affect me like this? Why did I let him? It was like he barged his way into my life, giving me instructions. When he came around, I felt like he took away my choices. But yet, he was a necessary evil in my world to get where I was going.

"Hey, ya'll." I heard his voice before I saw him. Even over the blaring music, I heard him. Turning around, Will stood before me and my stomach jumped; I was caught up in the rapture, Anita Baker style.

I swallowed. Butterflies? For Will?

He wore a cream sweater with a gold link necklace. His jeans were crisp, and his sneakers were fresh; not a scuff in sight. The earring in his left ear gleamed bright, and when he smiled, his white teeth blinded me. He was so tall, I never noticed how tall he was. The day in the cafeteria when we fell into each other, I looked up at him and into his eyes. Something about gazing up at him and him peering down at me made me feel protected. But now we were arguing, and I didn't know what to believe or what to think. But damn...he looked good.

"Hey, Will," Mila and I said at the same time. I glared at him too—just in case he was still mad at me.

"Is Malachi here?" I looked over Will's shoulder.

"No, we didn't come together. What's everyone drinking?"

"My man," Jaxon walked up and slapped Will's back. "Here's a cup, please enjoy yourself."

Will took a cup and grinned at Jaxon.

"Let's go. The cheerleaders are setting up a game of beer pong and everyone is lit." Jaxon gave a mischievous grin. The way he said lit made me cower; like he invented the word. The

room next to us erupted in laughter and cheers. Glancing around, the inside of the house resembled the outside. Hoards of teenagers with red cups moved about the home. It seemed the entire senior class was here tonight, squeezed into this mansion. Everyone had their own reasons for attending, but one thing we had in common was our need to hold on to high school, for one more minute.

Mila and I were doing the same, I suppose. Thoughts of the future worried me, even though somehow, I knew things would work out. I knew they would work out because I was going to do the work and make sure they happened. I didn't have a silver spoon like others, but I had a work ethic like no other and that had to be worth something, right?

Mila scanned the room for more red cups and when she found them, handed them out one by one. She was getting started.

"Thank you, me Lady," Elijah, a football player, said to Mila.

Mila giggled and shifted her weight. She kicked out her leg and her black stockings exposed a large run. I covered my mouth and stifled a cough.

"What?" she mouthed.

I pointed to the run in her stocking, and she arched her back to see for herself.

"Shit," she huffed.

The music already pounded through the house when someone turned it up even louder. I could feel the walls shaking in my chest. Was it the alcohol or the music? I wasn't sure.

"Indy," Will walked up and shifted his eyes. "Let's talk."

I nodded and followed him into the hallway where we stood in front of each other, eye to eye. This time I leaned in closer, hoping to smell his cologne like I had once before but he pulled away.

"We're worried about you."

Excuse me? "Who is worried? And about what?"

"Maybe you should…see someone. You know…like your mom." He looked down at his feet when he said, "like your mom."

"You think I'm like my mom?"

His eyes were wide. "N-no, that's not what I'm saying. I just think you should talk to someone."

I stared at Will. "You think I'm crazy, don't you?"

"Indy, you're so up and down these days and snapping at everyone. I don't know what to think. I just know we're worried about you."

"And who is we?"

"You know…us. Me, Malachi, Mila."

"You guys have been talking about me? Mind your fucking business." My fingers tingled and sweat sprang to my forehead. The gloss on my lips dried off, and I bit down on my bottom lip, tugging at the skin. The curse word spilled from my lips with disgust. I looked Will up and down as I enunciated each syllable; and I meant it. He was against me too, obviously. They thought I was crazy. I had a few outbursts, and I cried in the car with Will and…the voices…but he didn't know about those. Right? No, he didn't know, he couldn't.

I stomped back into the kitchen. Like your mom, Will had said. He mentioned that part for a reason. Coming from him, this was a gut punch. He was there when they first took my mom away. He was at my house when the police showed up and said there had been an accident. When they said accident, my heart skipped a beat; she had gone and gotten herself killed. This would devastate Sidney. It would devastate me too, but Sidney was younger. I was older and could take it. But she didn't get herself killed and she gave no rhyme or reason for her behavior.

So many times, when I didn't know I needed someone, he always showed up to save me. When Will and I were freshman

127

in high school, he came to me with a crazy idea for us to take each other's virginity. It made sense at the time—to get the whole thing over with, and to say we did it. Mila poked fun at us for not having done it sooner. I trusted him and had even considered the idea, but I decided against it. We were friends and I didn't see him in that way. Not then at least. Did I now? Not long after, I started dating Malachi, and we never broached the subject again. But I considered it.

My best friend now challenged my mental state. He thought I was nutty. Will knew a lot of things about me, but he didn't know everything. He didn't know that even if I was like my mom,—as he says—I couldn't just go "see someone." At the stroke of midnight this coming month, we didn't have any health insurance. Dad's hours at the center were reduced and with that went his coverage. Sidney was okay—her dad took care of her. But me and Dad, we lost insurance. Dad said we would apply for the state aid, but when I searched online, it said there was a 90-day waiting period. I guess I could call now for help since there were still two weeks left in the month, but what was the point in going through all of that and not being able to finish? College wasn't just my future and opportunities. It was access to mental health. Will was right about one thing; my moods were up and down. I wondered if seeing someone was the best thing for me too, but I had to wait. Being poor was a bitch. Still, who was Will to bring it up to me? And like this—at the party of the year we've been talking about since school started?

"I'll take two cups," Malachi entered the room. He was wearing his Tunica Rivers varsity jacket, jeans, and a baseball cap to the back. He resembled a black version of Jaxon.

"You are super ready, my friend," Jaxon handed Malachi two cups as he requested.

"One thing I don't play about is food and drink. I likes me food, and I likes me drink," Malachi rubbed his belly. He was mad corny, but it was cute. I wanted to grab Malachi right then and ask him to talk, but he was making his rounds around the room and greeting his other team members. My eyes followed him until he made his way to me.

"Indigo," he greeted me. Indigo, he said. Any other time it was Bae or Indy; today—it was Indigo.

"Can we talk?"

"Maybe later," he shrugged his shoulders.

"Later my man, later," Jaxon leapt over Malachi's shoulders and pulled him backwards. "He's mine tonight!" Jaxon grinned and pulled Malachi and me into another room of the house. This room was even larger than the kitchen and filled with trophies. Looking into the cabinets, I saw decades worth of golf awards lining the walls. A piano sat off in a corner of the room and the cathedral ceilings echoed at the bellowing music. I spotted Joya sitting on the piano and she was dancing in place. She had two red cups and was giggling; her eyes were low, and she nodded in my direction. I had just talked to Joya earlier when I confirmed the details for her appointment tomorrow. I didn't know she would be here too. I heard a few juniors say they would be crashing the party just because it was at Bordeaux Mansion, but I didn't think she would be one of those students. Not in her condition.

"You need another drink," Nico moved in front of me.

My eyes lit up with surprise, "When did you get here? I'm so happy to see you!" I threw my arms around his neck.

"Woahhh," he fell back. Nico was a familiar face, and one that was not mad at me. Even after I lost it on him.

"I've been here about an hour. Shit is crazy, right? Look at all these people!"

I wanted to tell Nico how sorry I was for my behavior the other day, but the music was so loud I was already screaming in his ear to talk to him. He tilted his head

towards me to hear better and he watched Leo, a football player, walk by him. Nico eyed him up and down before pulling away from me.

"Indy, I gotta go." He eyed Leo once more, and they retreated to another part of the house. I stood there alone. I looked around and observed people laughing, drinking, and some kissing. My head was pounding, and I steadied myself against the wall. The room spun. I watched Mila dance on an oval-shaped table. There were at least ten chairs around the room, and she flung each one out of her way—it was enough of a catwalk for Mila. She wobbled walking on top of the table, but soon she straightened up. The hole in her stockings had grown, and Mila in one swift motion kicked off her combat boots, rolled down her stockings exposing her bare legs and threw them at Jaxon, who had returned to the room. He and the football players cheered her on, forming a circle around her. Ever the performer needing attention, Mila walked more pronounced and sang now too. She gyrated on the table and twerked when Rihanna blared through the speakers. This time I didn't stop her.

"Here, take this." Jaxon handed me a joint.

I froze.

I drank at parties even though it wasn't my favorite—I didn't like the way it made me feel. But smoking weed, that wasn't my thing either. After a moment I thought, what the hell. I puffed Jaxon's small joint from his hand, and he gave me an approving smile. Feeling someone watching me, I glanced over my shoulder and saw Malachi peering at me intently.

Stumbling to him I asked, "Can we talk?"

He nodded and took another sip from his cup. He didn't want to talk when I first asked but liquid courage left him chatty. Malachi and I searched for an empty room throughout the house, but it seemed like there were teenagers everywhere, doing everything. "Oops, sorry," Malachi opened a door and quickly closed it. "My eyes cannot unsee that," he shuddered. We found an empty room at the end of the hall and it was the same size as my room, Sidney's closet, and Dad's bedroom combined. The gigantic bed rested in the middle and two chaise lounges were in corners of the room. The master bath had a large tub and separate shower with double sinks. It even had a small footstool in the middle. I didn't think people used those little footstool things, but today they proved me wrong. Malachi leaned up against the footstool, his sneaker perched on the cabinet.

"So, what's good?" He crossed his arms at his chest.

"I-I-I just wanted to apologize for our conversation the other day. I was upset, and it came out wrong. And for that I'm sorry."

"It's cool," his eyes were blank, and he didn't move.

"Are we okay?"

Malachi rolled his eyes. "You broke up with me for nothing, so it is what it is."

"You don't know what's going on!" I shrieked. My voice rose. "I have these thoughts and-and—I just don't know what to do with them."

"In the meantime, what am I supposed to do? I don't want to go to college, that's not my thing, and it's never been. I went along with it because of you. I love you. I've always loved you. Enough to even follow you to college. And I was going to, I thought long and hard about it. I applied to City College too, and I got in. But I can't."

I took a seat on the edge of the tub and sighed.

"I didn't know you got into City College."

Malachi shrugged his shoulders. "I didn't tell you. You were kind of on my back about it, and I didn't want to disappoint you. When I opened the letter and saw my name and congratulations, it didn't feel like me. It didn't feel like my story."

"What are you going to do then?"

He shrugged his shoulders again. "I'm not sure yet. I might just get a job. I'll figure it out along the way."

"So, no plan, huh?"

He laughed and his shoulders bounced. "Indy, every part of your life doesn't need to be planned. You're seventeen."

I pondered Malachi's words, but they didn't feel natural to me or like I could get lost in them. There was no ceiling in Malachi's house, and I needed four walls and a plan to keep things moving forward. I didn't understand this, "I'll figure it out jargon"—he might as well have been speaking Spanish because yo no comprendo. Malachi dropped on his hands and kneeled in front of me.

"We had a good run," I said.

"We did," he nodded.

A tear threatened to drop in the corner of my eye. I didn't feel sad though, I just knew I should have.

"Friends?"

"Friends," he half-smiled.

We rose at the same time and faced each other. Instinctively we fell into our routine and did what we had done the past year. He leaned in and kissed me on the lips.

I let him.

When I didn't stop him, he kissed me all over my mouth and my face. His hand slipped up my shirt, and I still didn't stop him. We kissed in the mansion bathroom quietly, and then quickly. I didn't stop him. My hand slipped behind Malachi's neck when I felt buzzing from his waist. I pulled back, and Malachi took his phone out of his pocket.

"Hello?"

I heard Malachi's mom on the phone; she was talking fast. I heard her say car.

"Okay, okay," Malachi shook his head. "I'll be there."

"What happened?"

"My mom got stuck at work and she needs a ride. I have to go pick her up."

"Doesn't she work close to an hour away?" I went with Malachi and his mom a few times to her job, and it was far. Malachi tried introducing her to Uber or Lyft but she was old-school. She saw her beloved Chris Cuomo, who she swore was Black on the inside, reporting on a string of ride-share attacks. She watched the same thing every night in rotation. It was the usual suspects: Jeopardy, Wheel of Fortune, and CNN. She decided women weren't safe

to travel this way and alas; Malachi was his mom's Uber.

"Yes," he sighed.

"Do you want me to come? You've been drinking."

"I'm good, I got this."

"Malachi, you've been drinking," I repeated. "A lot."

"I'm fine. We good though, Indy?"

I wiped my mouth and applied lip balm from my pocket. Knowing this would probably be the last time I kissed Malachi for a while, I batted my eyes at him and said, "We're good."

Malachi and I walked outside to his car and he said, "I'll text you on my way back."

"Be safe and text me as soon as you get to your mom," I slapped the hood of his car.

I glanced up at the house. The windows were open, and the rooms were lit up. I had an unobstructed view into each room, and it reminded me of those open doll houses. I peered into each room. This would be a good night; I could feel it.

I stood there in a trance and spied everyone. My breathing became shallow, and my ears rang, as my thoughts returned that quickly…I see them, but they don't see me…I could easily get to one of them in the house. They're all high and tipsy, anyway. My mouth curled into a sly smile. My thoughts were

uninterrupted and running wild with visions of how I could hurt one of them. Anyone would do.

In the distance, Joya was walking down the gravel road alone. What was she doing? I squinted to see better but couldn't. Cars were everywhere, but it was dark out here. I hollered down the road in her direction, but soon, a familiar silver car with tinted windows pulled up next to her and shut off their lights. Joya leaned in the window, throwing her head back and laughed. The same laugh she gave at the park months ago. She walked to the passenger side and got in. The car rode past me kicking up dust all around, until it was gone.

CHAPTER 15

BACK IN THE house, Mila was slumped over a couch playing on her phone.

"What are you doing?" I plopped down next to her.

"I drank too much. I'm trying to get it together."

"We've been here an hour," I giggled.

Nico was now on the table, sandwiched between two football players. His shirt was off, and he had one of the cheerleader's bras wrapped around his head, wearing it like a hat. I laughed, looking up at him. These are the days that we would remember. I took brain pictures of it all.

Will came from somewhere and plopped on the couch next to me. Mila's body twitched when he sat down, but his body warmed up sitting next to me. My head leaned on Mila's and my leg bounced against Will's when I smelled his cologne. Maybe Will and I could...no, he dated Mila. He was off limits. Girl code 101. But he smelled so good. I closed my eyes as I inhaled his scent.

"No resting, no one is resting! This is over—let's go," Jaxon turned the music back up.

It blasted through the house and this time; Beyoncé and DJ Khaled blared from the speakers. Jaxon pulled me and Mila to our feet and he gave us more red cups filled with something else that smelled like it could grow hair on my chest. I took a swig of this cup and it tasted worse than the one before. We were mixing liquor. even I knew that was a no-no. The room swayed, and I stumbled to stay on my feet.

"Oh shit, looks like Miss Perfect, isn't," Jaxon grinned.

Mila was giving her best white girl dance, swinging her head and hair to the beat and shaking her shoulders. I did the same, but with a little more flavor. Will still sat on the couch and watched us dance. His legs were perched open, and he leaned back on the slumped couch. His eyes were on me, and Mila's eyes were on him. He didn't break his gaze, and Mila didn't take her eyes off of him. I knew he was watching, and I didn't care—I kind of wanted him to. His cologne still tickled my nostrils and every time I swayed, I smelled him. I danced harder and became more pronounced with my movements. Swaying my hips and moving to the beat, my long curly braids swung at my waist.

Will sat up straighter on the couch, and I knew I had his attention. The way he gazed at me; it was like he saw me—really saw me. He had to have the same thoughts I did—he just had to. I could see it in his eyes.

My stomach fluttered, and this time, it wasn't from the red cup. Why did I care that he saw me? Our friendship had changed, just like he screamed it at me one summer night in Chicago over the phone. No, he isn't looking at me that way; I shushed my nerves.

But he is. But he is.

Will and I locked eyes as I swayed to the beat as he full-on stared at me, and his mouth was slightly open. I could see his tongue rolling in his mouth.

"Asshole!" Mila screamed. She tossed her drink in Will's face, and just like that our spell was broken.

His eyes bugged out and the football team chanted, "Yo fight, fight, fight!"

"What the fuck, Mila?" He jumped up and his cream-colored sweater was covered in red juice.

"You're always looking at her!" Mila exclaimed. "You always loved her."

The three of us said nothing; the elephant in the room was no more—Mila slayed it.

I inhaled sharply. "Mila, what are you talking about?"

"Just tell her, Will—tell her."

The football team stood behind us, whooping and hollering. Mila turned to me, "You've known all this time. He loves you; he's in love with you. He loves you," she repeated, this time softer. Mila was hurt, I could see it in her face. But her anger wasn't towards me, it was towards Will and a red sweater once cream-colored.

Will did love me, and we both knew it. He was quiet. His shoulders were slumped, and he looked like he was holding his breath. The anger I felt towards Jaxon, towards a lot of things in my life, built up. The feelings I tried to hide were bubbling over and seeping through my pores. They were almost on full display, ready to be unleashed at any moment. Even though Mila's words were the truth, they incensed me.

Will and I are friends. And regardless of what we both felt—that's all we would ever be. I had too many other things to worry about. He was my friend—my best friend. Anything more was too confusing right now. The thoughts ran through my mind, but I also knew they weren't entirely true. Something in me belonged to him. But I wouldn't give it up without a damn good fight. Besides, he thought I was crazy anyway. Mila didn't have to throw a drink on him, but in sidekick fashion, I'm glad she came and interrupted the moment.

137

"I'm leaving," Will snapped.

"Where are you going?" Mila questioned.

"Home! Do you see me?" he glared at his now red sweater.

"Go then, Will. Let's still not talk about it," she jabbered.

Will glanced in my direction and opened his mouth, starting to speak. He shook his head, scowled once more at Mila, and walked out.

"Ohhhh, another one bites the dust," the football team chanted.

"What is going on over here, ladies?" Jaxon returned with more cups. "You ladies are running all of my guys away. This is turning into a real chick fest. Oh well, more honeys for me," he giggled walking away.

"What's your problem?" I said to Mila. "Why have you been acting like this? The shit with JT—and now this. What are you thinking?" I demanded.

"Shut up, Indy," Mila shook her head. "You're too busy trying to get rich or die trying that you don't even realize Will has been in love with you for like, forever. Did he ever tell you that's why we broke up? Because he's in love with you. Always has been."

My eyes widened at Mila. "No," I shook my head. "That's not true."

Mila snorted. "Indy, have you convinced yourself it's not true? He could never be with me because his first and only love has always been you."

Somewhere in me knew that was true. Mila was kicking nothing but facts tonight. I didn't have time for this, not for Will and these feelings. I wasn't trying to get rich or die trying. I just wanted what others had. Was that so much to ask?

"Ladies, no fighting," Jaxon interjected. "Will set another game of Beer Pong before he left." He handed us more red cups and this time I drank the whole thing, finishing in two gulps.

"That a girl," Jaxon grinned. He took one of my braids in his hands and palmed it. "These are curly like macaroni and cheese."

My hair was funny to him. I pushed him away and the football team roared once again.

The rest blurred and I'm not sure what happened. Minutes turned into hours. I came to, and drool seeped out the sides of my mouth. Jaxon stood in front of me in the bedroom with his phone. The flash made me shield my eyes. Where is everyone? I peered around.

"They're not here. It's just us," Jaxon said.

We played Beer Pong like Jaxon had begged, and the next thing I knew, everyone was kissing. Mila and I stayed late into the night when, one by one, someone would tire and leave or retreat to a room in the house.

Now, Joya lay across my lap motionless, and I wondered when she had returned to the party. The click of the camera made me jump, and Jaxon moved in circles, snapping pictures of me and Joya.

I struggled to stand and stumbled to the bathroom as the music pounded my ears. It was still blaring from the speakers and the pain cut through my temples. I heard a loud groan, and when I peeked out of the bathroom, Mila came shuffling into the room. Jaxon's hand was placed in the arch of Mila's back and her hair was disheveled, and she was missing a shoe. Her eyes were bloodshot red.

"Whoa, whoa," he slyly smiled while I leaned into the bathroom doorway to steady myself. The room was spinning, and I was concentrating on not vomiting all over this expensive looking tile. I slid down to the floor, gravity getting the best of me.

Malachi, I thought. Shit. He was gone. Will—Will was surely here. Shit, he was gone too. His sweater. The bathroom had wet washcloths on the floor, and I slipped on one and fell on

my back. I hit my head on the floor tile under me and I saw stars. The pain ripped through the back of my head and I howled in pain and my eyes were blurry. Feeling around for my phone on the floor that had slipped out of my pocket, I cringed as my hands landed in the cold wetness that came attached with a smell I was familiar with, urine.

My hands landed on my cell phone, and Jaxon kicked it away and chuckled. He took my phone and pulled his out. The flash of his camera burned my eyes and I struggled to see.

"A day in the life of Indigo Lewis," he joked.

I gritted my teeth. My stomach turned so bad, and I didn't fight him for my phone. My curls that I had spent hours rolling, were wet.

"Uh-uh," I struggled to find the words before I blacked out again.

CHAPTER 16

"**P**UMP THE GAS, Ma!" I screamed.

Mom floored it, and my head slammed against the back of the seat. The old man came into our sights; the closer we got, the more he was real. He had a cane, and he hobbled across the road, unaware he was target practice that day. Mom and I glanced at each other and grinned. She wanted to see how high he could bounce, and so did I. He was older and walked too slow for his own good; they could spare just one. We were yards from him when he arched his back and turned towards us. He dressed like an old man and walked like an old man, but his face. His face was Jaxon's.

My body jolted in my bed and I sat straight up. My throat was dry. I found a half empty water bottle on my dresser and I cracked it open and sucked it down, but it did nothing for my thirst.

I vaguely remember Joya taking me home last night, but I distinctly remember vomiting in her car. She was returning later to pick me up for her appointment and it was my stomach that was in knots. My eyes burned and I rubbed them until I saw stars. The sun peeked through my small window, but it was still too bright. I laid back down and covered myself in the blanket. Balling myself into the fetal position, I closed my eyes.

My phone buzzed, and a text from Joya came through. She was picking me up in one hour. I thought I had more time to rest, but she was on her way. Last night I had three intentions: have a ball with my friends at the party, talk to Will, and clear things up with Malachi. I accomplished one, but maybe it was the one I shouldn't have. Will's words were still in my mind, "You know, like your mom." Tears flowed from my eyes under the blanket where I was getting hot, so I peeked my head out and let some cool air hit my face. Fat tears rolled down my cheeks, and I returned my head back under the blanket where I wiped them away.

An hour later, Joya and I rode in her new Audi in silence. I still smelled the stench from vomiting last night and Joya had the windows down, letting in cool air and the foul smell — out. The car was gorgeous and it glided down the highway whizzing past everyone. I wore large blacked out sunglasses, and I had my hoodie up. Joya was also wearing sunglasses and she had a large iced coffee in her cup holder. It was the biggest size and it had whipped cream at the top. I eyed it, pissed that I didn't tell her to grab me one too.

"Do you want some?" Joya pointed to the coffee.

My mouth watered looking at it. "I thought you'd never ask," I replied as I grabbed the coffee and took a long sip. The cold liquid quenched my thirst and felt so good in my mouth. I laid my head against the headrest and closed my eyes, trying to focus on not vomiting up the savory drink that was so needed right now.

"Are you okay? I wasn't expecting to see you last night at the party." I finally asked. I sucked down Joya's coffee with fervor.

Joya sighed and pulled down the blinker button hard.

"A few of the football players invited me, and I didn't want to stay in my house. My parents were having one of their 'what are you doing with your life' conversations and I just didn't feel like being there anymore."

"I saw Mr. Chestnut pick you up last night. Did he bring you back too?"

Joya was silent. Her eyes looked distant as she gripped the steering wheel tight. "He knows I'm going today. He said he would have come with me if…you know. He could. I guess I'm okay though. I shouldn't have gone to the party; he came to tell me that. He's mad that I went."

"Why? Did you…hook up with anyone?" I eased into the question cautiously, trying to see what she knew. My memories were still fuzzy from the night before. I really wasn't a big drinker, and it didn't take much for me to start feeling it. I knew the ropes—Mom didn't raise no fool. Never accept a drink from someone you don't know. Don't go anywhere alone with someone you just met. Always be mindful of your surroundings and your crowd. Mom ran down the rules to being a woman when I was young, but yet last night I still went against everything she had taught.

Visions of my mom followed me everywhere. Her voice followed me everywhere. I knew it was her—it was her words, her tone. Sometimes she just sat there and commented about my day. Other days she was angry when someone did me wrong. She sang and danced. But lately, she told me about different ways to end them. I did a good job of pushing the thoughts out of my mind, but now that they forced me to share air with Jaxon Green, Mom pitched a tent and set up camp in my head. Mom was always there, cursing someone for me, threatening someone for me. I wondered if she came to Sidney like this. No, I fussed. Sidney would tell me if that were the case.

"No, I didn't. I was drinking, but you were the one tossing them back!" Joya gave a half smile.

I held my breath before I asked her my next question. "...Did I...hook up..."

"You don't remember?" She shifted her eyes from me to the road and back again.

I shook my head.

"After Will and Malachi left, the party did get pretty wild with Jaxon. He and your girl, Mila, disappeared for a few hours and I'm not sure what they did, but you were in your own world. We were in the bathroom at one point, before I took you home. You kept saying, 'Leave me alone, Mom. I don't want to do that to them.' You were so upset I thought you were talking on the phone with someone, but nope, you were talking to yourself," she giggled.

Saliva collected in my mouth and I had to concentrate to keep down the bile that was forming in my stomach and throat. She heard me talking to Mom, to the voices. Shame washed over me, and I pulled the drawstrings on my hoodie tighter onto my face.

Joya and I rode the rest of the way in silence until we made our way to a small building with no names or windows. My eyes bugged out of my head when I saw a group of older white women standing outside of the building with signs that read 'Babies are a gift from God,' and 'Say no to abortions.'

One of the women held a bullhorn, and she screamed, "You don't have to do this, choose another option."

Joya stared out of the window at the women as she parked, and soon she began breathing harder and wringing her hands. "Why are they out here? Why would they do this?"

I didn't have answers as they continued their protest, and the woman on the bullhorn screeched, "You have options, we can help." By now the line was getting longer, and once Joya and I hurried to the end, we were still behind at least ten girls. I stared at the girl in front of us. She looked about our age, and she gawked at the women yelling up front. When she moved, I saw her round belly even from the back. How far along was she? I studied the other girls around us, and while they looked like different versions of terrified and annoyed, they didn't *look* pregnant yet.

This girl's petite frame looked alien-like against her round belly. An older woman who shared the same face, nose, and aghast look, clutched the strap of her purse and stood next to the girl, staring at the women up front still shouting. I peeked at Joya and she stared at the woman next to the young girl; maternal instinct passed between them. Joya's gaze was piercing and for a second, I thought she might vomit. She pulled her sunglasses off of her forehead and snapped them over her eyes when she saw me looking.

The security guard at the front checked IDs admitting people into the facility and every so often he looked over his shoulders at the women behind him. By now, one of the women was on her knees with her arms outstretched, praying. She said, "Dear Lord, please let these girls know we love them. They are not alone, and they don't have to do this. All lives matter."

"Excuse me? What the fuck you say?" A heavyset Black girl with her bonnet on in the front of the line yelled.

"Good morning, I hope you are doing well, beautiful child. You don't have to do this, you have options. All lives matter, and I would love to talk with you more to explain why. You were meant for more than this," the woman held a rosary between her hands. The line moved slowly and everyone paced and talked to each other with sharp voices.

"You don't know me! Don't tell me what options I have, and don't tell me all lives matter, Karen!"

Other girls in the line grumbled at the women, and their ringleader got on her bullhorn again. "You have options. Don't be mad at us—Jesus saves!"

145

"She don't know shit about me!" The girl before Joya and me in the line screamed. Two more security guards rushed outside with their hands on their hips clutching at nothing. When they arrived, the girls in line settled down but the women continued with their protest.

Joya kept her head low, but I observed everything around me with wide and curious eyes. I was glad I decided to come with her, hangover and all. No girl should have to experience this. Joya and I entered the building, and for the next three hours we sat shoulder to shoulder with dozens of other girls. The office played a painful song and dance of calling up Joya, verifying insurance, sitting back down, calling her back up again to check a million little things. Joya's insurance covered the procedure today, and she could thank her parents for that one. I looked around the room at all the different faces. The women were young and old. Some looked like they had been out partying the night before, like Joya and me. Others looked professional. They wore slacks, work shoes, and they clutched their designer purses and wallets, waiting for their name to be called. Some of them stared off into a faraway place and were lost in their thoughts. Others conversed with their friends who came along for moral support. From what I could see without looking too nosy, there were only two women here with their male partners.

Just two. Just like Mr. Chestnut, the men were able to skate out of the hard part and left the women to deal with it. None of the girls were crying.

Joya and I waited in a corner of the room, and we were shivering because it was so cold. The frigid air blasted out the vents through my hoodie above us and my toes were numb as I crossed and uncrossed my feet trying to get the blood flowing while we waited. I looked around the room and most of the seats were taken and there was nowhere else for us to sit. I saw Joya shaking every few minutes and I couldn't tell if it was because it was freezing in here or she was nervous. Maybe both.

"Joya Ranks?" A nurse called.

Joya jumped at her name being called and grabbed my hand. "Can my friend come back too?"

The nurse's face softened, and she gave Joya empathetic eyes. "Sure, Miss. Ranks. She can come with you to change but not into the operating room. She will be waiting for you in the recovery room."

"Okay," Joya said, her eyes glassy.

My stomach was in so many knots. We passed a water cooler in the long hallway and I grabbed a triangle cup, pressed the button, and cold water came out. I gulped it down as fast as I could and took a deep breath, following Joya and the nurse.

A few minutes later, I held Joya's hand once more in the recovery room. She was groggy from being sedated and her voice cracked barely above a whisper. She squeezed my hand so tight that I grit my teeth and dug into my toes in my shoes.

"Is it over? Is it over?" She breathed.

"Shhh, yes, it is." I held her hand and helped her to her feet.

"I want to go home and see my mom," Joya said with tears in her eyes.

I bit my lip, knowing the feeling well.

"Let's get you dressed, and we can go."

Joya ripped both the wristband and hospital gown off her as she struggled to get her jacket on. Nurses milled about the large room refilling saline bags and checking on other patients.

All of the girls were crying.

I drove Joya home in her car, and she was quiet the entire time. She reclined her seat and lay back, looking out of the window, her hoodie up around her head now too, and her arms were crossed. Her brown face was lined with streaks

from where she had been crying. The ride home seemed much longer with both of us quiet.

When I finally got home, I had made a decision. Dad was coming home from work at eight o'clock tonight. At dinner, we would talk about whatever was going on in my head. Soon we wouldn't have insurance, but surely, there had to be programs or something—right? I think it was time to talk to someone; I sighed. I reached for my phone and googled "hearing voices." Different mental health agencies popped up, and I scrolled until I found a place on the expensive side of Tunica Rivers.

I dialed the number, and my heart beat out of my chest. I climbed into my bed under the covers and into the fetal position.

"HeartSprings Counseling, how can I help you?" the chipper receptionist answered.

"H-hi," I said. "Uh, is this the palace where you go to uh, talk to someone?"

"Yes, it is. How may we help you?"

"I uh—would like to talk to someone."

"Okay yes, what kind of insurance do you have?"

"Uh, I'm covered right now, but in a few days I won't be. My dad is applying for state aid though," I said too quickly.

"Oh," the receptionist's voice changed. "Well, we do see patients without insurance, but you would just have to pay the out-of-network fee."

"And how much is that?"

"One hundred twenty-five dollars per session."

I gripped my phone and my knuckles turned white.

$125?

I'm sure I heard her wrong.

"You said $125?"

"Yes, ma'am I did."

This wasn't going to work. Why did I even get my hopes up like this? "Thank you, I'll let you know."

"Okay, well you give us a call back anytime. We 're always here for you at HeartSprings Counseling."

Sure. For $125.00, I sulked.

I slammed my phone onto my nightstand. The house was quiet as Sidney was with her dad this weekend and Dad was at work. I didn't even have to lie to Dad about going to the party—he was at work all night anyway. My thoughts shifted to last night. Malachi and I are officially broken up, and while that bothered me, what hurt more was the thought of him scrounging his life away, not wanting to go to college. What else would he do? They stacked the odds against kids like us, and we had to be extra special or athletic to do anything different. Malachi looked good and he played football, but there was nothing special about him that screamed "I got this."

And Will…even if there was something between us, we ruined it last night. He thought I was crazy, I scoffed. He may be right, even so; he called my crazy out. Funny thing is, Mom didn't have a thing to say about that one. She let him live. Literally. The past few months when I looked at Will, I saw something different. I noticed the lines in his face when he laughed. The way he walked down the hallway when he was running late for class. I especially remembered his face when he picked me up in front of the school and I cried in his car. But how could this be? He still dated Mila. Yes, for only a few months, but despite that, they were my best friends. And Will said, "We're worried about you," meaning the three of them. So, they had been talking about me amongst themselves and decided I needed help.

Mila—her words rang in my mind. "He loves you!" she yelled. I stayed silent, but I knew the truth.

I recalled the last time I was happy, really happy. Sidney and I went to the pottery studio with Mom. Mom was throwing a large round pot, and her hands were covered in clay up

149

to her elbows. Her hair was tied up in a tribal headband and brown ringlet curls fell over her forehead. The music was loud throughout the studio as she danced to Sheila E.

"You hear that bass, SidRock," she shimmied. Mom grabbed my hand and pulled me to her where we danced and laughed. "Come on Sidrock, you too!" she yelled, motioning for Sidney to come to us.

A smile spread across Sidney's face and she jumped off the counter where she sat and darted to us. We danced and two-stepped. Mom was showing Sidney how to do the Butterfly when her hip hit the pottery wheel and the pot collapsed.

Sidney and I stopped dancing and eyed Mom waiting for her to be angry, but she threw her head back and let out a roar of laughter. Mom looked so beautiful and carefree that day. Sidney and I looked at each other and began laughing too. Senior year was supposed to be fun, but I was ending mine boyfriend-less and friend-less. Just less. I grabbed my phone again and texted Mila. She responded immediately.

> **ME:** Wyd?

> **MILA:** Laying down. Girl, my head is spinning.

> **ME:** Mine too. Did you hook up with Jaxon last night?

I pulled the blankets up around me tighter and waited for Mila's response. I closed my eyes and yawned, the events of the night before and today finally catching up with me. I closed my eyes and on this seventh day, she rested.

CHAPTER 17

MILA NEVER TEXTED me back, and once I woke, I knew exactly where I wanted to go. Ms. Montague's studio was small, and it sat in a strip mall in downtown Tunica Rivers. On the left was a fried chicken joint, and on the right was a massage parlor. Mom used to say, "Happy endings all around us."

I called Ms. Montague before I arrived to make sure she was there—I needed to clear my mind.

"Lawd, you look just like yo' Momma, girl, "Ms. Montague opened the door for me. "Her little twin."

My heart fluttered. The only other person I heard say I resembled Mom, was Dad, but when he said it, it was with sad eyes.

Ms. Montague's eyes roamed me up and down. "It's only been a few months since I last saw you. Let me get a good look at you." She stood back and looked me up and down.

I paced nervously.

"And your braids are so long and beautiful. What's going on here?" she peered closer. "Were you trying to take your hair out?"

I looked down at my braids in confusion. A handful of them were cut and Ms. Montague noticed. I didn't see it when I hopped out of bed or while with Joya today. Now in the late afternoon, it looked like someone chopped off a bunch of waist length braids and they were unraveling.

"Uh, yeah. I was taking them out," I lied. I flipped my head over and put my hair in a bun on top of my head with the scrunchie I kept around my wrist. The shorter cut braids poked out of the bottom of my bun and I didn't have a bobby pin to secure it in place. What the fuck? What happened to my hair? And who cut off my braids?

I checked my phone. Mila still hadn't responded to my last text about Jaxon..

"I thought you might like to throw a piece today," Ms. Montague's eyes gleamed.

"And you guessed correctly," I smiled.

"You can head down to your favorite spot, and I'll get everything ready." Ms. Montague wore an oversized business suit at all times. She prided herself on her large scarf collection and today she wore a leopard print cloth tied around her neck. She was the epitome of a cat lady, and her office was filled with pictures of her many felines.

I sat down at Mom's favorite potting station. Behind every station was a corkboard with pictures from various studio events. Mom was in one of those pictures, her bright smile shining through the newspaper clipping. She stood with her hand on her hip and another hand holding a large vase.

She looked happy.

I wondered when was the last time she felt that same happiness or if happiness was an inside job these days. Ms. Montague shuffled back, and I met her halfway to carry the large piece of clay.

"Thank you," she huffed.

"Do you need help with anything?"

No, I'm fine, thank you," I shook my head.

"Okay, holler if you need anything else." Ms. Montague walked away, and I stood at the workstation kneading the clay. After washing my hands, I grabbed my headphones and popped them into my ears as I worked. Nicki Minaj's voice boomed, and I kneaded the clay harder. I grabbed a mallet and banged at it, slapping and tossing it until it was warmed up and flattened. I searched through the basket underneath the table and retrieved shapes I wanted to carve onto the piece. Once the clay was soft, I sat down and loaded it onto the wheel.

"That's right, my girl," Mom said. *"Open your legs a little more, feel the weight of the wheel. Don't be intimidated. You control it. It doesn't control you."* The clay felt slippery between my fingers and it dried quickly. I had to keep my hands wet and moving in a circular motion or it would harden and crumple on my fingers. My hands wrapped around the clay mass, and it spun in slow circles. My fingers moved with it, gently. The machine hummed a shallow song, and it suspended my eyes with the clay. I used my fingertips to spread it out and make it larger in some sections. I pinched my thumb and forefinger together to make divots in other parts. Yeah, it looked like something Mom would make. Ms. Montague walked up, leaned on the wall and crossed her arms. She mouthed something but I couldn't hear her with my earbuds in. I pulled them away and wiped my hands.

"You know you have your mom's talents," she repeated.

I grinned at her.

"Oh, Ms. Montague, Mom keeps saying to check out the person who bought her vase. I didn't get a chance to ask you at the last art show. I'm not sure what that means?"

"Ha, she's a hoot. An old industry trick we used back in the day. We had to vet the people who bought our pieces. It was

about mixing energy. The energy it took to create her piece, would be mixed with the energy of the person receiving it. We liked to make sure our creations would be somewhere they were loved," she explained. "We don't do it as much these days, everyone is just happy to make a sale regardless where it goes."

"Got it. More crazy shit," I thought.

"She mentioned it a few times in her letters, and I wanted to make sure I checked it out." I now stood up and leaned over the tubular shaped piece. It rose to my waist, and I bent over it, thinning it out even more.

"Listen, Indigo, while you're here. I want to give you something."

I turned off the wheel, and it slugged to an end. Removing the piece from the wheel, I gently placed it on the workstation and washed my hands.

"I'll go get it," Ms. Montague walked away. She was back in a few minutes with an envelope. "Here, open it," she pushed.

I tore into the envelope and pulled out three different letters. The first one said "Firstborn Children of Incarcerated Parents Scholarship."

"I found this at an event I attended a few weeks ago in Birmingham. I thought of you. They give out a grand prize of $15,000. It's not much, but it could help."

Not much she said. It was damn near millions to me. I grabbed Ms. Montague and threw my arms around her neck. Tears sprang to my eyes again, just as they did this morning. "Thank you, thank you so much," I cried.

Ms. Montague huffed and fixed her business suit. "It's the least I could do, your Mom was one of the most gifted women I knew, and it's a shame how things ended," she shook her head.

I now see why Mom loves Ms. Montague. Things hadn't ended with Mom because they were continuing with me and Sidney. This is what they would never understand. I didn't have time to play around; I had to move forward—for Mom and for Sidney.

"Oh, and I checked the records. About who bought your mom's piece? The last name said Green. A Jennifer Green."

"I know her. Did she know it was my mom's piece?"

"No, she didn't. I remember she had on the most god-awful perfume and I had to close the deal for Casey because Casey went into a sneezing fit around her."

My fingers turned cold as I cleaned up my area.

Green.

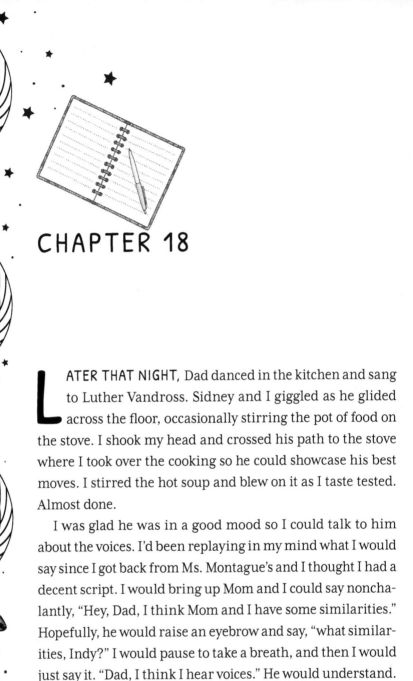

CHAPTER 18

LATER THAT NIGHT, Dad danced in the kitchen and sang to Luther Vandross. Sidney and I giggled as he glided across the floor, occasionally stirring the pot of food on the stove. I shook my head and crossed his path to the stove where I took over the cooking so he could showcase his best moves. I stirred the hot soup and blew on it as I taste tested. Almost done.

I was glad he was in a good mood so I could talk to him about the voices. I'd been replaying in my mind what I would say since I got back from Ms. Montague's and I thought I had a decent script. I would bring up Mom and I could say noncha-lantly, "Hey, Dad, I think Mom and I have some similarities." Hopefully, he would raise an eyebrow and say, "what similar-ities, Indy?" I would pause to take a breath, and then I would just say it. "Dad, I think I hear voices." He would understand. He would help figure this out. He would take over and make decisions like Dads do. That's what I needed him to do.

The doorbell rang and Sidney ran to get it. I heard a wom-an's voice, and Dad took off his apron and smoothed his jeans. That's when I noticed he was wearing jeans. I had only seen him in his uniform and work boots the past few months. Sidney and a tall, heavyset woman entered the kitchen. Sidney's eyes were wide, and she peered up at the woman and then at Dad.

Dad turned down the music.

"My girls," he said. "I would like you to meet Arletha. We met at work, and we've been seeing each other. I thought it was time for my woman to meet my girls," Dad gave a pensive smile.

Sidney and I looked at each other.

"Hi girls," the woman gave a wave. "I've heard so much about you. I made a cake."

Sighing, I waited for Mom's voice — I knew she was coming after this one.

"Indigo, right?" Arletha's eyes were wide and confident. She stared at me. "Your dad says you like pound cake," and she pushed one in my direction.

I froze.

"She does like cake," Sidney palmed the cake from Arletha's arms.

I was thankful for Sidney. The night went by in a blur, and I truly didn't know what to say. I looked around the house while Ms. Arletha was there, and things seemed odd. First of all, it was too clean. Our house was never dirty, but it definitely had that lived-in look. But now that Ms. Arletha was here, it was spotless, not a speck of dust anywhere. And Dad's jeans? He wore his work uniform so often I felt like I was gazing at someone else. He took the time to iron them and there was a thick crease running down the center of his pants. He ironed his clothes for her. The house smelled good too, and Dad rushed around fumbling, lighting candles.

"I'll do that, honey," Ms. Arletha took the candles and lighter from him and delicately lit them — only like a woman would. A woman's touch. That's what it was, that déjà vu feeling I had looking around — Ms. Arletha brought a woman's touch.

"So, Sidney, I hear you like field hockey?"

Sidney glanced at me before answering, and I nodded at her. "Yes, I play field hockey."

"Want to hear a secret? I played too when I was your age."

"You did?" Sidney's eyes were large.

"I did," Ms. Arletha beamed. "I got a scholarship to go to college actually."

This now piqued my interest. "And what happened?"

"My mom was sick, and I had to stay home and care for her. When she passed, it was too late for me to get another scholarship, and I couldn't afford it. So, I stayed here, in Tunica Rivers where I got myself a good job and met your Dad." She looked over at Dad and patted his hand.

Wow, I thought. Ms. Arletha said a mouthful. She stayed to take care of her mom. She articulated exactly what I didn't want for my life. I didn't want to stay in Tunica Rivers and care for anyone. I wanted to leave and see the world. Let the world see me. I had to get out—I just had to.

"Are you still any good?" Sidney asked.

Ms. Arletha shook her head. "Oh heavens no, I'm done with all that stuff. But I can help you with some of your moves," she said with a smile.

Ms. Arletha and Sidney happily chatted throughout the night, building something that with the help of cake and talk of field hockey—would last. Dad said nothing, but he stole glances at me. I didn't have any issues with Ms. Arletha, but I was definitely surprised. Dad worked all day long, but even with him working I forgot he was a man. A man whose common law wife, the only woman he possibly ever loved, was locked away for the foreseeable future. Dad still had needs too.

Ms. Arletha's words stuck in my head: I had to take care of my mom when she got sick, and I wasn't able to go to college. That wouldn't be my story.

Dad spent the next few hours washing dishes at the kitchen sink and bumping butts with Ms. Arletha. He laughed out loud and asked if we wanted to grab ice cream in a few.

He was happy. I couldn't tell him about the voices right now, I just couldn't.

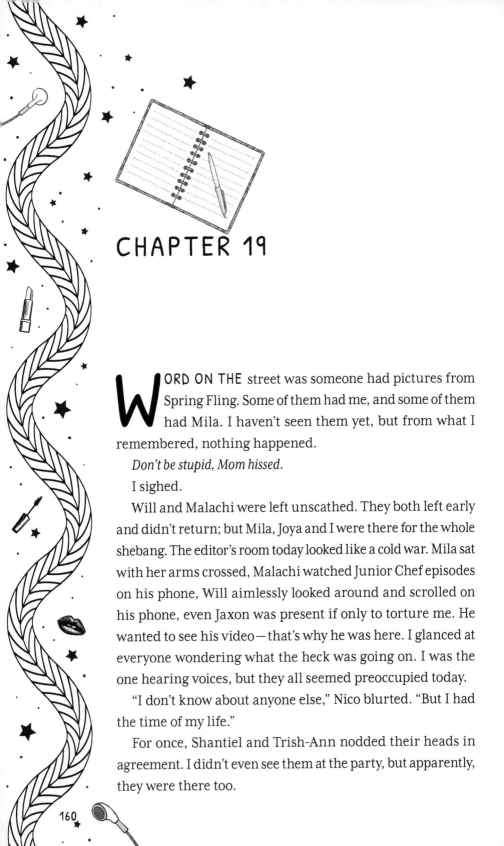

CHAPTER 19

ORD ON THE street was someone had pictures from Spring Fling. Some of them had me, and some of them had Mila. I haven't seen them yet, but from what I remembered, nothing happened.

Don't be stupid, Mom hissed.

I sighed.

Will and Malachi were left unscathed. They both left early and didn't return; but Mila, Joya and I were there for the whole shebang. The editor's room today looked like a cold war. Mila sat with her arms crossed, Malachi watched Junior Chef episodes on his phone, Will aimlessly looked around and scrolled on his phone, even Jaxon was present if only to torture me. He wanted to see his video—that's why he was here. I glanced at everyone wondering what the heck was going on. I was the one hearing voices, but they all seemed preoccupied today.

"I don't know about anyone else," Nico blurted. "But I had the time of my life."

For once, Shantiel and Trish-Ann nodded their heads in agreement. I didn't even see them at the party, but apparently, they were there too.

"And you, Jaxon?" I raised an eyebrow.

"Hey, it was lit for me. Only thing I'm waiting for now is my grand debut," Jaxon made eyes with me.

Mila rolled her eyes at him.

"You'll have it today," I nodded. "Malachi and Trish-Ann, are all the articles lined up for the last print run?"

"Sure are. I'm just waiting on Malachi's article and then we're done," Trish-Ann reported.

Malachi was writing an article about school lunches and how they could be improved. The lunch ladies let him taste test their arsenal of soups and salads, all right up his alley. "It's coming, it's coming," Malachi sat his phone on the table. Will said nothing to anyone. He and Mila still weren't talking because of Mila's outburst from the party. Will and I avoided each other's eyes and still hadn't talked either.

Once the room cleared out, Jaxon and I sat down to look at his video. I used the Fresh Prince of Bel-Air theme music and opened the video with Jaxon's house. From the front entrance, not the back where I had to come in. His eyes lit up.

The next two minutes of the video explored Jaxon's family and school day. It highlighted the fun Jaxon and the strong Jaxon. It mentioned nothing of his reading incapability. Jaxon's blue eyes gleamed through the video, and it closed with a family portrait of him, his parents, and brothers sitting in front of their house, smiling. Mr. Green's hand was on the shoulders of Mrs. Green, and she sat in front of the boys. They looked like the picture-perfect family — at least on video. But then again, isn't that what most people want anyway, to look the part on social media? It's one thing to struggle behind closed doors, but no one wanted other people to actually see it.

"This is great," Jaxon grinned. "My parents will love it."

"I'm glad you liked it," I gritted my teeth and hushed Mom away. She was fighting to be heard again and wanted to discuss

payment for the video and my still broken camera. I searched FAQs on the library's website for information on damaged equipment. It said in bold white letters all loaned items that are damaged will be charged the full liability insurance deductible. I didn't know exactly what that meant but I know it didn't sound good. It was getting harder to distinguish between my actual thoughts and Mom's voice. These days they were the same.

"I'll get your letter of recommendation from my mom—she'll love this," Jaxon put on his jacket. "Thanks Indigo," Jaxon looked me in my eyes, and it made me pause to be seen that way, by him.

I cleared my throat and started. "And about payment, I know you said $100 but I was thinking $200 is fair. Being as though your friend did break my camera, and I had to take off from work, and I had to find my own ride home, and…"

"Indy, I get it," Jaxon interrupted. "I'll ask my mom, but I can't make any promises." Jaxon was back to scrolling through his phone, and his gaze held mine no more.

I smiled back through pursed lips. In my mind, Mom whispered, *"don't trust him…"*

"Hey, am I too late?"

Jaxon and I turned around, and Joya stood before us.

"Well, what do we have here?" Jaxon gave a devious smile.

I cringed. Every part of my body reacted to him. I took all of his words personally.

"Hey, we're just finishing up," I smiled at Joya.

"Oh okay, can I talk to you for a second?"

"Girls talking? On that note, I'm out," Jaxon gathered his things and gave us a peace sign.

"Sit down," I pointed to an open seat.

"I finished my poetry pieces, and I brought a hardcopy for you to check out. Also, Malachi asked me to help him with his article, I forgot to tell you. I have that one done too." Joya shifted her weight and bit her lip. I checked out her nails, and they were also bitten and chewed. Joya wasn't even a part of the newspaper club, and yet Malachi had her writing articles. Sigh. His laziness once again would screw us.

"Joya, you didn't have to do this. If I had known he was getting other people to write his stuff, I would've never authorized this."

"No-no, I don't mind, really. I enjoy writing. I was thinking about joining the team next year myself."

"Really?"

"Yea. I started journaling, and it's not half bad."

"How are you feeling?" I reached out to Joya a few times after her procedure, but she never responded. This was the first time I saw her in a few weeks. I couldn't explain it, but I felt connected to Joya. Even though she was only one year younger than me, she reminded me of Sidney, and I wanted to look after her.

"My dad says we should just put the whole thing behind us. I'm fine, and I even got a car out of the deal," she chuckled. It wasn't a funny chuckle; I don't think she found anything funny. It was a sarcastic chuckle, like she couldn't believe where her life was taking her. I couldn't place her humor, and I thought about each of her words. Was she laughing or serious?

"What have your parents said? I know you got the car — but how do they feel?"

"They act like everything has been a nuisance to them. I dared to disrupt their plan for my life by being pregnant. They act like everything's okay, but at night, — at night — I hear them arguing about it. They don't know that I hear — but I do." Joya wiped a tear from her face and dug in her bag. She retrieved her article and placed it on the table in front of me. "Like I said, here is the article. I hope we can keep this conversation between us," she gave me blank eyes.

Like Jaxon and his reading...like Joya and her...whatever this was...I didn't spill the beans about her bean.

"Of course." I nodded. "Of course."

PART THREE

DESCENT

CHAPTER 20

"**A**ND WHO ARE you, Big Face?" Ez yelled.

"I'm Arletha. I'm dating Benjamin."

Ez looked Ms. Arletha up and down. "Humph. Do you know my daughter? Looks to me, you date him, but he don't date you."

Ms. Arletha inhaled and turned to Dad. Another Saturday morning at Ez's house. Dad was with us today with Ms. Arletha in tow; and this was his first mistake, bringing a stranger along. Ez was in a mood.

Ms. Arletha visited Dad at our house at least four times per week. Some days they would be in the kitchen cooking, and they would jump away from each other when Sidney or I walked into the room. Other days they sat on the couch side by side watching movies. When we walked into the room, Dad placed the big popcorn container between the two of them.

Ms. Arletha was decent, and I wouldn't throw her under the bus. Dad was smiling again, and he and Ms. Arletha searched for new jobs for Dad, so he didn't have to work so many hours. She also cooked dinner and made the meanest pound cake I've had since Mama Jackie's. But she wasn't my mom.

I wrote Mom three letters since Ms. Arletha showed up, but Ms. Arletha didn't show up in my letters to Mom. I didn't have the heart to tell her what she already knew. So, I didn't. Dad thought it a good idea for Ms. Arletha and Ez to meet today, and he didn't call to warn him. In Dad's defense—Ez didn't have a phone anyway. Ez said, "If I need anything I'll come looking for it. And if I don't come looking for it. You come looking for me."

Dad's voice snapped me out of my thoughts. "Ez," he said with a stern face. "This is my lady…" Dad's voice trailed off.

Ms. Arletha nudged him.

"This is my lady, Arletha Wilson."

"Pleasure to meet you, Mr. Ezra. I've heard so much about you," Ms. Arletha pursed her lips.

We already went through this part, but Arletha introduced herself again. I cringed. Ez. was not the 'meet new people' kind of person.

"What's that thing on your head?" Ez demanded.

I winced.

Ms. Arletha had a rather large, darkened birthmark on the side of her head. It covered her left forehead down to her temple and eyebrow.

"It's a birthmark, Mr. Ezra," Ms. Arletha explained. She didn't flinch under Ez's word assault. She must get that question a lot. Sidney stood next to me, her eyes fixed between Ez and Ms. Arletha. Sidney was team Arletha since she cooked and helped her with homework, but Ez would always be her first love. She was between a rock and a hard place, and it positioned her between her love for her grandfather and her need for a mom.

"Ez, it's cold. Can we go in?" Sidney begged.

Ez's shoulders relaxed. "I'm not in the mood for his shit today," Ez erupted at Dad.

"I'm not in the mood for you either, Ez. But you know what we have to do today. If you'd get a phone, I could call, and we could've planned this better. The city says you have to clean up the house or they will deem it unfit to live in."

Sidney cut her eyes at Dad. His voice echoed off the nearby trees, filled with exasperation. His brief show of strength must've been because Ms. Arletha was there. It surprised even me.

Ez hopped around his porch, and the floorboards creaked under him. "I don't care what that city says. Tunica River got my daddy blood on it," he spewed. "You let them try to come take this house here. It'll be an old-fashioned hangin'! Only it won't be me," Ez gave an evil cackle. He threw his head back, exposing many missing teeth in the back of his mouth.

Ms. Arletha gasped.

Ez was off the hook today. I haven't seen him this escalated in months. And Ms. Arletha wasn't seeing the best out of him. No...no, we had to stop this.

"Do something, Indy, do something!" Mom screamed in my head. Mom's voices were coming through loud and clear the past few days. I didn't fight them anymore, and I let her lead when I didn't know what to do.

"Ez...it's okay, we can come back another day," I offered. I retreated from the front step, and Ms. Arletha took a step back with me.

"No, we're staying," Dad insisted. He was blunt.

"You get out of here, boy," Ez sneered at Dad.

"Ez, we are coming in today. And do not call me boy." Ez and Dad stood almost nose to nose. Ez had white spit forming in the corner of his mouth, and he was sweating. His hands were balled into a fist at his side.

Sidney slid between the two and whispered, "Ez." He looked down at Sidney and let out a low growl before he turned

around and stomped into the house. The rest of us sighed, Dad included. Ms. Arletha and I peered at each other as we walked into the house.

An enormous pile of shoes sat in the room's corner, covering the great window Mama Jackie used to open and gaze out of. Ez had newspapers taped to the windows, and as I looked closer, they were all from the sports section. Cats licked into open cans of food, and the refrigerator door hung off the hinges. Ez must have tried to secure it because grey duct tape flapped on the side where the door had fallen. Old pizza boxes littered the floor, and cats, so many cats, roamed the house, with cat food and droppings everywhere.

Ez enjoyed those pre-moistened toilet wipes, and he gave us money to purchase them for him when we went food shopping. Ez had his own stockpile of wipes, and they covered the foyer, stacked up against the wall. The mound was almost the same height as Sidney. I looked on incredulously. Ez refused to drive most days and lived his life out of a small cabin on the lake, but he was stashing wipes like it was nobody's business. In a matter of months, Ez had accumulated triple the amount of items he normally collected.

"Mind your business, nosy girl," Ez eyed me, staring at his arsenal of wipes. "An old man likes to be clean too."

"Grandpa Ez…" I whispered and looked around "… and this is clean?"

"Oh, my!" Ms. Arletha put a hand over her mouth, stifling a cough.

The smell burned my eyes too, but I didn't cough. I was almost used to the smell but not my eyes.

"Don't be doing all that coughing in here woman," Ez yelled.

"Ez!" Sidney shrieked.

Turning around with wide eyes, Ez raised an eyebrow at Sidney. Ez stomped ahead and let us further into the house from the closed-in porch. The living room wasn't much better; Ms. Arletha grabbed a trash bag and a pair of gloves out of her pocket. She also dug out four masks, and she handed them to us.

"Thank you," I took mine. We never had masks before when we cleaned. That was smart and probably thanks to a heads-up from Sidney.

Ms. Arletha began sweeping the floor when Ez stormed across the room at her.

"Stop it, Ez! You have to stop this Grandpa Ez!" Sidney cried. "Stop treating Ms. Arletha badly, and Dad too. Stop treating Dad like this!"

Sidney said Dad. Sidney had called Dad, Dad.

The room was quiet except for the cats purring around us. One meowed around my leg. I kicked it as hard as I could and thought about burning it later, if I had time.

"This is my house!" Ez yelled. "You can't just come in here and do what you want."

"This was Sonia's house too. And Mama Jackie's. You can't keep living like this, Ez," Dad said. "I could see if the house was always like this, but this behavior is new since Mama Jackie passed away. You can't do this, Ez. You'll lose the house if you keep this up."

I saw tears in Ez's eyes, and my chest heaved. The last time I saw him cry was after the very first time we visited Mom at Trochesse. He sat in the passenger seat and cried all the way home. Dad had to drive home that day.

Wiping my eyes, Sidney grabbed my hand. I glanced down at my baby sister, and she had tears pooling in hers too. On my right, Ms. Arletha stood with one hand to her chest and palm at her mouth. She also had tears in her eyes.

"This is me and my wife's home, and ya'll dare come in here every month and tell us what to do. I do the best I can.

I tried to cook the food on the stove like them people ya'll sent over here showed me. I can't figure out how to get one of them stove things on and the other stove thing on, and I have to stir the pot at the same time, and if I use the oven...I just forget! I can't do it all at the same time. I don't know how to do none of that stuff. So, I eat out of them cans over there. Is it the cleanest? No, I guess it ain't. But these cats—these are my new family. Y'all are here, but sometimes, y'all be talking too much. The cats talk back in their own way, and I listen. My Jackie is here with me, right there." Ez pointed to the far wall and a large picture of Mama Jackie sat perched over top of the dusty fireplace. "My Jackie don't say nothing about this here house. And believe you-me, she would. She be coming in my dreams."

Dreams, Ez had dreams...I wondered if his dreams were like mine. Ez didn't talk about Mama Jackie; I guess the memories were too painful for him, like memories of Mom were too painful for me. Or maybe both memories were too painful for him. Both of his ladies, gone in one way or another. They took care of the life things so he could live the way he wanted. I wondered if it was partly Mama Jackie and Mom's fault Ez was the way he was.

"I don't drive that car because it's too many buttons and knobs and things to worry about. Matter-of-fact, before you stormed in here with your punk squad, I was fixin' to say Indy should just take the car because I'm okay with my canoe."

What? Ez was giving me his car? My heart beat faster.

"But now I change my mind," Ez sneered.

Sidney took a step forward and peered up at Ez. He was so much taller than she was, and his shadow loomed far behind her, even in the house.

"That's Indy's car, Ez. That's The Bus." Sidney furrowed her eyebrows.

"I know it, I know it, SidRock. Get out my face, girl."

The floor under my feet creaked, and I noticed the boards were sagging in the area I was standing. I moved Ms. Arletha and Sidney to another area of the room, but that side wasn't much better. The floor was giving out, and I wasn't sure how much longer it had.

"Grandpa Ez," I said. "This floor…" I looked down at my feet.

"Move from over there, Indy. Me and Mama Jackie don't go over there. It's on the way out."

"Are you going to let us clean?" I asked him.

"I'm not staying here for this tomfoolery! You do what you got to do, and I'll be back." With that, Grandpa Ez stormed outside.

Ms. Arletha glanced around the room. "Oh my, oh my," she breathed.

Dammit, man…how could I broach the subject of me seeing someone about my mental health with Ez like this? No time seemed like a good one. Dad and Sidney couldn't take it if something was going on with me too. I bit the inside of my lip until I tasted coppery blood pooling in my mouth. I grabbed a trash bag and positioned my mask over my face ready to clean.

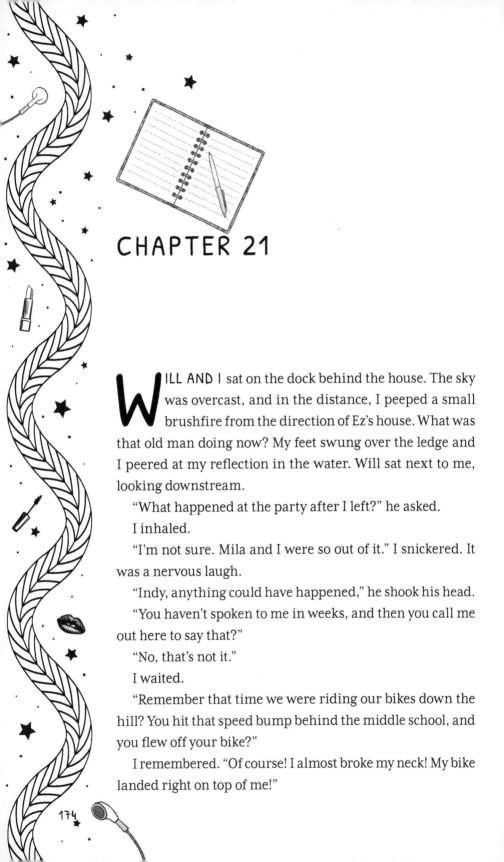

CHAPTER 21

WILL AND I sat on the dock behind the house. The sky was overcast, and in the distance, I peeped a small brushfire from the direction of Ez's house. What was that old man doing now? My feet swung over the ledge and I peered at my reflection in the water. Will sat next to me, looking downstream.

"What happened at the party after I left?" he asked.

I inhaled.

"I'm not sure. Mila and I were so out of it." I snickered. It was a nervous laugh.

"Indy, anything could have happened," he shook his head.

"You haven't spoken to me in weeks, and then you call me out here to say that?"

"No, that's not it."

I waited.

"Remember that time we were riding our bikes down the hill? You hit that speed bump behind the middle school, and you flew off your bike?"

I remembered. "Of course! I almost broke my neck! My bike landed right on top of me!"

Will threw his head back and laughed. His sideburns were cut to perfection. I knew that made him happy. He got a haircut every weekend, faithfully. My mom always said, "A man is only loyal to two things, his football team and his barber." Will's loyalty lay in a lot of things. I hoped I was one of them and that's why he summoned me outside today, like the old days.

"I remember you were going so fast. Your legs were peddling and spinning, and you were glaring and gripping the handlebar at the same time." Will imitated me holding onto the bars and riding my bike.

"Shut up!" I giggled.

"When you went flying, I was so worried."

"You know what I've been thinking about?" I said.

"What?"

"Remember when we were in middle school and you called me from Chicago and cussed me out?"

A large smile spread across Will's face and he chuckled. "First of all, I didn't cuss you out. Woman, I couldn't believe you. We went from seeing each other all day every day that summer to nothing. And I rode my bike all the way to your house to drop off a slip of paper with my phone number on it before we left, and you never even called. I couldn't believe it. I was like, did I do something?" he grabbed his chest and feigned hurt.

I giggled. He was Drakin' and it was cute. "And how do you feel now?" I held my breath.

Will looked at me. "I don't know. I don't have words for it."

"Try."

Will sighed. "You, Mila, and Malachi—it's been us four for a while. I mean, yes, Malachi came later but...you and Malachi dated. Mila and I dated. Everyone has dated...except..."

"Except..." I repeated. I couldn't say the words myself.

"Whatever you're going through Indy, I want to help you. I don't know what's going on, but I want to help you figure it out."

175

How did you tell your best friend that you heard your mom's voice every day in your head? How did you tell your best friend you fantasized about slaying others, and sometimes emotions overcame you that were so strong, and so angry, that it scared even you? And the worst one of all, how did you tell your best friend that sometimes these feelings made you feel powerful and in charge? That you smirk when you daydream about wiping out Jaxon?

I wanted to explore things with Will. He was right, something was there. But what if I had these bad feelings about Will too? They came on for Jaxon out of nowhere, and I couldn't risk hurting Will.

He looked at me with thoughtful eyes, and I wanted so badly to return his gaze. I wanted to turn to him and say let's try. Let's make two weeks our limit—no more than that. Let's go ride our bikes like we used to and laugh about Chicago. But I couldn't. Something bigger was taking over me and I didn't have control over it. Something would suffer, and I couldn't let it be Will.

"I-I don't know, Will. It's a lot to think about," I lied.

He looked at me with surprised eyes.

"Indy, I-I. I wouldn't mind…I want to be there. For you." Will stumbled over his words. I wanted him to grab me and say everything would be okay while I cried. But I also wanted him safe and I'm not sure he could be that with me—not right now.

"And I want you to be. As friends." I lied again.

Will stood and wiped nothing off his jeans. "It's cool, I just thought I would throw it out there," he half smiled. His eyes were different now, cold.

"Wait, are you leaving already? I don't have to be at work until later today. You can stay if you want?" *Please stay…*I thought.

"I have to get going, I have to get home." Will's keys clinked. The planks creaked underneath me as I hurried behind Will.

"I'll call you later," Will gave a wave and weak smile. He got into his mom's car and pulled off. Tears dropped from my eyes, and I wiped them on my sweatshirt sleeve as he pulled off. What was happening to us?

Later that day at the funeral home, I worked beside Mr. Dennis. I haven't seen him in a few weeks, and Tyson and I have been holding it down in the basement while he took care of the families upstairs. Mr. Dennis wore oversized suspenders hanging from his too long pants. A brown fedora hat sat on his head, and that, too, was oversized, and it slid around his head as he talked. I tried not looking at it when he spoke, but it was hard not to.

"Indigo, did you clean the tanks last night? I didn't see it noted on the contact log?"

"I did, I had to start a new sheet. We filled the other one."

Mr. Dennis was cited by the health department a few months ago. He swore someone downtown was picking on him because it was his first citation in twenty years. "They're trying to buy me out and make us move," Mr. Dennis said. I overheard him and Tyson discussing it one day in the office. I hoped they didn't buy him out while I was still working here; I needed this job, and I didn't want to go back to Ms. Montague's studio. I needed the money now that I had Ez's old clunker fulltime to fill up weekly; money was non-negotiable.

"Now, I want to show you something," Mr. Dennis wrung his hands. "Do you know how to work the internet?"

I giggled. "Yes, Mr. Dennis, I know how to work the internet."

Mr. Dennis rummaged through his file cabinet and retrieved a piece of paper. "Good. Put this in the search row," he pulled his glasses up from the lanyard around his neck.

I typed the website into the search bar and a crematorium website loaded.

"I'm thinking about buying us a new system," Mr. Dennis grinned.

"That's great news, Mr. Dennis!" I shouted.

Tyson and I spent many days sitting and waiting for the incinerator to finish burning. It hummed loudly, and even though Mr. Dennis told Tyson and me not to turn the temperature all the way up, we did it anyway to cut down on time and we regularly pushed it past fifteen hundred degrees Fahrenheit. We didn't tell him that part, though. I was thrilled that he was thinking about purchasing an upgrade because this place needed it. He compared himself to the funeral home down the street, and they upgraded to all new systems a few months ago. If Mr. Dennis wanted to stay in business, he had to upgrade his business. He didn't listen to me, and he didn't listen to Tyson. But when it started affecting his money, Mr. Dennis acted.

Mr. Dennis grinned, proud of himself. I watched him describe the new machine and all the bells and whistles it came with. His eyes lit up with anticipation and he pointed at the screen on his old desktop computer in his dated office. I surveyed the room; his office looked straight out of the 1980s. The curtains hung limp, as if they hadn't been changed in years. The carpet was a matted shade of brown and the ends of his desk were worn down to the metal. Pictures of Tyson when he was a baby lined the room, hanging crooked on the walls. Mr. Dennis looked like a good dad. He did what most dads thought was the extent of doing a good job. He went to work.

Mr. Dennis' enthusiasm kept him young and agile. He was older than my dad, but he had so much more life to him. Sure, Ms. Arletha was spending even more time at the house, but I couldn't help but notice when he arrived home late into the night he hobbled, crouched over in pain. The other night, he took off his work boots and Ms. Arletha made him sit them outside; she almost vomited because of the smell. Ms. Arletha didn't have any children, and she spent most of her days at church, or at our house cooking and cleaning. Dad and Sidney ate it up; she was just what they needed. Dad wasn't a 'get up and go to church' kind of guy, but every Sunday, Ms. Arletha made him put on his Sunday best and take her out. Those days, I noticed his eyes the most. He seemed so tired all the time. I hated to see him like that, and me going to college would be our ticket out. I'm not sure how, but whatever they threw my way, I knew I could handle it.

Dad and Arletha made French toast together yesterday morning for Sidney's birthday. Ms. Arletha also baked Sidney a big chocolate cake, and Sidney ate the whole thing just like that fat kid from *Matilda*. Mom didn't come to me then. When I thought she would scream into my ear or wake me from my dreams, she was quiet. But when I wanted her to go away and let me figure things out on my own, she put on her director's hat and said, "Action."

Work kept me busy these days, and I hadn't been to Trochesse to see her. Plus, I still haven't told her about Ms. Arletha. If I wanted to call a Spade a Spade, Mom was the one who told me about Ms. Arletha—so technically she already knew.

Dennis and Son's Funeral Home was dark when I locked up that night. I set the alarm and grabbed Ez's keys—my keys. It would take some time to get used to saying that. I opened the door and plopped into The Bus, as my phone chimed. Glancing down, I saw an email header from Titus University, Admissions Department. My heart skipped. I submitted my application weeks ago and had heard nothing.

179

Until today. I hesitated and looked outside. My hands shook, and I rolled down the window to let cool air in. I tapped on the Titus icon, and the screen jumped and turned black. A GIF with balloons and streamers opened up. *Congratulations, and welcome to Titus University*, it read.

I screamed, banging my hands on the steering wheel. The horn beeped and beeped as I pounded it. I did it! I got into college, and my very first choice too! Maybe things would work out. I just had to get my thoughts under control. Next stop would be college! I had to be mentally prepared for the role.

I started up The Bus and headed home with a grin. Wait until I tell Dad and Sidney...Ms. Arletha too. They would be so happy.

A few minutes later I screeched into the driveway at home and was surprised to find Sidney, Dad, and Arletha home. Good, I didn't have to tell the story over and over again.

"Dad! Dad!" I yelled, barreling out of the car. Ms. Arletha came running out of the house with flour all over her apron and hands with Dad right behind her. "I got in! I got in!" I jumped. I scrolled through my phone until I landed on the email. I opened the GIF and the balloons, streamers, and congratulatory noise played.

"Ahhh!" Dad and Ms. Arletha screamed together. Sidney came outside and looked at us like we were crazy.

"She got in, baby! She got into college!" Ms. Arletha nudged Sidney. Sidney's face broke into a smile, and the four of us began jumping and shouting on the front step. "This calls for a celebration! A fresh lemon pound cake coming right up!" Ms. Arletha shimmied in place and clapped her hands together before heading back into the house.

"Hold on, I want to help!" Sidney ran after her. "Congrats, Indy!" She screamed over her shoulder.

Dad and I stood outside smiling at each other. Tears formed in his eyes as he looked at me. His gaze made me nervous as understanding passed between us.

"Your Mom would be so proud," he said. "So proud."

"I know Dad. She is."

And I knew that she was.

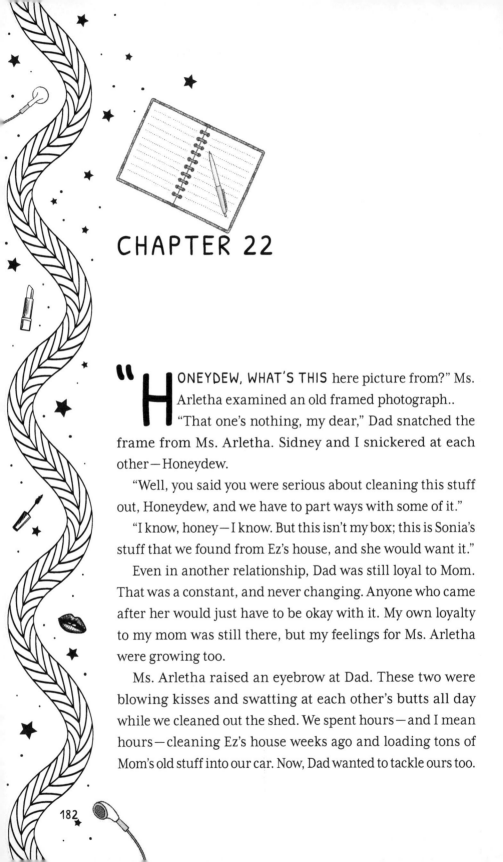

CHAPTER 22

"**H**ONEYDEW, WHAT'S THIS here picture from?" Ms. Arletha examined an old framed photograph..

"That one's nothing, my dear," Dad snatched the frame from Ms. Arletha. Sidney and I snickered at each other—Honeydew.

"Well, you said you were serious about cleaning this stuff out, Honeydew, and we have to part ways with some of it."

"I know, honey—I know. But this isn't my box; this is Sonia's stuff that we found from Ez's house, and she would want it."

Even in another relationship, Dad was still loyal to Mom. That was a constant, and never changing. Anyone who came after her would just have to be okay with it. My own loyalty to my mom was still there, but my feelings for Ms. Arletha were growing too.

Ms. Arletha raised an eyebrow at Dad. These two were blowing kisses and swatting at each other's butts all day while we cleaned out the shed. We spent hours—and I mean hours—cleaning Ez's house weeks ago and loading tons of Mom's old stuff into our car. Now, Dad wanted to tackle ours too.

In our bathroom currently sat Ms. Arletha's toothbrush and some hair grease. You know, the old-fashioned Blue Magic grease. Once she greased her scalp at the kitchen table and heated the hot comb on the stove, I knew it was official; she was here to stay.

"Well, you invited me over, and I'm just doing what you asked, Honeydew."

Dad's jaw tightened. "I know I invited you because I invited you. It's just…those are her things."

Sidney and I stopped packing boxes and peered at Dad and Ms. Arletha. She crossed her arms at her chest. "I'm getting a drink."

Dad was caught between two women. One woman wanting to be his future, and another controlled his past. His past was always there; even locked away in a shed, it was there. I walked across the room and peered into the box Ms. Arletha and Dad were bickering over. The box contained dozens of handwritten letters and some of Mom's old clothes were haphazardly stuffed inside. The letters were frayed at the ends and yellow. Mom's handwriting.

"What's all this?" I whispered.

"Nothing," Dad kicked the box away from me.

I squinted. His eyes were large and fearful. "Dad. What's in the box?"

"Those are your Mom's things, Indigo!"

Indigo, he called me Indigo. I glanced at Sidney and she sat on the floor cross-legged, staring at us.

"Dad," I rose to my feet, "…what's in the box?"

"Those are your mom's things!" He repeated.

I crept closer to my father, and we now stood inches apart, breathing heavily.

"Y'all, everything okay?" Ms. Arletha cocked an eye at us. She was wiping her hands with the dish towel from the sink. Mom's dish towels.

183

While he turned to Ms. Arletha, I dashed for the box and snatched a handful of letters.

"Indigo! You know what, do what you want," Dad threw his hands in the air. "Maybe you're old enough—at least you think you are!"

Dad's last words stung my soul. At least you think you are. He sounded tired of me. He was the one keeping secrets locked up in a box like some Nancy Drew novel, and he was annoyed with me. Holding the letters tightly under my arm, I hustled to my bedroom, shutting and locking the door; Dad didn't chase me.

I plopped on the bed and opened the first letter.

JUNE 1990, NOT SURE WHAT DAY IT IS.

Mom and Dad…how much longer do I have to stay here? It's already been three months, and you guys said if I improved, I could come home. I've done the cycle class, and I even took the Jazzercise class. (That one was fun) We made a little singing group, and I convinced Ms. Shelton (our camp counselor) to let us compete in teams. That's the good.

I haven't had any more of those thoughts…the bad ones. I promise you guys, that cat they say I burned, I didn't! I will keep saying it, I didn't do it! I don't know how it ended up with the lighter fluid on it, but it wasn't me.

I will take all the knives out of my bedroom, and you can take my Walkman at night. Hopefully, that will stop with the voices, I promise Mom…I promise. Can I come home now? I'll do better. I'll try harder. We wake up at 5am and run through the desert. They have us on this weird diet. They said in order for the voices to go away we have to change what we are eating, so we eat grass. I

swear that's what it is. Not really but it's definitely all this healthy stuff that's disgusting. Worst of all, the doctor keeps holding me down and spilling water onto my face until I say I don't hear the voices anymore. I hate that part.

Please come see me or write back,
Love, Sonny

SEPTEMBER 1990

Mom and Dad:

The summer is over and enough is enough. I can't take these people anymore. The dorm is loud, and these girls in here are disgusting. We don't have any pads. Do you know what we've had to use instead? No one cares what's going on, Mom. My roommate, Audra, said her parents told her this is not summer camp; it's conversion camp. Conversion Mom. And I'm saying Mom because Dad says nothing anyway, so I'm talking to you. You sent me to a conversion camp? I told you I would take the medicine! I just didn't agree with that word they said. Schizophrenia. I'm not that word! It sounds like Schitzo and I'm not a Schitzo and I don't even know how to spell it. And I told you I didn't set that cat on fire, and even after you asked me in your last letter, I didn't burn down that laundromat! My phone time was changed, and it's now from 6 p.m.–7 p.m. Please call me soon, and I'll explain more. I have to get out of here.

Please write back,
Sonny

OCTOBER 1990

Mom, this will be my last letter. You lie too much. I told you I would take the medicine, but you insist on trying to make me complete the full course, so I had no choice. You and your bad parenting skills brought this on yourself. Is Jackie even your real name? I don't know why I have these thoughts! I just do! I thought I was doing the right thing when I told you and Dad, but you used it to stuff me away so these people could abuse me! Yes, I said abuse! You control Dad; he is your little slave, and he goes along with everything you say. Well, no more, I won't do it either. He doesn't even respond to my letters anymore, and I know it's because of you.

Ben is coming to get me tomorrow, and we're leaving. Please don't try to contact us. We will be happy and away from the people who believe the lies that others tell them and try to control our lives. We'll be nineteen soon and out on our own. Audra got me an audition with her cousins-friend's-fiancé's band, and I just may just go on tour.

PS: Thank you for sending my dress for our prom here. It was still not a real prom, but it was fun, I'll admit that.

-Sonny

The letter dropped out of my hand and fluttered to the floor. No…no, it couldn't be.

Stomping across my bedroom floor, my feet smacked against the hardwood beneath me.

"Mom was Schizophrenic?!" I screamed. I said it even before I swung the door open. My voice echoed into the hallway.

Dad, Ms. Arletha, and Sidney eyed me.

"Is. She *is* Schizophrenic," Dad corrected. His voice was stern and measured, like he was waiting for me to storm out of my bedroom with these questions.

"And no one thought to tell me and Sidney…! Tell me!?"

Dad's jaw tightened again. "Indigo. There are some things children just should not know about their parents. I didn't know if you could handle it."

"What does that even mean? Why couldn't I? I have a right to know!" I yelled.

"Children shouldn't know everything about their parents." Dad repeated.

"Have you read these?" I screamed, tossing the letters at him.

"Most of them, yes. Some I couldn't get all the way through…" Dad breathed.

"Because of what they did to her," I blurted.

He nodded.

"And what is it? Mama Jackie and Ez sent her to a conversion camp?"

Dad nodded his head yes again.

"Why?!" I cried. "Why would they do that?" Tears streamed down my face.

Ms. Arletha stood uncomfortably in the room's corner amidst a family feud.

"What's that mean, Indy? That word you said?" Sidney quizzed.

"Schizophrenic. It means Mom was crazy. Exactly what we thought, but no one told us."

"Don't talk about your Mom like that!" Dad snapped. "She couldn't help those feelings. They came on quickly. She turned into a different person when those other people got into her head. When she was good, she was good."

"And when she was bad, she was bad, I guess." I was belligerent.

"Indigo!" Dad boomed.

"She is gone because she killed someone! Killed Dad! You never talk about it; ever! You don't go see her anymore! You don't do anything anymore! You act like this is normal life, but it's not! If Mom has mental health issues, that is our right to know!" I screeched. The tears continued falling down my face and my throat cracked. For years there was an elephant in the room that I wanted to talk about but didn't know how. All this time I felt like something was wrong and now it was confirmed. These feelings I had and these voices I've been hearing, Mom heard them too.

When Mama Jackie died from a heart attack years ago, Mom took it the hardest. She was manic for a long, long time. I learned what that word meant at an early age, earlier than most. Manic. They say it's when your mood is up and down. Sometimes you sleep too much. Sometimes you don't sleep at all. A couple years ago before she went away, Dad picked up Mom from crisis and she slammed papers on the kitchen table and stomped back to the bedroom, flinging the door shut. Eyeballing the paperwork, I found the word Schizophrenic. I didn't know what it meant, and I never even saw that combination of letters put together to form that word. How did you even say it?

I took brain pictures of the word and searched it back in my room. Everything that I read about that word sounded like my mom. So, this was it. There was a name for it. This is why she did the things she did. I dug deeper into my research, trying to figure out how to fix her. Medication? Therapy? Mom did none of those things they said would help, and if she did do it, she hid it well. I padded into the kitchen and plopped down next to Dad asking him about the funny spelling word that I saw. I didn't tell him that I Googled it and it sounded a lot like Mom.

"That's not your mom, Indy," Dad patted my knee. "Those head doctors write so many things in your file and it sticks with you for life. No worries, honey, Mom is okay."

So, I dropped it. I believed my dad because I wanted to. I wanted nothing to be wrong with Mom. But there was something wrong, and here was the proof. Dad had lied all of this time, and Mom was not okay.

"You know what Indigo; you think you're so grown! While we're on the topic, let's talk about Ez."

"Benjamin, no," Ms. Arletha stepped from the shadows in the corner.

Sidney perked up hearing Ez's name. "What about Ez?"

Dad swallowed. "We've allowed Ez to go on like this for too long. He needs help, Indigo. You know he does. The man doesn't have a cell phone, he leaves his car at our house, and his primary mode of transportation is a canoe? He needs more. And Ez is…sick. Ez is sick."

Sidney gasped. "Sick with what?"

"He has Autism. They say it's like high functioning Autism or something—like he can still do things for himself, but he has some quirks. Ez has gotten through life with Mama Jackie, but now that she's gone, I fear that he's not safe by himself. And don't forget the gun."

They've lied to me this whole time. I knew there was something wrong with Ez, I knew it! I had nothing to compare him

to, I didn't know much about Autism either—I'd have to search that later. Mama Jackie and Mom handled everything regarding Ez, and I thought that was normal for our family. We took care of the elderly because it was respectful. Or so I thought.

"Ez is Autistic," I wiped my eyes.

Sidney's tears quietly fell.

Was I Schizophrenic? Or Autistic? How did that happen? Were you born with it? Was it all genetics?

"How long have you known?" I muttered.

"All my life. All of your life."

Ms. Arletha crept to the couch and sat down carefully, afraid to make a sound.

"And why did no one tell us this either? He's our grandfather!"

"Indy, it never came up. We always thought, that's just Ez. He's just funny about some things. Sure, he could be OCD sometimes, but aren't we all? We knew Ez was different, but it never came up. No one talked about it, and Mama Jackie took care of everything while Grandpa Ez chopped wood all day."

"And how do you know?"

"Indy, I was here. Are you forgetting Mom and I went to school together? I saw it firsthand."

"Oh…right…"

"But he was in the army," I countered.

Dad nodded his head. "He was, but it didn't last long. It was too much for Ez. People screaming at him, the noises, everything really. He didn't last long before he was discharged."

I thought back to my childhood. I never remembered Ez going to work. He never talked about his own childhood or much of anything. He talked in riddles and it seemed like his life began when Mama Jackie came into the picture. My eyes were red, swollen, and my shoulders were slumped. So were Sidney's and so were Ms. Arletha's.

Not Dad's. "This is why something has to be done. You wanted to read those letters, so there you go."

"Mama Jackie and Ez sent Mom to a conversion camp? Why?"

Dad paused before answering.

"Grandma Jackie thought…Mom was fighting a demon. Your Mom skinned a few cats and lit a dog on fire. She heard voices, and Mama Jackie believed they told her to do it."

"My God…"

"It's not true, Mommy wouldn't do that!" Sidney shouted.

"She did, Sidrock. It's true."

"But we had Mayweather at my dad's house! She loved him! She never hurt Mayweather—she loved that dog!"

"I don't know, Sidney. I guess sometimes the feelings come and go. I don't know."

"I'm sorry, Indy, for not telling you. I thought I was protecting you guys, and I was wrong. I should have told you earlier. About Mom…Ez."

I sat down on the couch and wiped my tears. "So, I was right, this whole time. When I came to you years ago with that paper I found on the table and you told me it wasn't true. And when mom first went to Trochesse, you said she accidentally hit someone with her car—you lied to me." I sobbed.

Dad was quiet before he spoke. "One thing I am grateful for is that you girls are okay. You are both so strong and so smart. Just because your mom is struggling right now, doesn't mean you have to. Indy is going to college, and soon enough she'll be a big-time writer. And she's working now, making good money down at the funeral home. And us three…we'll be okay too," Dad grabbed Sidney's hand and Ms. Arletha's.

"Dad…I-I…" I began.

"Tell him, Indigo!" Mom hissed. I closed my mouth and kept quiet. I just read in Mom's letter that she regretted telling her parents about the voices, so why would I tell him, especially

right now? Six eyes peered back at me intently. "I-I love you guys," I half smiled. Swallowing away the words sitting on the tip of my tongue. It still wasn't a good time to talk about it; my own issues would have to wait.

Sidney held tight to Ms. Arletha.

Dad finally had tears in his eyes. "Come over here, girl!" Dad extended his arms and hugged me tight. Knowing that Sidney and I were okay was the one thing that brought tears to my dad's eyes. Like Mr. Dennis—he provided. He went to work and provided the best way he knew how. Only thing, we weren't okay. I wasn't okay, but by the looks in their eyes, they needed me to be.

Dad embraced me; my phone buzzed. I read the text from my lock screen.

> **JAXON:** We need to talk, asap.

CHAPTER 23

THE RAIN POURED and poured today; I almost didn't make it in. The Bus didn't start in the rain this morning, and Dad had to come outside and give me a jump before school. I was shitting bricks all day, imagining that I would walk outside, and the car wouldn't start again.

It roared to life like nothing happened. Now I was sitting in the salon chair getting my hair braided and it would take at least the next hour. After the party at the mansion, I found a few more nubs that were cut down to my scalp. That pissed me off—you don't cut no Black girl's hair. That was law. What made it worse, I didn't know who did it, why they did it, or the intent behind it. I just knew my hair was gone and someone was responsible.

I looked at my cell phone and noted the time. It was 3:22 p.m. I was supposed to meet Jaxon at 4:45 p.m. and I was cutting it close. My heart plummeted at the thought of canceling on Jaxon. I wanted nothing more, but he and I had not talked since his text message, and he still hadn't paid me the $200. I didn't know how to bring it up, so I didn't. Mila finally admitted that she hooked up with Jaxon and called it the "the best party-ever."

She wasn't even worried about pictures or someone potentially seeing us in compromising positions. Maybe she didn't care but I sure did. I didn't want anything to disrupt me getting into college. I saw people on social media losing scholarships and offer letters because of videos and pictures of them doing crazy things. I wasn't stupid enough to let my ticket out of town be squandered away by pictures. I shuddered at how easily Mila and I had been persuaded by the life and times of the rich and famous teens of Tunica Rivers. The things we didn't have were flaunted in our face. A cookie was dangled and instead of being who we are, we got caught up in the moment and went along with the group.

The time on my phone ticked away. I already had my hair appointment set up when Jaxon texted me yesterday and I couldn't cancel. It would be another two weeks before they had appointments open, and my braids were rough. I was using edge control to gel my edges, but they curled up as soon as I stepped foot out of the house and into the April humidity of Louisiana. I tried to squeeze all of my errands into one day, but I was still behind as I watched the clock in anticipation. I bit my lip and stole glances around the room to calm my nerves.

"Finished," Sheeda said, spinning me around in the seat.

I glanced at my hair in the mirror and felt my scalp where she replaced the missing braids.

"There weren't too many gone, only about ten or twelve. But they were cut all the way down to the root. Those spots will have to grow back."

I grimaced with her words. Paying Sheeda and rushing out of the salon, I jumped into the car, turned the ignition, and nothing happened. Pausing, I turned the ignition again, this time pumping the gas pedal too.

The engine was quiet.

"Nooo, nooo!" I shrieked.

"*Indigooo, Indigooo,*" Mom screeched in my ears with an English accent.

"Shut up, shut up, shut up!" I fussed—banging my hands on the wheel. Tears streamed down my face. Please God, not today, not today. I had too many things to do, and I couldn't deal with Jaxon or Mom right now. I shouldn't have to deal with Jaxon or Mom right now.

"*My dear daughter, why do you deny your destiny? How about you come visit me on the weekend love? I told you about my dream.*" Mom's English accent sang.

"Stop talking like that!" I yelled.

Sheeda had another client in her chair, and she was shaking a bottle of hair dye, watching me from the window. I gritted my teeth and exhaled…wiping my face, I turned the ignition and pumped the gas again.

Nothing happened.

I screamed and banged my hands on the wheel. Why today of all days?

Another voice somewhere in me—this time not mom said, "*Calm down. Give it a second and try one more time.*" This voice was quieter, softer. I breathed and wiped my face again. I rolled down the window. Ez's car still had old school roll down windows. The cool air hit my face, and I rested on the headrest behind me. After a few seconds, I leaned forward, pressed my foot to the brake, and started the engine.

The car roared to life.

"Thank you," I said out loud. The sky opened once more and fat raindrops fell onto the car as I pulled out, rushing to meet Jaxon. Sheeda still watched me from the window.

A few minutes later I pulled into the park; the same park Jaxon and I met months before to discuss his college video.

Jaxon's black JEEP was already there, towering over the smaller cars parked near. He didn't pull into one parking spot; his ride was spread out, covering two spaces. His windows were rolled up. I couldn't see him through the tint, and the rain didn't help.

Hopping into his car, he had the nerve to look annoyed. "I've been waiting seven minutes," he tapped his phone.

"I'm sorry, I got caught in the rain," I half lied. "What's up?"

Jaxon squinted as Future's voice blared through his speaker. He turned the music down, and rain was pounding the car, making the conversation for us — as awkwardness took over. "I'll get right to the point. Jaxon's voice was hard. "I took some pictures from the party...I think you might like to see them."

Pictures...Mila and I heard rumblings about pictures, but no one produced any yet. I thought it was high school rumors, but Jaxon knew otherwise. He scrolled through his phone and held it up to my face. I instinctively extended my hand so I could hold his phone.

"No — I'll hold it," he swatted.

Jaxon scrolled through the pictures, and my eyes widened. He had pictures of Mila and I topless. Pictures of me wrapped around the toilet, red cups strewn around. Vomit sat in the corners of my mouth, clearly visible. In one picture Jaxon held up a pair of scissors and was smiling, holding them close to my braids. He had a video of me dancing on the table with Mila. I didn't remember dancing at all.

My face flushed.

"I've thought about this for a while, and I thought, instead of me worrying about these papers and things they want me to write, I figured you could just write everything for me. And, if it works out, maybe we could figure out something beneficial for both of us for college too. Also, I never asked my Mom about increasing your payment to $200. She would

have had too many questions and I figured there was no point anyway, after this." he gave a crooked smile like he figured it all out. "I still forgot your money though; I will bring it soon."

Jaxon was the pied piper, and he was here to collect.

"E-e-excuse M-me?" I stuttered.

"I guess I have to spell it out for you. In order for me to not show these pictures to anyone, I want you to do all of my papers from now on. I think it's fair. We only have a few weeks left of school before we graduate. Then we'll be out of each other's hair. And if it works out, maybe we can plan for college too," he repeated, his time with a grin. He nodded his head like — like he already decided and was waiting for me to get on board. Like this was a good decision for both of us. Like I should be thankful. Like he was waiting for a thank you. "I think this will be good for both of us. It can be beneficial." He talked like he discovered gold on the moon — he was truly proud of himself.

There he was. The real Jaxon. The one I knew was in there somewhere. I felt guilty these past few months because our interactions were so strained. I thought maybe I was being hard on him, and no one saw what I saw because nothing was there. I tried to convince myself that nothing was there, he didn't know any better. He was a teenage white boy who had no thoughts about a Black girl from the other side of Tunica Rivers. Well, something was there...I saw it. Even if no one else did, Mom tried to warn me, but I didn't listen. I saw him. I sighed.

"What happened to my braids, Jaxon?"

He grinned again. "I kept thinking they looked like macaroni and cheese, and I wanted to see for myself. I was so messed up." Jaxon looked out of the window and snickered like he was remembering a wonderful memory. He cut my hair because he was curious about Black girls, and he acted as if it were no big deal. He cut my hair, and he grinned. I waited for him to say "fun times" with a knee slap, because that's the face he was making.

"Jaxon, fuck you."

"I was hoping you wouldn't act like this. No need getting all upset because it's really not that serious."

"It's not that serious? You're blackmailing me with naked pictures and you're telling me it's not that serious?"

"Blackmailing is a strong word," he gave a chuckle. And there! There was the knee slap, in real life! "This is an opportunity for both of us."

"And what's in it for me?"

"I won't show the pictures to anyone, obviously." Jaxon shrugged his shoulders. He shrugged like that part should have been already understood. But I didn't understand. I didn't understand any of this.

"Wait, so if you have pictures of me and Mila, why are you coming at me? Does she know?"

"Mila is weak," Jaxon said matter-of-factly. "People expect these things from her. You know actually, I'm surprised you two are even friends—she's a roady. You hit once and hit the road." Jaxon giggled. "And no, she doesn't know; no one knows for sure. I know rumors have gone around, but I spread those."

He smirked. "I came to you first after I came up with this idea."

Jaxon's words hit me like a ton of bricks. He expected this from her but not from me, and therefore he came after me. I was being condemned for doing the right thing. What was the right thing anymore, anyway?

"*My dear daughter,*" Mom interrupted my thoughts with her usual English accent. "*Now is your chance. No one is even here. Just one swift slash to his neck. Look around for a pen or something sharp.*"

I did as Mom instructed and searched the dashboard for a pen or something. I saw nothing. "Fuck you, Jaxon," I shouted again. I stumbled out of the car and shielded my eyes from the rain; it was now coming down sideways. Jaxon started his car and smirked at me.

The drive home was a daze. Malachi and Will texted me, both checking on me during the rainstorm. How dare Jaxon blackmail me? I knew I was messed up that night, but I didn't know it was that bad. When had he been able to take all of those pictures? I couldn't afford to have them get out. Jaxon could expose me. I just got into college, and something like this would hurt me—hurt Dad. Jaxon's family was rich, and they knew people. Hell—they easily called my job and made them make me write an article for Jaxon. Who knows what stunts they could pull at the insistence of something Jaxon said. Jaxon would always be believed over me. It's just the way it was; he would rebound and be okay. He would get pats on the back and high fives. I would be vilified. It would be some way and somehow, my fault. They would say I shouldn't have been there anyway. I let myself get so smashed. That's what they would say. It was a cruel cruel world, and for a girl like me with everything to prove—it was icy.

"*No…No Indy, I don't like this one Indy,*" Mom said, still in her English accent.

"Shut up, Mom, shut up!" I banged on the steering wheel again. I couldn't see through the rain, and my heart shuddered when the car hydroplaned. I pulled over on the side of McTaugh Road. Cars whizzed by splashing water on my side and I cried.

I cried for Mom.

I cried for Dad.

I cried for Malachi, Mila, Will.

I cried for the thoughts screaming at me in my head.

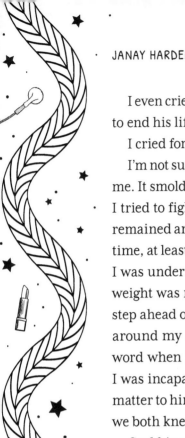

I even cried for Jaxon, because I wanted nothing more than to end his life.

I cried for $200.

I'm not sure what it would take to quell this feeling living in me. It smoldered with every passing day. I tried to put it out. I tried to fight it. I even tried talking back. But the thoughts remained and whispered to me how fun it would be: just one time, at least. The feeling sat with me and attached itself like I was underwater with weights. The weight was Jaxon. The weight was my future slipping away and Jaxon, always one step ahead of me. He wasn't afraid to have his parents move around my schedule without telling me or go back on his word when I needed a ride home or cutting my hair when I was incapacitated. None of that mattered because I didn't matter to him. I was disposable to him, and the sad part was, we both knew it.

Grabbing my cell phone, I called Malachi. I gripped the phone tighter with each ring. No answer. I called him again.

No answer. I called Will, and like Malachi, there was no answer. I sat my phone down on the seat beside me. I couldn't let this get out. And Jaxon was right, we only had a few weeks of school left, and I could get by and be done with him. Wiping the last tear from my face and knowing that I would have to go at this alone, I picked up my phone. So many things hinged on getting this college thing right. I opened my texts and sent one text message to Jaxon.

> **ME:** I'll do it.

CHAPTER 24

IT WAS OFFICIALLY the first weekend I was working by my-self at the funeral home. Mr. Dennis and Tyson produced some sort of certificate which said I was eighteen and I was licensed in funeral home preparations. Mr. Dennis and Tyson had been training me for a few months now on the entire process, start to finish, and today, I was officially on my own.

It was easy money, and I didn't have to deal with people today which was good because I wasn't in a talking out loud mood anyway. Upstairs was closed to the public while I worked, but downstairs, downstairs was different. The bodies talked to me. I studied their features, and I made up stories about their lives and things they had gone through. Had they hurt anyone? Had they meant to do it? Especially the young ones. Why did they pass so young? I made up so many wild stories in my mind that they became my friends. I popped in my head-phones and covered myself in an apron. Tyesha, a slim Black woman lay across from me on the table, her body covered by the long white sheet. I would work on her next, but first this week was poor Ms. Abigail Foster. Abigail was thirty-eight, according to her chart, and she passed away by a sudden stroke. What makes your body have a stroke at thirty-eight? I drained each orifice and started the body cavity process asking myself this question.

"Indigo, make sure you brush my hair." Ms. Abigail Foster said.

I looked down at her on the table. Her eyes were closed, and she looked like she could jump up at any moment. Her pasty white skin was almost translucent, and it felt like leather. Her hair was still a bright shade of blonde and all things considered, her mane was her best attribute. "I got you Ms. Abigail." I grabbed a brush from the prep table and brushed her hair as soft as I could.

"And to answer your question Indigo, who knows why someone has a stroke at my age. I didn't always eat right, I had diabetes. I let my family stress me out and you know in the days before this happened, I had just decided I was going to go back to school and finish my law degree. I told my husband, and he said, we couldn't afford it, and I was too old anyway."

"Well, baby, tha' sugar will take you out anytime. I don't play with that," Tyesha said, from the table across the room. "I saw it take my mama's foot. It swelled all up and the gangrene got it. They had to take it off. No ma'am, I don't play with tha' sugar."

I peered up from Abigail's skin examination and smirked at Tyesha. "Hi, Ms. Tyesha. How are you feeling?"

"I'm okay. Make sure not to use that brush on me; I need a comb to run through these roots girl."

I snorted, "We have combs. I'll even put it into some braids if that's what you want. I'll try to talk to your family about it when they come to see your body."

"Yes, please and thank you because they want me to wear one of those beauty supply wigs with the bayang and I cannot spend my days looking baby Jesus in the eye with a bayang.

Chile, they ain't bout to be talking about me in Heaven—no they won't."

I squeezed my eyes together and laughed out loud from my gut. It was the first time in months I let out a hearty and genuine belly laugh, and it felt nice to do.

"Be careful over me with all that laughing" Ms. Abigail warned through her own laughs.

"How did you pass, Tyesha?" Abigail asked.

I finished Abigail's skin examination and moved to the sink. I filled it with warm water and added a few drops of lavender essential oils just the way Mr. Dennis liked it.

"It was my ex-boyfriend. I broke up with him and he wouldn't leave me alone. He broke into my house one night and did this with one direct chest wound."

"My lands! Did you try getting a restraining order? Did you tell someone?"

"Ms. Abigail, I went to the courts. I sat there all day and the judge said he didn't see a reason because we antagonized each other."

"Antagonized each other?" Ms. Abigail repeated.

The water was almost filled in the deep steel sink, and I left Ms. Abigail and Tyesha talking while I turned on Shelby in the other room. We had a cold one in the freezer and his family chose something different for his final resting place.

When I returned to the room, they were still discussing their demise. "That's my question, too, Ms. Abigail. I posted on Facebook that he was following me, and he printed it out and brought it to court. Told the judge I was slandering his name. I guess that judge agreed."

"That's ridiculous! Did you speak up? Did you make the judge see?" Ms. Abigail asked. Her words were slower as she tried to comprehend.

"Of course! I tried to. He didn't want to hear it."

"I still know some people from the law world, what juris-diction is this?"

"Um, jurisdiction? I don't know what that means, but it's the city."

"Tunica Rivers City Court? Not the borough? Or the township?"

"You mean where all the rich, white people live? No, it was definitely the city, Ms. Abigail. Our judges in the city aren't so quick to listen to us Black girls," Tyesha said matter-of-factly.

Ms. Abigail said nothing.

"You ready for your bath Ms. Abigail?"

"I'm ready, Indigo. Before we start, hear me and hear me good. You keep yourself safe, and wherever life takes you, make sure you go all the way."

"Facts," Tyesha said.

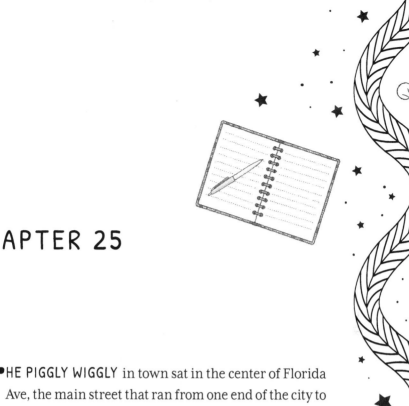

CHAPTER 25

THE PIGGLY WIGGLY in town sat in the center of Florida
Ave, the main street that ran from one end of the city to
another. It was the third exit off of a roundabout circle.

"Shit!" I gripped the steering wheel tighter. I never drove
a roundabout by myself and I missed the exit, rounding the
circle again. I turned the wheel and peered at the exit harder.
As I put on my blinker to cut over and turn off, a car came up
out of my blind spot and blocked me.

"Shit!" I screamed again.

"Bitch, what is you doing?" Mom giggled in her English accent.
I heard her over the radio. I turned the dial all the way up.
Circling for a third time, my underarms were sweating, and
my eyes darted back and forth between all the signs pointing
in different directions. *"Take it slow, Indy,"* Mom instructed.
*"Merge over now and give yourself some time. Don't merge at the last
minute."* I did as she said, and I took the exit. I relaxed my now
tightened shoulders.

Throwing the car in park, I grabbed my backpack. My
phone buzzed and saw a text message from Jaxon flash across
the screen.

I gritted my teeth.

> **JAXON:** Can you pick up my dry cleaning? I need it before my date with Jill tomorrow.

> **ME:** NO. I agreed to what I agreed Jaxon. And nothing more. This is crazy. And where is my money?

> **JAXON:** I thought we were past this. No reason to get all angry Black woman on me. We only have a few weeks, and you know the alternative. And I got it! Let's meet up soon. Jaxon sent a GIF of a white boy shrugging his shoulders.

I slammed my phone down on the seat and ran inside the grocery store. I grabbed the first set of tulips I could find; Mama Jackie's favorite. They were right in the front by the entrance, and I was glad. I hated walking all the way inside. I felt like people stared at me, or maybe I was imagining things — Grandpa Ez worked at the Piggly Wiggly for a couple months, and everyone asked about him when I went in, even though I barely remembered him working anywhere. From what Dad said, Grandpa Ez walked three miles every day to and from work, because there was no water access to use his canoe. Mama Jackie put in the application for him, got him dressed, went to his interview with him, and went in there with a straight face and told them people that he didn't like to interact with large groups of people, but he would be good in the back stocking the shelves. They took one look at his broad shoulders and heavy arms and he became their new stocker. The other employees loved Ez and his quirks. He talked about guns and fires and food and anything else that his life consisted of that day. He was genuine, and they loved him for him.

The day Mama Jackie passed, Ez was at work. Mama Jackie and Ez's neighbor called and said Mama Jackie was sitting on the front porch in a chair not moving, where she and Ez usually sat and watched the road. Imagine—being at an age where watching the road was a thing. But that was their thing. Dad got the call too and he went to the store and picked up Ez. Once we got to the hospital, it was too late. Mama Jackie had a heart attack, right there sitting on the front step with no one home. When she died, Ez quit his job and didn't work again. He was convinced she passed away because he wasn't home, so now he spent all of his time at home. In some ways, Ez died too, right along with Mama Jackie.

"India?"

The voice stopped me dead in my tracks. It was the same voice that made me move my car to the back of their house so the neighbors wouldn't see.

"Hi, Mrs. Green," I nodded. She stopped right in front of me with her cart blocking my way. I tried to go around her, and I kept my eyes down, hurrying.

She stepped in front of me. "I've been meaning to call you."

Two taller boys walked up behind her, and I recognized them as Jaxon's brothers, from the photos hanging on their walls at home. They were shoving and punching each other in their shoulders. They all looked alike, the three of them. These had to be the older brothers that Jaxon spoke of. He mentioned they both attended prestigious colleges, and they would live the good life. Yes, Jaxon actually said that.

Why did it seem like only my people didn't expect to live a good life and get a decent job? Ours was a guaranteed fight

and a steep climb. They could still be in college and know what the future held because they had options and the mindset to explore it. Luxuries I didn't have. Time, I didn't have. Her son was blackmailing me. The only thing I needed was for the next month of school to fly by.

Jaxon was now texting every few days and adding things for me onto his to-do list since he was officially accepted into UGA: write his English paper, complete this application for college, email so-and-so. UGA was taking part in a mandatory email pen-pal program with their college roommates. Jaxon had me corresponding with his roommate daily, pretending to be him. He couldn't be bothered to get to know me, his future roommate, or anyone else of no importance to him. And I went along with it so I could have those same options too. It was a sordid situationship.

"The article you wrote about Jaxon was very well done. It even surprised me a bit," she let out a little giggle.

"How so?"

"Well, you made him sound so smart, so talented. I think you and I both know Jaxon needs a bit more help than others," she leaned in and whispered like she had shared a dark secret with me. I inched backwards and the back of my knees hit the stand where the flowers sat. I was still boxed in. "How did the letter of recommendation work out for you?"

And with that—I smiled. "It worked out well. I got in."

"Beautiful!" She gave a little clap. "I'm just so proud when you girls take initiative and go at life with gusto. You guys have had it so hard." She shook her head and tsked-tsked.

I cringed. "I have to go, Mrs. Green."

"Mom, she has to go." The older boy said, annoyed. This one looked like a taller version of Jaxon. His hair was slicked to the side with gobs of gel, and he wore shorts and man flops just like Jaxon. Was that a family trait? The man flops. Or was it an "I have nothing to worry about so I wear and do whatever I want" trait? The world would never know.

"Wait-wait," she said. "One more thing."

"What's that?" I gave Mrs. Green a quizzical look.

"Listen," she inched closer. "I've been on this diet, and I've been doing okay for the past month. I've lost three pounds so far, but I haven't weighed myself this morning. I'm supposed to eat lots of leafy green vegetables and fiber. I've been buying fresh collard greens, and I know you gals like them. I'm sorry, India, I mean they are just so bitter. I don't know how you gals eat that stuff—I just don't. So, when I saw you in the market today, I had to ask…how do you eat them?"

I felt myself getting a headache. "How do you cook them?"

"Cook them?" Mrs. Green's eyes bugged out of her head. "I wasn't cooking them, I thought they were like spinach, you could add them to salads and stuff."

Mrs. Green's sons roared with laughter behind her and her face turned bright red.

"Mrs. Green, I have to go," I shook my head and scowled.

I moved her cart from in front of me and went to the register. She really had nerve. *You gals? India?* The apple really didn't fall too far from the tree, and I don't know why I expected anything less.

"Thanks anyway, India, let me know if you need anything else."

"Indigo. My name is Indigo."

A dense fog settled over Tunica Rivers in the mornings. It hung there, thick and brooding. When you live here your entire life with nowhere to go and nothing to do, you notice the subtle changes. So many people didn't make it out. I noticed the kids' parents at school; they were proud to be first born and raised here. The same way Dad was proud. They didn't care what happened to them; they made their

choices and were living the effects of them. Choosing to stay home where life is as it always was, and for some that was a welcomed treat — a warm blanket on a chilly night. For others, it enveloped them like smoke. It fumed around them, getting into every orifice in their body as it invaded their lungs, brain, most of all — heart.

Sitting at Tunica Rivers graveyard, Mama Jackie's gravesite was in front of me this Saturday morning. I brushed some old leaves away from the headstone and laid down the new flowers I just got from the Piggly Wiggly. Some people would do anything they could to get out and make it. And sometimes, those same people came back. But when they did, they were different. It hardened them. They didn't dream anymore; they didn't laugh. They worked at the glass plants in town, backbreaking work — but it was steady and always readily available. For someone returning from putting their dreams on the line only for it to not work out, that became the highlight: stability and consistency. Always knowing where your next check came from and working for the next forty years didn't sound so bad. Not when you had met the alternative.

I didn't want it.

I had to change my reality. Saying yes to Jaxon would help me do just that. I wrote two papers for him last week and one the week before that. It wasn't too bad, and the words came easily for me. It was simpler than having to answer questions about those pictures. Besides, I already decided when this was all over, I would convince Jaxon to delete them all. From his iCloud, too. How — I didn't make it that far yet, but that was my plan. Through this process, what angered me the most was I still told no one his secret. I still told no one that he couldn't read, could barely write, and his family was covering for him. He dared to blackmail me when I had dirt on him too. I guess that was the difference between us. I held his secrets, and he exploited mine.

I didn't want to be one of those people who came back to Tunica Rivers with nothing to show for it. I watched my dad break his back day after day and he too had nothing to show for it. That couldn't be me. It wouldn't be me.

I applied for the scholarship Mrs. Montague gave me. There was a box on the application which asked if your guardian was a single parent. I didn't know how to answer that part. Was Dad considered a single parent? Was it even fair to assume that he was? Mom was technically still around, even though she wasn't with me every single day. In some ways, I had both of my parents, and in other ways I didn't have either of them. And in the most scary way of them all, I had no one.

I kept Mom in my head to myself. Dad and Sidney were wrapped up in Ms. Arletha. It relieved me that Dad and Sidney had her; they needed something to look forward to. I had something to look forward to—college.

Controlling Mom was becoming easier. I googled symptoms of Schizophrenia, and it said to keep a mood journal. I noted the times I heard her voice; she always came when I was with Jaxon and when I was nervous. She was missing from my happier and quieter moments. She was never there when I was with Malachi or even Will. That was how I deduced that she didn't come during happy times. If I just stayed happy, she went away. I had to stay happy. Had to. How did someone stay happy, though? Was it possible? I wasn't sure, but I had to learn quickly. At least when I made it to college, I could see a professional there. I checked the Titus University website and they had a counseling department; I would make an appointment as soon as I got on campus. There was no use saying anything to Dad right now. We still don't have insurance and truthfully—he was happy right now. Happier than I had seen

him since before Mom went away. I kept my mood journal, and I thought I was doing a good job of managing the thoughts. In a few months, I could handle it on my own, and he would be none the wiser. I didn't want to leave Tunica Rivers and come back with a mental disorder. I wanted to simply—leave.

I was so deep in my thoughts I didn't hear her walk up. Her shadow enveloped me, and I saw the outline of her shapely silhouette.

"Hey, Mila," I smiled without turning around.

"Hey, girl," she sat beside me at Mama Jackie's grave.

"You are a real-life stalker," I giggled.

"Well, that is the point of your location being turned on your phone, correct?" she snorted.

Mila and I had a running habit about showing up to where the other was if our locations were close.

"Where were you?"

"I met JT before his game."

I groaned. The Mila and JT show continues.

A tear fell from my eye. I'm not sure where it came from, but a cold feeling accompanied it and Mila wiped my cheek. Mila wouldn't care about pictures coming out. That wouldn't bother her. In fact, the party wasn't the first-time the senior class saw Mila dance on tables, or topless. If someone was going to give Mila attention and create a scene in which she could be the star, she always took the opportunity. She had joked that she should forgo college and instead attend NBA All Star weekend and land herself a baller. She was content being the trophy wife and the life that came with having pretty privilege. White privilege, too. No, she didn't care about pictures. They helped her get to where she was going by getting her attention, albeit negative attention. Attention was attention for her. Everyone wanted to get where they were going in a sense, and everyone was subtle in the ways in which they went about it. Jaxon blackmailed me, Mila used her body and me...I planned and plotted and used other people too.

"I didn't get in."

I was confused, but soon, I knew what she meant.

"City College?"

"Yeah. I got the letter the other day. They said my SAT scores aren't high enough. They offered some sort of remedial program. I go to the summer program, take a few placement tests, and they'll admit me on a trial basis." Mila and I had taken the SATs together last year, and she didn't do well. Mila is notorious for not being able to take a test without some dramatics. During the SATs last year, I watched her get up and go to the bathroom at least three times. I mouthed "What's up?" and she pointed to her butt and her eyes got big.

Diarrhea.

Mila's nerves were so bad she had diarrhea during the SATs. When the test time was up, she wasn't even halfway through finished because she wasted so much time.

"You don't sound excited," I inquired.

Mila plucked at the grass beside me. "Maybe it's just not for me. I'm not the college kinda girl. You know I applied because you made me," she shoved my shoulder.

"I didn't make you; I just strongly encouraged," I shrugged. "So, what are you thinking? What will you do?"

She shrugged her shoulders and said, "Mom says that she can get me a job downtown at Dr. Rasner's office. I can do some secretary work for right now, you know, until I figure it out."

My heart sank for Mila. For my friends, they were dropping like flies. It's not that I think they have to go to college, but I know whatever it is they are looking for, they wouldn't find it in Tunica Rivers.

"Have you heard about Joya?" Mila lowered her voice like someone could hear us. She changed the subject easily.

"No, what?"

"Word on the street is she and Mr. Chestnut are messing around."

"Really?" I thought back to our conversation at school.

"Yeah, someone saw them together and now wheels are spinning. Can you imagine? Sleeping with an old man?"

"I thought he was in his thirties?"

"That's old," Mila nodded. "They say, that's why she got that new car, he bought it for her. To keep her quiet."

"I-I..." My words caught in my throat. I started to catch Mila up about my semi-friendship with Joya and what I knew but my loyalty to Joya was there too. I told her I would keep her secret—just like I would keep Jaxon's. Mila studied me waiting for my reaction. She loved the gossip and sometimes I did too. I knew way more to the story, but it wasn't mine to tell and I had too many other things on my mind.

I swallowed.

"That's crazy," I said flatly. I tried to go for no emotion so Mila wouldn't follow up with questions.

She kept right on talking, babbling on for a few minutes, but I really wasn't listening. After a while she quieted and didn't bring it up again.

I said my goodbyes to Mama Jackie and climbed into the car. Mila followed behind me in her white Dodge Neon.

We passed the hill, and I smiled. Mila, Will, Malachi, and I spent long afternoons there racing up and down the hill. I would miss it. I stared at the buildings. Tunica Rivers Pizza, the nail salon, the skating rink. The pottery studio. I spent many days as a child stomping through these establishments, and now may be some of the last times I do that before college.

So many of these places I went to with Mom. I remember one day Mom took Sidney and I to Tunica Rivers Pizza and she ordered an entire party sized pizza tray. We ate until it stuffed us. Mom ordered more and more pitchers of soda, and we ate like kings. When the bill came, Mom told the manager we didn't like the pizza, and the soda tasted funny—therefore we wouldn't be paying the tab. The manager and Mom argued, and she had to call Dad to the rescue.

Another time, Mom volunteered to chaperone my class trip to the skating rink. She got on the mic in the DJ booth and began rapping and singing over the Macarena song. They had to wrestle the mic from her. Back then it was embarrassing—it still is. But was that the last time I would have her in person, outside of Trochesse? If I knew that then, maybe I wouldn't have been so embarrassed, knowing my time with her would be limited anyway.

Did Mrs. Green know her son was blackmailing me? Dangling money in my face? I'm sure it wasn't something they discussed over dinner. Jaxon's mom steamrolled me—just like he did. I was indispensable to them, clearly. When they boxed me into a particular place, even if it was only a section of the supermarket—that's where I had to be.

Jaxon's older brothers looked like Dumb and Dumber. They were tall and stupefied. Out of the three of them, I could see they were the brains of the operation and how Jaxon could be looked at as the black sheep of the family. The Greens chose favorites, and in their world, Jaxon made their lives harder because he actually required help with anything resembling hard work. That's right. Jaxon's problems made them work harder, and they had to overcome his shortfalls by calling in favors. Make someone write articles for them; help their son jump through hoops to get into college. I didn't know if she knew what her son was up to, but the way I saw it—she was guilty too because she had birthed and created the monster that stood before us, over eighteen years of never holding him accountable. It was her fault. And they completed all of their hardest work on the backs of little people like me.

CHAPTER 26

MAY 3RD

Hey Mom,

I hope you're okay. I'm sorry I haven't been to Trochesse in a while, but I don't have good news. I went to the pottery studio and I think I found out who bought your piece. I do know the people who bought the piece. We can talk about that in person, there's too much to explain. I have all the brain pictures you can think of. Oh, and I went to Mama Jackie's grave too. It felt nice to sit there and talk to her.

Remember the last time we were all together when Mama Jackie was alive, and you were home? I remember. We were at the house grilling. It was the 4th of July and everyone was home. Sidney was young then, lol. She kept running to the water's edge and trying to jump in. Even Sidney's dad stopped by, remember? Things were good then. When the fireworks started that night, Ez grabbed his gun and howled at the moon. It's so funny now, thinking about it.

I'm not happy, Ma…things are…happening with me.

Things that I don't know how to explain. How are you sleeping? Do you have dreams? I'm not really sleeping well. I found an old box of

your letters you wrote to Ez and Mama Jackie — when they sent you to that camp. I'm so sorry they did that to you. You were different, and people don't know how to deal with that. I guess they don't know how to deal with girls like us. But Mom, I'm not sure how to deal with me yet either. The thoughts are keeping me up at night, and I envision how I could hurt someone else. Sometimes the feeling lingers inside of me and it screams so loud to be let out and unleashed. It's getting harder to hold it and I've been thinking, maybe just let it out… at least once and see if it will scratch the itch. Who knows, it could be a one-time thing… right? Maybe the next time I visit, we can talk about some of this stuff? I have so many questions. I hope you are ready to, because I sure am. See you soon.

Love, Indy

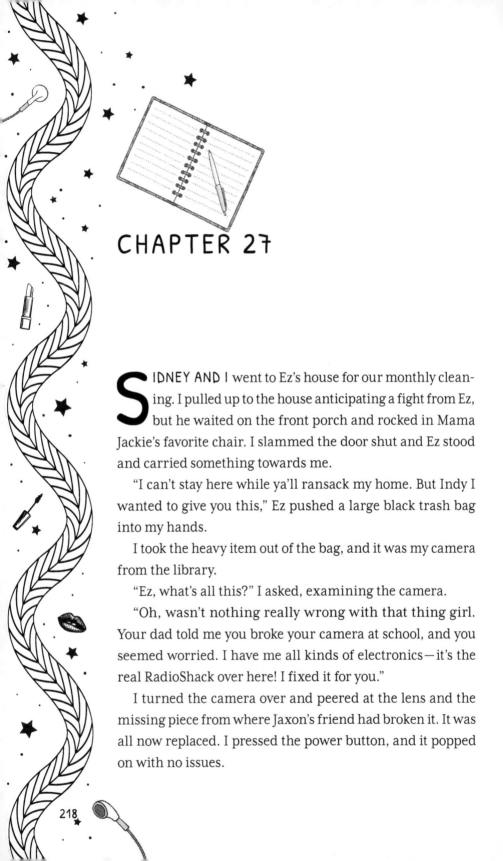

CHAPTER 27

SIDNEY AND I went to Ez's house for our monthly cleaning. I pulled up to the house anticipating a fight from Ez, but he waited on the front porch and rocked in Mama Jackie's favorite chair. I slammed the door shut and Ez stood and carried something towards me.

"I can't stay here while ya'll ransack my home. But Indy I wanted to give you this," Ez pushed a large black trash bag into my hands.

I took the heavy item out of the bag, and it was my camera from the library.

"Ez, what's all this?" I asked, examining the camera.

"Oh, wasn't nothing really wrong with that thing girl. Your dad told me you broke your camera at school, and you seemed worried. I have me all kinds of electronics—it's the real RadioShack over here! I fixed it for you."

I turned the camera over and peered at the lens and the missing piece from where Jaxon's friend had broken it. It was all now replaced. I pressed the power button, and it popped on with no issues.

"Thank you, Ez. Thank you so much!" I jumped up and down. I didn't know who to thank first, Dad or Ez. I was worried about receiving the money from Jaxon so I could pay for the camera damage fee. Now I wouldn't have to worry about that, and I could stop dodging the library's calls.

Ez patted my head and put his hat on. "Now I'll be back soon. If I can't find my stuff when I get back, I'm whipping your tail. Bye, Sidrock." And with that he grabbed a paddle and trotted off to the water.

Sidney and I glanced at each other and shared a smile. We entered Ez's house and moved quickly throughout the rooms, but the mess seemed never-ending.

I looked around at the clutter that still loomed before us. I stopped at the dollar store before we came to Ez's and bought trash bags, but we still managed to almost go through the entire box. It seemed like every month we went through more and more. The sad fact was that Ez was accumulating more stuff. Before Grandma Jackie passed away, she taught Ez how to use the Home Shopping Network. Every week, he stood in front of the television with the house-phone, barking his order into the receiver. They mailed home a bill for each purchase and between me and Dad, we made sure it was paid. We couldn't keep up anymore.

This week I noticed he was stockpiling engine parts. Random nuts and bolts were strewn throughout the house and I swear he had an entire engine sitting in the living room. Why did he have this stuff? I tried not to touch them, these were probably some of the parts he used to fix my camera, and I was grateful.

Hearing a car door close, I ran to the window and peeled down newspaper Ez had taped up. Malachi, Will, and Mila stood outside, supplies and trash bags in tow. They glanced

around at the mess that was Ez's yard. Will had been here
before but not Malachi or Mila. They peered around the
most. My heart skipped a beat at the sight of them! They
were here — for me. All three of them, at the same damn
time. Between us sparring for one reason or another, it had
been at least a month or two since we were together outside
of school. My friendships with them are important to me,
but lately, I wasn't sure how they felt. Them being here right
now told me they cared too. They still cared.

I ran to the front door and carefully pulled it open so as
not to knock over Ez's pile of empty cans that the cats were
eating from. "What are you guys doing here?" I asked with
wide eyes.

Will stepped forward. "Your dad called. He said you haven't
been sleeping well, and he asked why we haven't been to the
house in a while. He said we could find you here….I called
them up," Will pointed to Malachi and Mila. "And well, here
we are." My dad came through for a second time, and my
heart swelled with pride.

I ran to Will and threw my arms around his neck. He stumbled back onto his mom's car and dropped a bag filled with
bleach, gloves, and cleaning supplies. Will grabbed me back,
tighter this time. I inhaled one more time and he smelled of
teakwood, shea butter, and a hint of love for me. Will's arms
were around me, and they felt tense and jerked slightly. Like
he didn't want to let go but he wasn't sure if he should. I didn't
want him to let go, but not in front of Malachi and Mila.

Hugging Malachi and Mila next, my heart was so full. I
didn't understand Malachi's reason for not wanting to go to
college, and I didn't understand Mila's relationship choices,
and Will…well, I understood nothing about what was happening with me and him — but we were here. All four of us.
They didn't know how much that meant to me right now.

"So, what's going on?" Mila asked, looking past me up at the house. She and Malachi had never officially been to Ez's house, and when Will came before, it looked totally different because Mama Jackie was still here to take care of things. Will glanced around, his face scowled, and he said nothing. By the looks of it, Will knew Grandpa Ez was not okay too.

"So, this is Ez's house." I waved my hand around, showing them the property. Cats meowed and the old front door creaked and groaned as it banged against the frame. It was a little windy and stench from a combination of old food and the cats wafted in the air. Malachi glanced around while placing his hands in his pockets. He pulled out a small vial of hand sanitizer and squeezed some into his hands. Mila was quiet as she took in what she was seeing. Some of the homes in the trailer park where she lived accumulated tons of stuff in their yards too but seeing Ez's house along with all of his land which was equally as covered, I'm sure shocked even her.

"Where is Ez?" Mila questioned.

"He's out on the water somewhere. Said he didn't want to be here while we ransacked his house," I shrugged.

"Ransacked?"

"That's the word he used," I chuckled.

Mila's shoulders relaxed.

"So, what do you need us to do?" Malachi stepped forward.

I looked around the property at all the work we still needed to get done. Ez started a small bonfire of some magazines that were in the house. *Too many words,* he had fussed. Cats still roamed the land, flushable wipes littered the yard, and Ez's clothesline hung from rope extending from the house to a tree. As I looked around at the mess, my eyes filled with tears. My Grandpa Ez, Sidney's Grandpa Ez, was not okay, and I didn't know what to do about it. I hated that my friends saw him like this.

221

I sniffled as tears ran down my cheeks. At the same time, Will and Malachi stepped forward—both inching closer to me with arms extended. Will was the furthest away because he stood next to the car, but he moved fast, not backing down. Malachi was closer, but truth be told, I didn't see him. I saw Will only. He was so tall. So strong. Malachi glanced between us and slowed walking. Will made it to me in one swift motion and before another tear dropped from my face, he was there—like always.

"It's okay, it's okay," he held me.

I cried for Ez.

I cried for me.

I cried for Mom.

I cried for it all.

Mila came up behind me and placed her hand on my shoulder. I heard footsteps, and soon Malachi was at my side, his hand on my right shoulder.

My friends. Mine.

I wiped my tears into Will's shirt and glanced up towards the house where Sidney was staring out of the papered-up window, smiling at us. "Sidney is in the house. We needed more trash bags too, I'm so glad you're here," I joked. "We can head inside."

"Copy that," Will nodded. He and Mila walked inside, while Malachi stood in place looking at me.

He grinned.

My stomach fluttered, and my face felt flush.

I grinned back.

When my head wasn't somewhere hearing voices, it spent hours thinking of Will. But my body...my body whispered a language only Malachi was fluent in.

"Ms. Lewis," he inched closer.

"Yes, Mr. Reynolds?"

Malachi said nothing but palmed a few of my braids resting on my shoulder. His touch was soft — like he was taking in the moment. I inched closer and sniffed his cologne. He only wore cologne when he went to work, so I knew he just finished his shift down at the movie theater. I inhaled, remembering days when I left with his scent on me.

"Girl, go in the house!" Mom's voice shrieked.

I jumped back, startled.

"Let's go inside," I breathed.

Malachi snickered and put space between us while Will watched from the porch. My phone buzzed, and I sent Malachi ahead of me. I blinked and stared at the header.

It was an email that read: <format>You have been admitted for the 2021-2022 Freshman Class.

I was accepted into Virginia State University.

223

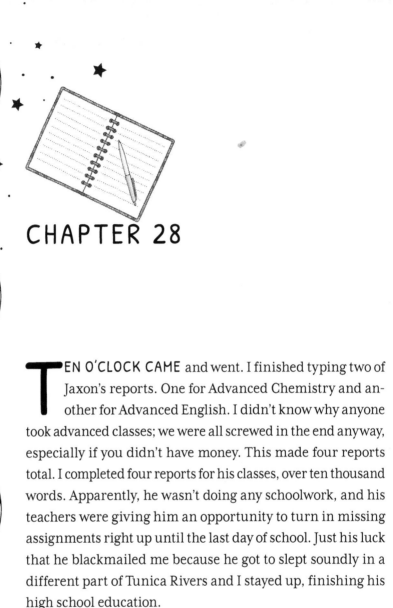

CHAPTER 28

TEN O'CLOCK CAME and went. I finished typing two of Jaxon's reports. One for Advanced Chemistry and another for Advanced English. I didn't know why anyone took advanced classes; we were all screwed in the end anyway, especially if you didn't have money. This made four reports total. I completed four reports for his classes, over ten thousand words. Apparently, he wasn't doing any schoolwork, and his teachers were giving him an opportunity to turn in missing assignments right up until the last day of school. Just his luck that he blackmailed me because he got to slept soundly in a different part of Tunica Rivers and I stayed up, finishing his high school education.

I woke up this morning, and I wondered what it felt like to be a spy. A fly on the wall. Change the game and spy on Jaxon for a change. Yesterday I thought I could be a singer like Mom. Sidney and I dressed up in her old clothes we fished out of the shed from when we cleaned. Sidney and I giggled at the old clothes, but I also imagined what Mom was doing when she wore them. How she felt. Was she happy or sad? Was I happy or sad? Today was the big day, and I didn't know if I felt happy or sad. Mom seemed to have a good time at Trochesse — she seemed so happy when we went to visit. Maybe she was happy there. Maybe I would be too? I wondered if they had room for me in their band of misfits.

I giggled out loud to myself and looked in the mirror. My eyes stared back at me, but the rest was Sonia Lewis herself: Mom.

I giggled again and waited for the voices.

What are you doing here, mom?

Waiting for you to do what you know you have to do.

And what is that?

Mom smiled back through my own eyes with a sinister grin but didn't answer. My eyes shifted until soon I couldn't tell them apart; Mom's eyes and mine were the same.

Sidney stirred in her closet of a room. I giggled again. I wondered if she was tired-tired or just regular tired. I always wanted to learn to play chess, and I thought she and I could learn together. Oh! I had a better idea. My car wasn't starting again, and I've been meaning to check the oil. Ez taught me how to do it a few years ago. One of the few life lessons from Grandpop Ez himself. How did Ez let Mama Jackie send Mom to that camp? Surely, he was smarter than that. Who was anyone these days, anyway? Dad hit the nose on the head. There were some things children shouldn't know about their parents. Well, there were some things parents shouldn't know about their children either.

Random thoughts spilled out of my mind. My body had to move, had to think, had to process. I danced in front of my mirror and my fingertips tingled and felt numb.

Dad couldn't control the thoughts in my head; I would have to go at it alone. And if I did hurt someone…well, who was I to interrupt fate?

I looked at the clock again. It was 12:47 a.m. I always wondered why they called midnight the next morning. There

was nothing that made me equate morning with midnight, the darkest part of the day. The house was quiet, and I heard nothing except crickets and slapping water outside. *I wonder what Ez is doing.* Maybe I would go see him. I never paddled the entire lake by myself, but maybe I could try tonight.

My mind raced thinking all the thoughts known to man. Different voices ran circles in my head as I lay on my back on my bed staring at the wall. The words spelled themselves out on the ceiling as I looked on. I saw the words so clearly—they painted my ceiling with different colors and fonts for different people talking. Some voices were nice and soothing. Others were harsh and demanding. The voices said the same thing, just different ways. *Kill him, run him over, you'll feel better, just do it once, see how it feels.*

When I finally crawled into bed, the sun was coming up. It peeked through the window in my room and landed on my face. It was bright, but I turned over and pulled the covers over my head. My mood wasn't sunny. Today was the big day, and the sun wouldn't wait for me. My presence was expected.

Graduation day.

The day brought a flurry of activities, hugs, and tears. Months before, I only applied to two places: Titus University and Virginia State University, and I got into both. I was proud of myself for that. Everything happened the way it was supposed to happen. At a time when so many things were being taken away from me having a normal senior year, I was happy that I got to experience that. My decision was easy. Titus University was closer to home; I still wanted to be around for Sidney.

When I confirmed my attendance for school, it took me two full weeks to gather all the documents they required. My shot record—which cost me $15 from my doctor's office. A place I haven't been to in months due to insurance. A $200 dorm room deposit, and if you had a car that you planned to bring

well, they needed all of that documentation too and a paid permit slip. They always made it sound so easily done when they send you the documents: just print, sign, and send back, and boom you're finished.

I went through the process in my head about how I would get it done. I would go to Ms. Shondra's down at the corner. She had a printer and an old dial-up computer in the back. She and Dad went to school together, and she said I could come and use it anytime I needed. After I printed all of the pages, the signing part was straightforward. Then came the next hurdle—sending it back. I had a few options: I could go back to Ms. Shondra's and send it old-school, buying a stamp and an envelope. Or, I could take a picture of it and email it back, but it was at least fourteen pages that I would need to sign and return. I tried to do it twice, and I got so frustrated when I began mixing up the forms and some pictures were taken twice. My next option, I went to the Tunica Rivers Library and used their old 1990s copier machine even though I was still trying to lay low from the library these days, after the camera fiasco. Before that, I spent long afternoons scanning important documents to various bill collectors when Dad didn't remember. This machine costs thirty cents per page, and I had fourteen. Everything costs money these days. Everything. The coins jiggled in my pockets; my worth tied to their song.

But I did all that.

I went through all of that and jumped through the hoops, and despite all the things that stood in my way, I got it done. It was a moment that I would be proud of for a long time. I wore my hair in a high bun on my head, and I opted for the largest hoop earrings I had in my collection. I gelled my edges with special attention, I clipped small gold beads to my braids, and my face was beat for the Gods! My pink eyeshadow shimmered

in the sun and my highlight accentuated my already defined cheekbones. I applied a nude lipstick which matched beautifully with the rest of my makeup.

Within a few hours and under a fiery Louisiana sun, our Principal screamed, "Indigo Lewis!" and Ms. Arletha, Dad, Sidney, and even Ez, beamed at me from the crowds. Ez was wearing a buttoned up checkered shirt, and he waved and tugged at his neck. Dad had tears in his eyes, and Sidney and Ms. Arletha clapped as hard as they could. My heart burst with pride for my family—Ms. Arletha included.

The day folded into the night, and Will had a large party at his house. All of Will's older relatives were there, eyeing us youngins.

"Baby, that's a lot of lipstick," Will's grandma said to me. Mila covered her mouth and stifled a giggle while Malachi made choking noises.

"She looks just fine, Grandma," Will said, staring at me hard. His gaze made me shudder.

Plates filled with all sorts of savory dishes and delectables were moving around three different large tables. Rice, chicken, steak, french fries, hot dogs, hamburgers, corn on the cob, spareribs, cakes, pies, ice cream. We laughed, we danced. Mila showed off her dance moves, and Malachi was in his element, surrounded by a smorgasbord of food.

Under an oak tree off to the side, I sat in a lawn chair watching everyone. Will pulled up a chair and sat next to me.

"Penny for your thoughts?" He said.

"Look at all of this." I gazed around. The night was surrounded by nothing but friends and family. There was a lot of love in this space right now, and I was here for it all.

"It really is amazing isn't it?" Will grinned.

"And how are you? Really?" I turned to Will. He was always there for me, and I hope he understood what his friendship meant to me.

Will sheepishly looked away. "Indy...I love you. Mila is right, her and I were never going to work out because it's always been you. I meant what I said. I want to be there for you with whatever you're going through, but you have to let me in."

I inhaled sharply, surprised by his words. "Will...I-I, I think I love you too. No, I know I love you too. Whatever goes on with us, and I'm not sure what that will be, I want you around."

Will grinned and his perfect, white teeth shone in the moonlight.

"You're going to be a big-time college girl, you sure you want me around?"

I pondered Will's words considering I would be three hours away. I nodded my head. "I don't know what to say Will, I really don't. I do have some things going on right now, but I'm working it out. I don't know what will happen, but I'd like to try."

"Well, I'll be here whenever you call. Just like Chicago," he smirked.

"That's our limit! We don't go more than two weeks!" Will and I exclaimed at the same time.

"Deal?"

"Deal," I grinned.

The plan was for the four of us to get together tomorrow night to really celebrate. There was a new club in Baton Rouge, and we planned to have a good time just the four of us—like we used to. I laid my head on Will's shoulder and took mental pictures of everything. I didn't want to rush this moment; it was too perfect.

My phone buzzed, and the smile immediately left my face.

JAXON: We should meet? I have your money. And some other things too. Tomorrow?

ME: I have to work. Meet me at Dennis and Son's 6 a.m.

JAXON: The funeral home?

ME: Yes.

JAXON: Wow, that sucks. Okay.

CHAPTER 29

JAXON: Can you come here?

ME: Excuse me?

JAXON: My car is getting custom seats put in, I won't have a ride.

ME: Get on your bike like the rest of us poor people. You live less than two miles from my job. No, I won't pick you up.

JAXON: Fine. I'll be there in a few.

M Y OWN CAR broke down the week before and I had to take two busses to get to work on time. He complained about a quick bike ride; I jeered. He was lazy but willing to wake up and meet me at work at 6 a.m., that wasn't a good sign. I was exhausted from staying up at Will's graduation party. The voices were still coming to me, mainly at night now—preventing me from sleeping.

Minutes later, Jaxon arrived sweaty and out of breath. He wore sneakers on this day, and not his usual man flops, and sported a small drawstring knapsack on his back. He must've been desperate to talk, and that made me nervous. What did he want this time?

He took a step forward, invading my space while we stood in the foyer of Dennis and Son's. "I have to show you something."

"Get back out of my face, please." He was so close my reading glasses fogged up.

"What?" He extended his arms as if I was the problem. He sat his bag down in the visitor's chair next to the front door. I peered out of the small window, hoping no one saw him arrive.

"Look at this." Jaxon shoved a course syllabus in my hand. The names read Jaxon Green and another person's name I didn't recognize.

"This will be for me and my friend at college....He and I talked, and I told him what you do for me, and we thought you could do it for him too. Maybe we can work something else out. I'll pay you. That's what you want anyway, right? I'm not stupid. I saw your car; you could use the money." He looked at me with curious eyes and he palmed my braids—the new ones I had to have replaced because of him. He came closer again and placed his hand on my shoulder and licked his pink lips. "Oh, and I have your money too, sorry for the wait." Jaxon dug in his bag and pulled out a fresh one hundred-dollar bill. "How bad do you want it?" He smirked and pulled the bill back. He gazed at my face, studying it up and down.

I felt like a piece of meat. I studied his face too, only I was disgusted. I felt like I would vomit, staring at him, hearing his words, and feeling his intent.

This time, I knew he didn't mean schoolwork. Jaxon wanted to taste the rainbow. He tried to sweep his palm underneath my chin and cup it before I pushed his hand away from my face. I wasn't the smartest girl, and I wasn't in advanced classes, but I was picking up what he was putting down. Sneering at him, I inched backwards.

"What's the big deal? You make everything bigger than it has to be." He sucked his teeth. "You want this little bit of money, take it then." He took the bill and flaunted it in front of my face.

"I make everything bigger than it has to be? And you're asking—no—telling me you want me to do your work in college, and now some of your friends too?" It wasn't even about the money at this point. This man continued to disrespect me. Jaxon stood in Dennis and Sons, and he was out of place. He never saw an actual day of work in his life, but he was holding me up from doing mine. It was still slightly dark outside as the sun was just rising. That would be a good thing for what I knew was about to happen.

I had one thing on my mind: Murder.

I glanced around the room; I had had enough.

Do it! Do it! Do it! voices chanted in my head. They didn't sound like Mom this time. Whoever it was knew what was up. It was time.

I turned away from Jaxon and I headed down the steps into the studio. He could see himself out or he could keep this up and lose his life. I'm not sure how, but today was surely the day. I didn't sleep last night, the voices kept me up and the sheer excitement from graduating high school had my adrenaline pumping. My eyes were bloodshot red, and now my temples were pounding. I could feel them pulsating as I gritted my teeth.

I took large steps across the shabby rug and Jaxon was hot on my heels.

I yelled, "I told no one your secrets! I told no one that you can't read. I held your secrets, and this is what you do!" I was fuming. Jaxon was not going to stop—we both knew that. Things had to end with me.

"Is this more of that angry, woman thing? C'mon, Indigo. Wait a sec," he grabbed my shoulder again. He touched me. Again.

"Arrgggh!" I screamed.

Jaxon's eyes widened in surprise. He stood behind me and I could feel his breath on my neck. In one motion, I turned and yanked his arm hard pushing him forward down the stairs. The building was old with steep, cellar steps. Right in front of us was a flat wall that I had to duck under every time I went down the stairs. I knew the building well from spending so much time here—but Jaxon didn't. I ducked, so I didn't hit my head but when I pushed him, his head slammed into the wall in front of us and he yelped, sounding like an injured animal. His head bounced back, and I didn't let up.

"Umph!" I kicked Jaxon as hard as I could while he held his forehead. His head slammed into the wall once more, and he slid down, trying to grab hold of the railings to steady himself. His hand narrowly missed the railing, and he tumbled down the steep steps, landing on each step harder and harder. One by one, he rolled fast and hard. It seemed like it was happening in slow motion, with each drop he winced in pain and cried out. When he hit the bottom step, he sprawled out into the studio, motionless. He didn't move, and I didn't see blood.

"Oh my God!" I screamed.

Loveee that chicken from Popeyes. That bird is cooked and finished! a voice in my head cackled. They all came through at the same time now. They were the same voices I heard in my room a few nights ago.

She did it!

Boy, our girl made us proud!

Start cleaning, Indy, check out the scene.

I moved quickly, as if I had prepared for this moment. As many times as I went over the scenarios in my head and how I would do it—I froze, unsure of myself. I panted heavily, and scrambled down the steps, looking around.

What should I do, Mom?

That's right, baby girl, Mama is here. What can you use that's around? Check out the scene first. Use what you have to get rid of the body. And look at the bright side. His car isn't here so that's one less thing you have to worry about.

I looked around and saw nothing, an empty foyer room which led into the studio and Shelby. I paced throughout the studio, looking for options. Think Indigo, think.

Our girl had her first kill. The voices still swirled in my mind. They all sounded like proud parents. Was this what things had come to? I was proud that I made voices in my head proud? I shut those thoughts down; I didn't have time for it right now.

My thoughts turned to Shelby. I walked the short distance and peered at her. Good, ol' faithful, never-stop-ticking, Shelby. I walked back into the studio and eyed Jaxon. He still lay motionless at the foot of the steps. I inched closer and knelt down.

He was breathing and his chest moved up and down slowly. I peered around again looking for something to help me finish the job.

End him, a voice said.

I obliged.

I stood and kicked Jaxon in his side. His eyes didn't open but a small whimper escaped his body. The asshole was still holding on and him being alive angered me. How dare he live? How dare he put his hands on me? I had let him slide one too many times. I wouldn't end up on one of these tables

like Tyesha and Ms. Abigail. I would keep myself safe and go all the way, just like I had promised.

I walked back into the furnace room once more and placed my hand on it. It was cold to the touch. I turned the knob all the way to eighteen hundred degrees. It would take approximately seven minutes for the furnace to get hot; hopefully Jaxon held off until then.

CHAPTER 30

I DARTED BETWEEN SHELBY and watching Jaxon and back again; in and out of each room every few minutes as I waited for the ready light to flash on Shelby. When the furnace timer finally dinged and the ready light switched on, I had to make a choice. Was I really going to do this? *Do it, do it, do it*, the voices in my head chanted.

This was the moment I feared but fantasized about for so long. This was the moment I tried to fight. The moment I tried not to think about. The moment I so desperately wanted more than anything to talk to Mom about. She wouldn't judge me; she would let me cry. But I couldn't cry now. I was on my own, and I had to make a choice. Actually, I guess in a way, Mom was always with me. Maybe not physically—but she was as real as all the rest of the voices.

Jaxon didn't move the entire time, and I was thanking the heavens above that I wore my sneakers today and not my work Crocs. I would need the extra support.

I grunted and pulled Jaxon's body from the studio. It was only a couple of feet to Shelby, but Jaxon's body was stocky. I tried kneeling down and tugging at one of his arms, but that

didn't move him either. I huffed at moving him only inches and fell back onto the floor when I lost my balance and my glasses flew off my face. I tripped backwards and I slammed onto the pavement. Tears sprang to my eyes.

What should I do Mom? What should I do? This was not going to work. I spied the room, looking for something to help.

Jaxon let out a sudden cry, and I leapt back and covered my mouth with my hands. I looked around the room for something, anything to quiet him. My eyes landed on the tranquilizers we used every once in a while. Mr. Dennis said sometimes the bodies resisted rigor mortis and would twitch by themselves. They were dead, but their skin jumped. Mr. Dennis would look at a body and say, "That one's fixing to make a comeback." We gave them another sedation shot until Mr. Dennis was satisfied the body had transitioned. My hands shook while I filled the gel-like solution into the syringe. Jaxon lay writhing, moaning, and groaning in pain behind me. I had to move quickly; each groan was stronger than the last. I inhaled and exhaled, trying to settle my nerves while I worked quickly through shaking hands.

I darted towards him, knelt down, and jabbed the syringe into his neck. Jaxon yelped once more while he lay in my arms. We stared into each other's eyes as he faded away. Finally, they rolled back in his head. I looked up to the skies with tears sitting in my eyes, and no sooner, another noise escaped Jaxon's body. He convulsed and foamed at the mouth. His pupils were larger than I had ever seen on anyone. I felt wetness on my lap.

Jaxon had peed himself.

Finally, he stopped moving. I uncradled him, dropped him back onto the floor out of my arms, and inched backward from his body until I hit the room's corner.

Shelby hummed from the other room, and I stood once more, this time huffing and puffing. I groaned and put all of my might into Jaxon's weight this time, knowing I had no other choice. I dragged Jaxon's body closer to Shelby. Sweat formed at my hairline and it sat on my nose. Running back into the studio, I grabbed the large metal cart we used to transfer the bodies. I laid the cart on its side and I groaned again while trying to roll his body onto the top shelf of the cart.

"Ahhh!" I grunted. Jaxon's weight was too much for me.

I tried placing my arms underneath his armpits to lift him but that didn't work. I tried to roll him onto the cart from the floor and that didn't work either. I took a step back and gathered my thoughts. I was breathing hard, and my throat was so hot. I spotted a two-by-four board standing upright leaning against Shelby. I grabbed the board and got down on all fours and hoisted it under him.

"Ughhh!" I rolled Jaxon onto the metal cart with the help of the two-by-four. I wheeled him into the furnace room where Shelby was hot and ready. His head and leg hit the side of the door entering the room, but I didn't care. I stood in front of Shelby, sizing her up. Jaxon lay on the cart and it came to my waist. How will I get him up there? The dead bodies we cremated were hollow and I moved them easily. Jaxon was still warm and full of shit.

You're going to have to do this, honey. Mom's voice urged above all the other ones. There was so much chatter in my head. So much screaming, so much shouting, so much everything—but Mom's voice reigned supreme over everyone else's. *Find the strength, Indigo. Lift him with all of your strength. You can do it; you have to do it…*

I opened Shelby's door and knelt into a squatting position. I grabbed Jaxon by the shoulders and screamed at the top of

my lungs as I struggled to hoist him up. I tried to stuff him into the furnace, but he was just too heavy, and my knees buckled under the weight of him. He slipped from my arms and fell to the floor. I screamed and closed the furnace door as the high heat singed my eyebrows.

What should I do? What should I do, I repeated.

Indigo! Mom's voice was stern. *You have to find the strength. You have to find the will. Everything depends on you. You have to finish him. I'm so proud of you.*

I mulled over her words. I had to finish this once and for all.

I opened the furnace door once more and squared my knees for more stability, setting my feet onto the cement beneath me. With a loud scream and in one swift motion, I hoisted Jaxon up again over my shoulders and shoved his body into the furnace door.

"Aghhhh!!" I yelled out. I grunted and pushed him into the hot flames, and I slammed the door shut behind me and locked it.

In seconds, I heard a blood-curdling scream, and Jaxon's hand slammed up against the small glass window. I turned the timer all the way up and soon, there was nothing but the hum of Shelby.

By my calculations, it would take at least forty-two minutes for his body to burn, and I wasn't sure if I had that much time. Mr. Dennis mentioned swinging by to sign some paperwork. He often did that on the weekends, before any funerals began for the day, to make sure I was there on time. Hopefully today wasn't one of those days.

I pulled up a folding chair and sat next to Shelby. When the alarm went off on my phone, I clicked off Shelby and let her cool for a long and painful five minutes. My leg shook back and forth. Waiting, just waiting. Weeks ago, Mom helped me navigate a roundabout. This day she helped me navigate a murder. I could only hear my own breathing; there were no voices now and no Shelby humming. It was just me. I waited a few more minutes for Shelby to cool before I opened the small door and found the remains of Jaxon Green. Ashes to ashes, dust to dust.

CHAPTER 31

SCOOPED OUT THE remains of Jaxon and put them in a zip lock bag. I raced around cleaning up any evidence that Jaxon had been there. Since his car wasn't here the only thing I had to get rid of was his bike. I chewed on the inside of my mouth and worried about what to do about the bike. I couldn't be seen with it, and since the sun was now up, someone probably spotted it already. The thought of someone spotting his bike made me pick up the pace. I had so many things to think about. Jaxon wasn't the type of person who could just go missing. He was a teenage white boy in Louisiana. They would come looking for him.

They won't find him though, you're already ahead. Think smarter not harder, honey, Mom interrupted. *Take that bike and shove it in the same place where you shoved Jaxon.*

I stood a little straighter—I hadn't even thought of that. Racing up the stairs, I burst out of the front door. Peering around, I didn't see anyone. If they saw me, they didn't stir. I wheeled Jaxon's bike inside the foyer and then carefully downstairs, narrowly missing the wall in front of me. It was rough getting it down those steep steps, but finally I walked the bike towards

Shelby, hoisted it up with the same strength I used to raise Jaxon's body, and shut the door. Shelby didn't need to reheat because she was hot and roaring to go. Another twenty minutes went by and I repeated the clean-up process, let it cool down, and then scooped out the remains into another zip lock bag. I looked at the bag and couldn't believe what I held in my hands.

I did this. I did this.

A smile formed at the crease of my mouth, and a new feeling I hadn't felt in a long time set back in. Happiness.

"What are you doing here?" I questioned Malachi. Joya dropped me off in front of the house, and after I showered and napped, Malachi popped up. Dad still lay snoring in his room.

"I told you I was swinging by after work. Remember my text? I just wanted to check on you. We haven't had a chance to really talk, just us."

My shoulders relaxed remembering Malachi's text message, but my heart still beat out of my chest. Did he know what I had just done? Did he see it on me? In my eyes…on my skin? On my face? The elation that I felt throughout my body startled me. My hands and stomach tingled. I did it. I had really done it. I was at the top of a roller coaster and I was gliding down. The excitement and jolt of energy coursed through me, and I thought of all the ways I could improve for it. Not that I was planning another time…but you know, just in case.

"Indy, you good?" Malachi interrupted my thoughts and looked at me with quizzical eyes. "Where's The Bus?"

I hadn't had a chance to tell him it broke down. I caught him up on that fiasco.

"You should get that looked at soon. It could be anything." Malachi instructed.

243

Standing on the front porch, I studied Malachi. The sun gleamed off his dark brown skin, and he wore a long-sleeved shirt and blue jeans. He licked his lips as he looked at me, and I had the urge to kiss him. I leaned in and did just that.

"Whoa," he said. "That's what I'm talking about, girl," his eyes flashed.

I grabbed Malachi's sleeve and pulled him towards me. Electric jolts shot through my body, and the voices in my head sent their congratulations. *Her first kill,* they mused. They sounded impressed.

My first kill.

I succumbed and gave into the voices in my head, but maybe they were the ones who were there for me the entire time. Maybe they knew my fate, and I was the one standing in my own way. The energy that I felt in this moment made Malachi look like a million bucks to me. His broad chest. His eyes were bright and staring at me. The same intensity and understanding running between us that always did. I held open the front door for him to come in, and I inhaled his cologne. Goosebumps formed against my skin.

"Where is everyone?"

"My dad is sleeping so you'll have to be quiet. Sidney's not here." I batted my eyes and took his hand.

"But won't he wake? He'll freak if he wakes up and I'm here."

"I don't know, and right now I don't really care," my voice was low and sing song-y.

He smiled and shut the door behind him.

My phone buzzed, and even though I didn't want to, habit made me look at it. A text from Will read:

> BRING YOUR CAR BY LATER TODAY,
> I'LL TAKE A LOOK AT IT.

I smiled. Will was always there when I needed him, but right now—in this moment—Malachi was right where I needed him. I locked the front door and tip-toed behind him down the hallway to my bedroom.

CHAPTER 32

THE VOICES SCREAMED in my head and it seemed they were having a party…they were so proud of me. I actually found myself humming in the shower. It was soft too—a Chaka Khan song that Mom used to sing to me and Sidney. She didn't sound half bad, and neither did I in the shower. I flitted around the house and my damp feet slapped against the bare, hardwood floors.

"Alexa, play Chaka Khan," I said out loud.

Alexa sprang to life and played the song that I requested. I hummed in the shower. I swayed my hips and sashayed into the kitchen from the hallway when I was done. I grabbed the broom and began sweeping under the kitchen table and moved the chairs out of the way. I let the broom guide me as I swirled and pretended it was a microphone. I sang that song like they had paid me to sing it. I sang that song like my life depended on it. I sang that song like Sonia Lewis sang it to a young Sidney and an older Indigo; she gave us the best love that she had. It filled my heart with joy. Electricity shot through my fingers and radiated down to my toes and all throughout my body. The feeling was intense, and my head felt calm.

Inhaling, I took in the apple pie Ms. Arletha made the night before. It smelled fresh and sugary sweet. She had placed yellow tulip flowers on the kitchen table, and I slid to them, closed my eyes, and inhaled. Their light, airy scent tickled my nose, and I cupped them and inhaled again.

I sang loud now and my voice cracked trying to match Chaka's moans. I sang for the voices in my head. For making them happy. I sang for Mom as she was the star of the show and would accept nothing less. The joy that I felt knowing Jaxon Green had succumbed by my own hands left me feeling invigorating.

I had more energy and when I got out of the shower and studied my face in the mirror; it looked aglow. My skin was moisturized and soft. My skin was clear, except for a few beauty marks. Either I was crazy or those were new too. You know when you don't feel good and everyone says 'drink some water'? I looked like I had been my drinking my water and everything was agreeing with me.

Maybe the voices had been trying to help all along. Why did I wait so long? They knew what I needed, even when I didn't. Did that sound crazy? Parts of me still wondered that, too.

I heard banging on the front door.

"Alexa, turn the music off," I barked. She shut down immediately. I pulled the front door open and on the other side stood a police officer. I looked at his badge: Jamison. K. Jamison.

"May I help you?" My words caught in my throat. I swallowed them away.

"Yes, I'm looking for an Indigo Lewis? Is that you?" he questioned; his voice was smooth. Nice. His eyes were kind.

"Yes, that's me." I gave nothing else.

"What I'm here about is the disappearance of Jaxon Green. His mom...uhhh..." K. Jamison flipped through his tiny spiral notebook. He licked his tongue and swiped the pages up quickly. "Mrs. Green alerted us you may have been one of the last people to see Jaxon Green."

My words caught in my chest, and I coughed a little hearing him say Jaxon's name.

"I'd like to ask some questions, if that's okay." K. Jamison studied me.

"That's fine, but my dad isn't here." I know my rights—Ez was funny about stuff like that. He couldn't hold down an everyday job and couldn't do many things all at the same time, but he knew the laws, and he knew his rights. Ez taught Sidney and me the rules, what it means to be Black in America, and possibly, a plan to keep myself safe. Thanks to him, I wasn't a dumb girl, and they wouldn't be questioning me today.

"And when will he be home?" K. Jamison pressed.

"He normally gets off from work around 9:00 a.m. Come back tomorrow morning."

"I'll be here," he nodded. He retreated to his police truck, tapped on the hood, and tipped his hat.

He would be back; I had no doubt about that. I read it in his eyes and knew he meant business. He didn't know I meant business too. He could come back, but the way I felt I wouldn't be able to guarantee that he would leave. I had a team around me that didn't play about me.

Pictures of Jaxon Green lined Tunica Rivers storefronts in town. Slicked hair, keys in hand, and shining teeth—his face glared back at me whenever I peered at him from the street. I went to the corner stores, the drug store across from Dennis and Son's—everywhere I went, I had to stifle a giggle and place my hands to my mouth to keep the smirk to myself. No one wanted to see the real smile hiding behind my eyes; but it was there. Could they handle the truth? There was one picture of Jaxon standing in front of his JEEP at the school wearing his man flops. When I saw that picture, I just about cracked up

right there when I remembered his love for that damn truck.
The picture had a sign with it that read, Jaxon Green missing
now thirty-three days.

That's right. It had been thirty-three days since he disappeared. I counted each day on my calendar in my closet door
at home. Since it was also was Sidney's bedroom door, she
heard me mark an x through each day on the calendar in
our shared space.

Dad and I were visiting Titus University this week. They
were having an open house and Dad wanted to, as he said,
"Get a lay of the land." I think he really just wanted to get a
good look at the place and decide if it was up to his standards.

Dads.

Today I sat in the editor's room at TRHS for the last time
and I paced, cutting into the rug beneath my feet with wick-
ed speed. The computer dinged, altering me to a new email
message, from Titus University. My eyes scanned the email
and they widened; this one left me with more questions than
answers. Should I call someone? Was there something I had to
do? I wanted to make sure I did everything right for what they
wanted. I wanted to be what they wanted. Jolts shot through my
fingertips, and I bit down on my bottom lip. Was this for real?

Will, Mila, Malachi, and Joya sauntered into the room. We
met to pack and prepare to shut the room down for summer
break. The last time we would all be in here together before
we all went our separate ways—whatever that was.

I could not contain myself. "I got it, I got it."

"What you got, girl? You pregnant?" Mila giggled.

"Don't say that!" Will swatted at her shoulder. Mila
stopped smiling.

"No, for real! Like—I got the email from the pottery studio
publishing house. I applied for a scholarship and they didn't
give it to me, but they gave me some sort of endowment. They're

going to pay half of my tuition for two years!" I screamed. "This is even more than the scholarship!"

Will lunged forward, and a sound erupted from him I hadn't heard before. He grabbed me in a bear hug, lifting me off the ground. My toes dangled to the floor. "Oh my God, Indy, oh my God, that's great!"

Malachi tagged me in my arm and jumped on Will's back. They both swarmed around me. As we grinned and laughed, somehow, I ended up between the two, and we crashed into the editor's table. Will on my left, and Malachi on my right. I laughed back tears and glanced up at Mila. Jealousy flashed in her eyes, but she blinked and smiled it away. It was so fast I wasn't sure I had even seen it, but her change in energy told me otherwise.

Joya waited for the boys to stop roughhousing before she extended her arms into a hug, "Congratulations, girl, you're going to do such great things," she whispered. She had tears in her eyes when she pulled away. Word on the street was that Mr. Chestnut and his wife moved away, rendering Joya alone. I didn't even know he had a wife. I didn't tell her, but I was glad he left, it was time to untangle herself from his clutches one way or another.

Mila's mom held up her word, and she got the job with Dr. Rasner. She would be working part-time at the office starting next month. She didn't say much about it, and I didn't pry.

Malachi cleared his throat. "I have news." We all turned to Malachi surprised. He never had news.

"As you know I'm not going to college like planned. But I did find something I like and well, I applied and was accepted into culinary school. I'd like to be a chef."

My face broke out into the largest smile, and one by one we all cheered and clapped for Malachi. He shrugged and looked slightly embarrassed but pleased with himself. I stared at Malachi for a second, amazed and proud of my ex-boyfriend.

Will, on the other hand, wanted to be a plumber, and I didn't know anyone who wanted to be a plumber. "No, no, hear me out," he said when I gave him incredulous eyes. A plumber? "No, no, listen, they've got the union, and all of those white boys are going to college for four years and leaving with all of that debt. And I'm going for the same amount of time and learning a skill that's going to make me the same money, if not more. You know I'm not good with that clickety clack shit and sitting-behind-a-computer type of stuff," Will explained.

I wondered what else his hands were good at? I thought about it a lot. I was happy that our friendship remained. He was my best friend. After what happened to Jaxon, I wasn't sure if I could still be considered a good friend, but Will made me feel like I was. When Malachi instructed me to get my car fixed when it broke down, Will came to the rescue and fixed it himself. It was one problem that two men approached differently. I had so many thoughts about what could be, and what needed to be explored, hung heavy. We would always kinda, sorta, be—unfinished business, Will and me. But I had other things on my brain too. I loved killing Jaxon Green. There, I said it.

Should I raise my hand and say it in the mirror five times? No, that's Candyman—I wouldn't do that. Or should I stand behind a podium and beg forgiveness?—Would people clap for me? Would people feel bad for me? Would they empathize with a seventeen-year-old Black girl from Tunica Rivers just trying to get to college? Perhaps my skin tone would tell on me and tell them things before I could even open my mouth. Would they decide who I was without even asking me? In some ways, they already had.

They would say Jaxon gave her an opportunity. He allowed her to write an exposé about him. He helped the poor little Black girl who came from a broken home, and this is how she repaid him. The stories they could come up with—you could believe those…and the stories I could tell you, well, you could believe those too. It would be me and dozens of voices in my head. Just our thoughts and perspectives, but nothing too crazy. Or on the contrary, maybe you could believe a bit of it all. The truth lies wherever your perspective led you. What's done is done and I couldn't bring it back—I didn't want to bring it back. Sadly, I had to take a life to get mine back. If this is what it feels like to feel life, I wanted more of it.

CHAPTER 33

"**S**HE WAS AT work. I believe we already said that." Dad said. His jaw was tight, and he said nothing more. K. Jamison shifted in his seat and stopped writing in his little notebook.

I wondered what else he wrote in that thing. He held onto it like it was the keeper of Tunica Rivers secrets. I peered down at my toes. I got a pedicure, and we painted them a clean and shiny white. They looked nice up against my beige sandals. My hair was braided in large passion twists and we had to add in pieces of braiding hair where Jaxon had cut mine all the way down. It looked beautiful and you could hardly tell. Summer was here and sweet smelling air returned to the scene.

The sky had been perfectly blue since Jaxon's demise. His parents still searched for him, and secrets lingered in the air, and some of those secrets sat in K. Jamison's book. My lip curled up, and I stifled a smile. The cops had been making their rounds talking to his friends and family. For some reason I really didn't think they would come and visit me and as each week passed, it didn't seem like they made any headway.

They wouldn't find him. They could ask all the questions in the world. They wouldn't find him.

That's the spirit! A voice in my head cheered.

Damn right, I nodded.

K. Jamison noticed my head nod, and his eyes flashed. "Ms. Lewis, do you have something to add?"

"She has nothing to add, she is a minor." Dad stood in his seat. Ms. Arletha stood behind him with her arm draped over his shoulder. Sidney stood in the hallway behind Ms. Arletha. Dad was my watchdog, Ms. Arletha his, and Sidney was hers. If I didn't know any better, we looked like a family.

"Don't ya'll have things for this, like phone records or something?" Ms. Arletha frowned. My head whipped from up admiring my white pedicure and I stared at her. Whose team was she on?

K. Jamison cleared his throat. "Well, it's not that easy, ma'am. Apparently, Jaxon had many different burner phones he used for a variety of things. We've only been able to track his account through his parents' phone contract which hasn't turned up any leads."

"My, my, he's something else, ain't he," Ms. Arletha shook her head.

"I do have one more question if you don't mind." K. Jamison glanced between me and Dad. Dad and I nodded at each other.

"Do you know anyone who may want to hurt Jaxon Green?"

I paused for a second. I revisited the jabs. Parking in the back of their house. Being left at school and having to find a ride home. My camera. Being blackmailed. Paying me only $100. His hands on me. Touching me like he was entitled to. Intervening with my job. He had to go, and it had to be by me. And that went for him and whoever else.

Even though K. Jamison was Black, he wouldn't understand my world or my reasons. In a world where they put white men on pedestals, I had to take my own protection seriously; I didn't have a team of people behind me. My team was right here in this room and a couple dozen more in my head.

"No-no, I don't." I shook my head.

"Thank you for your time," K. Jamison and Dad stood.

He and Dad were the same height. Two Black men; one in a police uniform, and another with steel toe, worn down to the ground, work boots. Funny, the way they stood in front of each other, you would think they were enemies, sparring with each other — reasons unknown. But out in the world, out against people who viewed them by different standards and different uniforms that they couldn't take on and off every day, they were just Black men. Their uniform was their skin color, and it spoke for them. They should have been on the same team, on the same side — but they went down two different paths and today, those paths converged, and they sparred off.

K. Jamison left the house and tipped his hat to us, only this time his eyes looked different. I couldn't place the thought, but I wondered if this would be the last time I heard from him.

Dad slammed the door behind him and turned to me. "And you're sure none of your friends know where Jaxon is? I know he played football with Malachi, right?"

I shifted my weight and flashed my most convincing, blank, teenage look. "No, my friends don't know what happened to him — Malachi either."

And with that, I didn't have to lie to Dad.

"Good," he nodded and grabbed his keys. "Ready?"

"Yep!" I skipped.

We scrambled out of the house and into the car. Dad drove, Ms. Arletha sat in the passenger side, and Sidney and I piled into the backseat. The university's family open house was today, and we were on our way as just that — a family.

"What do you think he wants with her?" Ms. Arletha questioned.

Dad held onto the wheel tight. Both of his hands were locked, and his knuckles were white. "I'm not sure. Apparently, they don't know what happened. I saw his parents on the news a few nights ago. The cops are saying he's a teenager and maybe he just ran away. His parents are calling bullshit and saying that he would never up and run away from home."

"And what does that have to do with our Indy?" Ms. Arletha countered.

Our Indy...I smiled.

"I saw it on Channel 6, too, Dad." I perched up from the backseat. "They used some of my footage from his college video. I guess that's why they came to me."

"I just don't like it," Ms. Arletha frowned. "You send a Black man to question another Black man and that Black man's child, about some little white boy? He probably did just run away. You know those rich families have they own secrets too. All kinds of stuff going on behind closed doors," she pointed out. But she wasn't wrong. Damn, she wasn't wrong.

I looked over at Sidney. She had said little since Jaxon disappeared. Not that she knew him, but when a white boy disappears into thin air, it was big news. Tucked away in Sidney's closet of a room under a floorboard, sat Jaxon's notebook. I started to burn it after I read through it and found nothing important. But soon, Mom convinced me to keep a gift for myself.

I did, indeed I did.

Sidney had her headphones in her ear, and she was swiping away. Her dad bought her a new iPhone, and it was her newest obsession. She paused whatever she was listening to on her phone and popped out one earbud.

"What?" she peered at me with confusion.

"Nothing...I was just looking at your ugly face." I teased.
She punched me in the arm. "If I'm ugly, your Mom is ugly!"
We fell into a fit of giggles.

"Two beautiful Black girls! Ain't nothing ugly about that. I
don't want to hear that nonsense!" Dad scolded.

"They're just joking, Ben, my lands," Ms. Arletha giggled.

"Well, I was wrong—three beautiful black women." He gave
Ms. Arletha lovey dovey eyes.

Ms. Arletha was taller than Dad by at least four inches.
Even watching them in the car, she towered over him. Their
height mismatch garnered a few giggles by people who didn't
understand the power of needing something that you didn't
even know you needed. Or wanting someone you didn't know
how or why you wanted. Like Will and I...shit, like Malachi
and me. I wanted each of them for different reasons. Malachi's
want came from a different place; a more visceral and primal place. Will's wanting came from a quieter corner within
me. I raced around the Monopoly board, collecting money
and tokens as I went, but he was always home base, always
there—and always for me. The voices in my head wanted
things too. The party died down, and the congratulations
quieted. They were thirsty for more and whispered about
the next time. They used words like, *again, after, encore.* Was
it me? Thirsty for myself? Or really—them? I realized that
I was them and they were me.

We were the same. When they wanted me to do certain
things it was really only because that thing already lived in
me. They were bacteria breeding in my body. They were there,
festering and wanting more. And they fed that need and now
lusted for more.

While at Family Day, I told Dad I had to meet with my college
advisor to pick my classes, but I didn't tell him I really wanted
to check out the campus wellness center. I checked my map

and it should've been in the front behind the student center. I walked through the campus, observing everyone.

There were so many different types of people—big, small, young, old. The campus had a mix of white and brown faces. They stood in groups and talked and laughed. Some played instruments while sitting in the grass, and others scarfed down hot dogs and red beans and rice from the nearby food trucks. Everyone was so well put together. This place would be my new life soon and I would be one of those well put together people. I found the Titus Wellness Center.

"May I help you?" a young white girl at the front desk asked. She wore a name tag that said Kate. Her smile was broad and genuine, and she looked me square in the eye when I walked in.

"Yes, I will be an incoming freshman for Fall semester. I would like to talk to someone about, uh, counseling sessions." My voice tapered off and my cheeks reddened. If I wanted to talk about this stuff, I had to at least stop feeling embarrassed by it.

Kate said with a smile, "No worries, you are in the right place."

"I don't have insurance. I read on the website I would be eligible for school insurance, as long as I'm a full-time student?"

"Yes, that is correct. Once you are officially enrolled full-time, you would be covered under Titus University Student insurance which covers mental health sessions among other things."

I exhaled a sigh of relief. Maybe I could get this thing on track. I gathered a few pamphlets as I completed a short intake form for Kate. One of the questions on the form asked which counselor I would like to meet with, and it had a list of eight different counselors to choose from. I didn't know any of them, so I tried to circle the names which sounded like someone Black. I ran across a T. Jenkins....Jenkins had to be Black, so I made sure to circle that one.

"Kate, you can take your lunch. I'll cover the front for you," a heavyset Black woman said to Kate.

"Thanks, Trenita, I'll be back in about an hour," Kate rose from her seat and grabbed her bag. I handed my forms and clipboard to Trenita as she looked it over.

"Indigo — what a beautiful name."

"Thank you, my mom named me," I smiled back.

"I'm Trenita, one of the counselors here. It's so nice to meet you." Trenita smiled and extended her hand. Her nails were painted royal blue and her hair was cut down short and tapered on one side. Her face was shiny, like she just put on lotion, and every time her hands moved, I smelled her sweet perfume.

I liked her.

I gathered my pamphlets and exited the center holding back a smile — this might work out.

Sidney was hot on my heels sitting at a nearby bench. We had been talking so long about college — the big, bad elusive college — that when Sidney finally laid eyes on said college, and realized with her own eyes that I had to live there and wouldn't return home every day, well, she clung to me like a kid clung to the last days of summer. Maybe I was her summer.

Later that night, after I showered and settled in, Mila called.

"Hey girl." I answered.

"You okay?" Mila asked. Rather, it sounded like a demand.

"Yeah, why?" My heart beat.

"I just saw Joya at the skating rink. She said she picked you up from work a few weeks ago. She said you looked high, and you were mumbling and rocking in the car. Almost...talking to yourself." Mila said the last words carefully. Like there were no other words in the English language that would convey

what those few words would convey. She had chosen the direct route and did not beat around the bush.

No, this bitch didn't....A voice said in my head. Only this time, the voice was my own. Mila had nerve.

"I was fine. I needed a ride from work. My car was broken down at the time. I work around dead bodies all day long. Excuse me if I was out of it one day," I scoffed. The words rapidly fired out of my mouth, sounding more rushed than the ones before it. I kept explaining. Mila put me on the spot, and I twirled one of my passion twists in my hand and picked at my nails. I was never one to tell what someone else trusted me with and even though I wanted to drop all of Joya's business out, right there on the table for Mila to take and run with, I would still keep quiet.

"And you were...talking to yourself?"

"I was not." I ached for my friends in my head, whom I had to deny to my friend in real life. They wouldn't understand, and I wasn't ready to have this conversation with anyone, and definitely not Mila.

Mila sighed. "Indy, have you been able to see someone, about what we talked about before? With Will?" Mila still thought I was crazy, that was clear. What did I do or say that made her feel that way? What gave me up?

I told the truth. "Yes, I have. We went to the university's family day, and I grabbed a ton of brochures and pamphlets from their mental health clinic. I met some of the staff and I think it'll be good for me." Honesty was sometimes the best policy, sometimes. Only if it fit the time, person and place. This time it did, and I wielded my truth like a full house.

Mila's voice became a high-pitched shriek. "Bitch tell me everything! How was family day? Why didn't you tell me you were going? Did you see any cute guys there? We're going to have to buy chastity belts. Tell me everything. Lawd the tea...."

I smiled into the phone, and my shoulders relaxed. Mila's shallowness easily allowed for her to chase me down rabbit holes. As the words spilled out of my mouth, I feared I had slapped down my joker card too soon.

CHAPTER 34

THE SUN WAS ablaze outside. Even at 7 a.m., it sat perched high in the sky, waking everyone and everything in its path. I heard Ez outside on the lake. He had a small battery powered radio and Martha and the Vandellas rocked about nowhere to run and nowhere to hide. Ez's loud, baritone voice sang on the water as he cut through the waves with no destination in mind. Just him and the water, spending time. Ez shared a love affair with the water that I didn't understand. It brought him solace and comforted him in ways that were foreign to me. I had to get to work in three hours, and I had already been awake the past fourteen hours.

Don't go to sleep, Indy, not yet. The voices whined.

Ordinarryyyy ppeoplleeee…another one sang in my head.

The busy array of voices, when they were at their loudest, sounded like a Saints and Falcons game. The noise was deafening, and sleep did not come easy.

Mrs. Green had shown up to my house the day before, with snot filled cries. She knocked on the door and clutched her pearls and held tight to her purse. Her knees and feet were locked together straight ahead. When Dad invited her in, Ms.

Arletha went into there's-a-white-woman-in-the-house mode, and turned the TV off, offered her some pound cake, and a glass of water from Mom's best china. We used regular cups, but Ms. Arletha opted for the good stuff. Only the best for Mrs. Green. Ms. Arletha didn't even know her and made the white woman entering our home feel comfortable instead of asking why she clutched her valuables in the first place.

"I got your address from the *Times*, you captured my son so well, I hope you don't mind" Ms. Green cried. "He was supposed to be interviewed for the school legacy committee. To get our family name dedicated into the school gym," she explained. She dabbed at her eyes even though I saw no actual tears. She sat with her purse directly on her lap. "I was hoping you could write a follow-up article. Something mentioning that he is still missing, and we are looking for him. That way, they'll still dedicate a brick to our family name, knowing that this is an active situation, and nothing nefarious is happening."

But something nefarious did happen, Mrs. Green, I mused. Oh, but something did.

She sat in our living room, her eyes darting back and forth between our dated furniture and a few panels missing from our drop ceiling in the living room. She refused to take her jacket off even though it was hot as balls outside. She looked down on me and us, even in her time of need. And to make matters worse, on this day she called me Indigo. Today, she knew my name, after months of calling me whatever she wanted. But now, she needed me, and she knew my name. Go figure.

"I'll think about it and send you what I come up with," I considered. I walked her out and shut the door behind her.

The day after Mrs. Green's impromptu visit, I struggled to find the words to accurately describe her son, what he meant to me, how his search party was going, and how people could

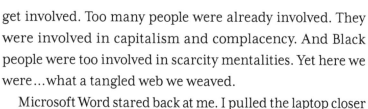

get involved. Too many people were already involved. They were involved in capitalism and complacency. And Black people were too involved in scarcity mentalities. Yet here we were…what a tangled web we weaved.

Microsoft Word stared back at me. I pulled the laptop closer and began typing.

Jaxon Green has been missing for forty-seven days at the time of this article. Jaxon forever lives in our hearts, and we are hopeful that his imminent return will answer many questions and restore hope in the hearts and minds of Tunica Rivers citizens and concerned parents.

Indigo Lewis, Times Writer

A few hours later, I rushed to Ms. Montague's studio. She emailed earlier mentioning she was leaving for vacation today, and she had a graduation gift for me. I wanted to catch her before she left and properly thank her for the studio's endowment. Thanks to her, I wouldn't need to worry about paying for college out of pocket for at least two years. Between her endowment, a small savings from Dad and a work-study job I would be assigned, I wouldn't have to worry about money for a while. I pulled into the parking lot as Ms. Montague's two-door white Mercedes pulled out. She had on sunglasses and all of her windows were down.

"I almost missed you!" I yelled out of my window. I parked, hopped out, ran over to her passenger side, and leaned in. "I wanted to thank you, Ms. Montague. You've done so much for me. Really, I…I…don't know what to say. I'm so grateful."

Ms. Montague's skin reddened, and her face turned a medium shade of pink. Her tan skin made the blushing more noticeable. "You go stand in the light, Ms. Lewis," she shook her head. A tear sat in the corner of her eye. "I left something for you, it's on my desk." She winked and pulled off.

I waved as she turned the corner.

Entering the studio, Ms. Montague's secretary ventured to the back and returned with a medium size brown bag. "Here you go," she transferred it into my hands. They wrapped it in tight cellophane and bubble wrap, and I couldn't make out what it was.

"Thank you," I said, walking out. I sat in the car and opened the bag. There was a small greeting card. I opened that first, and it read:

> *The buyers returned this. I normally don't allow refunds,*
> *but because of the circumstances, I allowed it this one time.*
>
> *- Ms. Montague.*

My heart skipped a beat…it couldn't be…

I tore into the cellophane with the sharp end of my keys. It took a while but once I finally got it opened, Mom's pottery piece sat before me. The one Mrs. Green had purchased. I held it to my chest and tears fell from my eyes. I wiped them, angry that they were there, but soon, I let them fall. I didn't want anyone else to see me cry, but they rolled down my face anyway. They were salty and traced the corners of my mouth and onto my chin and neck.

I had a piece of Mom.

I didn't know why the Greens returned the piece or what it meant, but I had a piece of my mom, and that was all I cared about.

CHAPTER 35

WHEN I WOKE up that morning, the birds were chirping, and the sun grazed my face. It was the first time I had slept in weeks. No voices, no intrusive thoughts. Just me, myself, and I. I snuggled closer to the warmth of the rays. I felt the sun shining through my closed eyelids and I smiled.

Today I would visit Mom at Trochesse. I brought prom pictures with me that I got developed down at the drugstore. I was worried about having money to buy a prom dress but going through Mom's things when we cleaned out the shed at Ez's house, I found an older, slinky white lace dress and a wilted corsage.

Ms. Arletha hemmed and sewed some of the frayed edges until it was just right. It fit my long torso perfectly and I kicked my left leg out, Sonia Lewis style. Up against my deep brown skin, it looked perfect. When the night came, I proudly wore Mom's high school prom dress to my own prom. I went alone — and it was my decision to do so. After the party, no one would be making decisions for me anymore, I made my own choices.

I was visiting Mom alone today. Sidney was with her dad, Ez wasn't interested — and I didn't ask Dad. He had Arletha, and that was answer enough. I waited and invited the voices into my head, but they didn't come this morning. Slinging back the blankets, I sat up in bed and planted my bare feet on the floor. I gave a loud growl and stretched my arms to the sky, extending my still asleep muscles. I welcomed the bad things into my head instead of shushing them, and they let me get some sleep. What an arrangement.

People lived in me, and sometimes I listened to those versions of me. I pushed them away, cursed them away. I fussed with them and let them fuss at me. I was a child of a Schizophrenic, and most likely, it had not skipped a generation like all the research I had done said should happen. No, it didn't skip a generation; it lived within me.

It felt natural. Primal. My, what evils girls can do — and we do.

I stood in line, inching closer to the front of Trochesse. Workers were on the left side of the building painting over the colored sign until it was no longer visible. I pulled my sunglasses up to get a better look, and I smiled. I watched them as I got closer, and I waved and said good morning.

I had left the house early to spread Jaxon's ashes on the land at Ez's house. He and the cats could get to know one another.

I put my braids up into a large bun on my head. I wore wine red lipstick and fake diamond stud earrings I picked up from the beauty supply store. It was a rare sight for me, but I was on some rare shit these days.

Entering the large rotunda, I clutched at my crossbody waist purse, and I nodded at Nurse MeanFace. She nodded back and studied me. I poked my neck out further, and I know the lights caught my earrings just right and they shined just like I shined.

Again, I heard her voice before I saw her...

"Whooaaa something on my mind..." she sang.

Mom stood at the top of the cathedral stairs in a floor length fur coat. She gave her best shoulder shrug, Tina Turner style, and shimmied down the steps, carefully, one at a time. Behind her from the left and right, background dancers emerged—wearing similar outfits. By the descriptions that Mom gave in her letters, I recognized the man on the right to be Minister, and the woman on the left to be Ruth-Ann. Ruth-Ann wore a fur vest and Minister a fur belt. The tips of his hospital shoes also had faux fur glued to them.

The trio made their way closer to the visitors, never missing a beat. Mom didn't even look down where she was walking. She pounded down the steps, not waiting for it to make room for her; she made room for it. The trio held hair brushes to their mouths, and they walked in front and behind of each other singing. It didn't take me long to see they were moving in a figure-eight pattern. Mom was teaching them all of her stage tricks. I nodded.

Everyone in the rotunda stopped to stare at the group making their way to us, giving their best Showtime at the Apollo moves. I peered at Nurse MeanFace in the bubble. Her eyes were wide, and her hands were to her cheek. She looked both stunned and humored, but she didn't stop them.

Mom and her group performed another number. This one was quicker in beat and required Mom and Minister to put their fake mics down, hold hands, and dance. Mom and Minister did some fancy footwork while people cheered and clapped around them. Mom beamed, and her hair bounced around her face. She leaned back and gave hearty belly giggles. She performed and worked the room like she was at the Grammy's and we were her adoring fans.

"Okay, Ms. Lewis, that's enough," Nurse MeanFace finally warned.

Security had walked into the room and placed their hands on their waists. Too many people dancing, standing, and moving at the same time was not what they liked to see, and they were itching to shut down any resemblance of fun. The crowd settled down, and I waved to Mom through the scattered people. "Over here!" I yelled. I sat down at the table and waited for her to sashay over to me.

Mom collapsed into the seat with dramatic fashion and dabbed at her sweaty hairline and brows. People were tapping her shoulders and congratulating her for her performance, and one person actually asked her for her autograph. I sank into my seat and waited.

When they finally left us alone, Mom turned to me. She wore mascara and eyeliner, and the darkness sharply contrasted with her wide and wondrous eyes. She shone with madness only I—her daughter—understood. I had a feeling what she would say before she even said it.

"So how was it?" she shimmied her shoulders and playfully cut her eyes at me.

"How was what?"

"Your first…kill right? Your first kill? How was it?" She leaned forward and curled her lip into a half smile.

THE END

Thank you for reading "Forty-Two Minutes." I'd love to hear what you think! If you enjoyed this book (or even if you didn't), please visit the site where you purchased it and write a brief review. Your feedback is so important to me and will help other readers decide whether to read the book too.

PS: Check out the next page for a sneak peek into Book 2 of the *Indigo Lewis Series* coming soon December 2021.

SNEAK PEEK

"**A**ND THAT, LADIES, is how you stay safe and not get yourself snatched up," the older Black woman repeated. She nodded her head with a dramatic pause. I checked my phone for the second time. It felt like I had already been there forever, but it was only an hour.

Dorm orientation for Titus University was well underway, and we were learning the ins and out of how-not-to-get-your-self-raped spiel. As if it could somehow be our fault and there was something we could do to prevent it. I was alone, everyone else was sitting with their roommates. The orientation instructions stated we line up by our floor and room assignments and spend the next few hours getting to know each other. My roommate seemed to be absent, and so I sat alone.

"She acts like we come to college and check off the 'I want to be raped box.'" A light-skinned, girl leaned close to me and smirked.

I giggled.

"Never have I ever thought, man, I want to go to Titus University, and get raped today," the girl dug a little harder. The way she rolled her eyes and sucked her teeth made me cover my mouth to hide my chuckles.

"I'm Naomi — Naomi Holland." she said.

"I'm Indigo, they call me Indy."

"I think I saw your name somewhere. You're on my floor; the fifth, right?"

Naomi and I paused for a second before we exclaimed — "on the fifth floor," and held up four fingers. Martin was life, and I hoped they had the channel here at Titus that I needed to watch it.

"What's your major?" Naomi asked. She motioned for me to follow her and we trotted back to the food table.

Titus University set up an elaborate spread to welcome the incoming class of 2025. Cakes, pies, fruits, coffee, and sandwiches lined the tables, and we weren't the only ones in line for second plates. They packed students inside the building and it was already a sizzling September day; the type in down south Louisiana when the old folks moved slower and quieter.

I knew choosing this college was a good choice. I only applied to two schools, but this one was only three hours away from home, plus I had The Bus and I could visit whenever I needed to see my sister, Sidney, and my dad.

Shrugging in Naomi's direction, I said, "Liberal Arts is my major right now. I'm not sure what I want to do, but I just know I'll find it in college." Silently, I cursed myself for saying that last part. Hopefully, I wasn't too forward.

She said nothing but nodded her head. "I feel the same. I'm majoring in Political Science, but I don't know the first thing about it." Naomi was heavyset with her hair pulled back into a tight ponytail at her nape. She had on these bad ass Jordan's that I could never afford, not with my sad work-study job the school assigned me. When I got the letter in the mail and it said I would work in the theatrical arts department this school year — my dad laughed and said, "They're gonna have my baby opening and closing the curtains." He and his girlfriend, Ms. Arletha, thought that was hilarious and fell out in stitches.

I hoped they weren't right.

"Then why are you majoring in Political Science?"

Now it was Naomi's turn to shrug. "Parents just don't understand, right?"

"If that ain't the truth. Where are you from?"

"New Jersey. Where are you from?"

"Right here in Louisiana. About three hours away in Tunica Rivers, even thought this place seems like an entire world away."

"Yea, it's pretty different from Jersey too," Naomi's face softened as she looked around and watched the other students.

The presenter was still upfront, teaching us girls how not to get assaulted and handing out condoms to the boys. Naomi and I carried our food to our seats. We found a small corner in the back of the room that wasn't taken and we spread our food across the table. We each had two plates topped with all kinds of sweets and sandwiches. I looked at Noami and she was already grinning at me and my plate — then her and hers.

I had a forkful of salad ready to devour and my mouth was watering when my cell phone rang.

Crap! I thought I put it on vibrate. A boy at a different table eyed me when my phone rang, interrupting the woman's shrill voice up front. "I'll be right back, can you watch my food?" I mouthed to Naomi. She nodded, her mouth full of chicken tenders.

"Hey Dad!" I breathed into the phone rushing into the hallway.

"Indy Lindy!" I heard different voices scream in the background at the same time.

I smiled. Dad, Ms. Arletha, Grandpa Ez, and Sidney were on the phone.

"What are you doing, Indy?" Sidney always wanted to know my whereabouts.

"I'm in orientation. They're teaching us how not to get assaulted."

"What now?" Dad blurted. I could hear him frowning through the phone.

"Who assaulted my Indy?" Grandpa Ez's voice boomed through the phone and I winced as my eardrum buzzed.

"Hush Grandpa Ez, I'm fine!"

"And what's this Grandpa Ez business girl? Don't go to that crackerjack school and start acting funny now."

Grandpa Ez insisted that Sidney and I call him Ez. Now and then, I would slip in a Grandpa on him but he quickly shut it down. "I ain't no old man girl," he would shake his head. He was tall, wide, and surly. Ez was muscular and his arms bulged from paddling his canoe up and down Tunica River where we lived. He still walked the woods and tended to the land every day. Ez resembled a retired offensive lineman, and if it wasn't for his salt and pepper hair and slight belly bulge, he could have passed for one too. All seven feet of Ez looked nothing like a Grandpa, but he was still mine.

I heard some muffled sounds, and Ms. Arletha's voice came through loud and clear. "Indy you tell them people you are team *hashtag Me Too,* okay?"

"Me too, what? I want it too," Sidney whined.

"You stay away from them parties, Indy. Me and 'Letha been watching SVU, and we know what goes on at the colleges on Thursday nights."

"Oh, hush boy and leave that girl alone!" Ms. Arletha cut in.

I smiled into the phone while they fussed at each other. This was my family. Hearing voices from the orientation, I whispered, "I gotta go, love you guys" as students began shuffling out of the room.

"We love you Indy! And have a good time in college," Sidney shouted.

"And you call me if you need me to tinker with The Bus, Indy!" Ez's voice cracked above the pack.

When I hung up and re-entered the auditorium, Naomi was still waiting. She had taken a napkin and placed it over my food for me and didn't let the cleaning crew come along and toss it. "Got anywhere to be?" She gave a devilish grin.

My plans comprised running to the store and picking up more stuff for my dorm room, and I wanted to walk around and figure out where my classes were so I wouldn't get lost when the semester started in a few days. I also wanted to search for a beauty supply store because, well — every Black girl needed to be within a five-mile radius of a beauty supply store — that was law. I also wanted to check out the arts theater and meet my supervisor. But the way Naomi looked at me, I knew whatever she had in mind was more fun.

ABOUT THE AUTHOR

Janay's passion for words began when she spent hours reading borrowed books from the local library where her love for words were homegrown. She served as the editor of her high school newspaper, and for years tended to her craft until she and it were ready.

Janay attended Rutgers University where she received a Bachelor and Master's Degree in Social Work. She is a Licensed Clinical Social Worker, School Social Worker and Mental Health Therapist. To date, she's held many titles, but her favorites are mentor, mental health advocate, and melanin story teller.

Janay is a native of Southern, New Jersey where she resides with her husband and daughter. She enjoys reading, spa days, and crab legs. This is her second published novel and her first is titled, *"Hey, Brown Girl"* available at all major retailers.

If you enjoy young adult stories about melanated characters navigating love, friendships, and family, please consider sticking around for Janay's collection of words.

Watch her make a SCENE!

Made in the USA
Columbia, SC
09 December 2022